UNDERDOG CITY

ALSO BY CHRIS NEGRON

Dan Unmasked

The Last Super Chef

UNDERDOG CITY

CHRIS NEGRON

HARPER

An Imprint of HarperCollinsPublishers

Library of Congress Control Number: 2023933480
ISBN 978-0-06-325187-8

Typography by Chris Kwon
23 24 25 26 27 LBC 5 4 3 2 1

First Edition

For my sisters, Lisa and Laura, who had to endure
my earliest stories about dogs, told from the way,
way back seat of our family station wagon.

For almost two months, the Red Devil has been waking me up at 5:00 a.m.

Okay, that's not exactly true. The first few weeks, back when sixth grade was still in full swing, my eyes would snap open like a reanimated zombie. One time, he even jolted me out of a dead sleep so suddenly I rolled right off my bed, belly flopping onto the floor. I keep a pillow down there now to soften my landing in case it happens again.

Which it won't, because I finally got used to the rooster next door's daily crowing—the same rooster that came with our new neighbors, Mr. and Mrs. Cortez, like the strangest package deal ever. If "gotten used to" is what you want to call my body clock being so trained I'm *already* lying awake in bed staring at the ceiling when the daily, first-thing-in-the-morning cock-a-doodle-do-ing starts up fresh.

As soon as the first crow ends, our house falls silent again. Until Dad, only half conscious himself, begins his slow shuffle down the hallway. It's still dark, so I can barely make out his outline. But I know it's him because, like me but unlike Mom, Dad is somewhat vertically challenged. Okay, I'll just say it: we're both short. Plus, his shape is round and jolly where Mom's is all long, sharp angles. I also know it's Dad because, after he stops in my doorway and rubs his eyes open, he whispers in my direction.

"Mortimer, you up?"

Is it after 5:00 a.m.?

Because, then . . . *yes. Of course* I'm up.

But it's too early for actual conversation, so I only manage a shadowy nod back at him. Dad mirrors my head bobbing before starting his countdown. Three fingers up and then, one by one, three fingers back down again, until all that's left is a gloomy fist. Which suddenly opens in a flash, his fingers spread wide. Because he and I both know an explosion is about to happen. And, sure enough, at that very moment, the Red Devil's *second* morning crow echoes through our house.

"Will you shut that Red Devil up?!" This answering yell—almost a scream, really—comes from Reginald

Brewster's deck. Another morning ritual. The big man himself always issues the first and loudest *human crow* of the morning. And, honestly, it's hard to say which is more grating to the ears: Red's piercing serenade or Brewster's screeching response.

Today, Red replies with a third crow. If I could see Dad's face, I imagine his eyes would be wide, as surprised by this uncommon outburst as I am. Usually our rooster neighbor takes a long break after sounding the first two alarms, like he's catching his breath or something.

This third one's so sudden and so loud, though, it sounds like Red's right here in my room with us, despite my window being as vacuum-sealed shut as possible. Which is just *great* in the summer when all you want to feel is the fresh morning breeze, all you want to hear are the sounds of your Townsend Heights neighbors greeting each other, all you want to smell are the afternoon hot dogs and hamburgers grilling, the morning bacon sizzling.

But even if my window were open, I doubt I'd hear or smell any of those summer staples, because they've been pretty absent from our neighborhood streets for a while now. For almost exactly two months, come to think of it.

The Heights used to have such an active community, full of happy chatter. Lately, though, it feels like the volume of Reginald Brewster's constant Red Devil crowing increases by the day.

Worse is the fact that his words have been spreading through our streets and hills like some kind of virus. Red Devil may have started out as a nickname only Brewster used, but in the past few weeks, the entire neighborhood's started repeating it. No one's bothered to ask what my new neighbors' pet's name is.

Our early morning ritual complete, Dad leaves, continuing his slow trudge toward the stairs. Mom, who was an early riser pre-Red, is surely waiting downstairs in the kitchen. So, too, is Dad's coffee.

Me? I might be awake, but I'm not *up* yet. It usually takes longer for me to be sure I'm ready to roll out of bed. Trust me, my knees don't need any more mishaps, and—emergency pillow or not—my belly would definitely prefer to undergo as little additional flopping as humanly possible.

People say you don't have to do much to take care of a hamster. All I can say is people, apparently, don't know enough about hamsters. They're a *ton* of work. Especially my helpless buddy, Cinnamon. I have to do practically everything for him.

Seriously, daily hamster maintenance is no joke.

Each morning, I go through my series of sticky notes, arranged in careful order on the wall behind his cage. Fresh water? Check. Remnant nastiness removed from food dish? Check. New food added? Check. General cage cleanup? Check. Make sure his wheel isn't stuck on any bedding? Check, check, and check.

I mean, good luck if that wheel ever gets jammed up

and you don't notice it. I named him Cinnamon in the first place because all he does is roll.

Okay, well, Dad thought it was funny.

Seriously, though: in Cinnamon-world, the inability to roll nonstop is an absolute, guaranteed 911 emergency. My hamster gets a crazy look in his eyes if that wheel doesn't spin like he's expecting it to.

As I complete each hamster-related duty, I crumple up yesterday's note—purple—and rewrite the same step down onto a new note with today's color. Yellow.

The color coding helps make sure yesterday's tasks don't get mixed up with today's. Because I can't miss a single one of these steps. Cinnamon is counting on me. And when someone's depending on you, you can't let them down. No matter what.

Bad things can happen if you get distracted and forget your job, even if it's only for a second.

The whole hamster-care process takes me about a half hour, which means by the time I make it downstairs, Dad's finished his second cup of coffee and started a new fix-it project.

Today's victim? Our toaster oven. It's in pieces, screws and metal brackets strewn all over the counter. I stop in my tracks as I enter the kitchen, staring at the poor thing like a fallen comrade.

Dad stares, too, his glasses dangling from his mouth.

He chews on the end of one arm as he peers at the toaster oven's remaining guts.

"Is it broken?" I ask, hearing the panicked tone of my question. It's just that I used the toaster oven yesterday to make pumpkin spice waffles, and the last two in the box were dancing in my head as I hurried down the stairs.

Mom, still nursing her first coffee while standing near the sink, shrugs and rolls her eyes, but Dad doesn't notice her expression. Instead, without turning around, he holds a perfectly toasted slice of bread over his head. As far as my eyes can tell, anyway, and I've seen my share of toast.

"This was not properly toasted at all," he answers with his face still buried in the toaster oven. "I'm sure it just needs a tune-up. Bit of maintenance. Back up and running in no time."

"Thanks for having a look, Nick," Mom says pleasantly. Dad's back is still turned to her, so I'm sure it's only me who catches a glimpse of her second eye roll in less than half a minute.

I understand Mom's frustration. Lately, a "bit of maintenance" means the loss of yet another appliance or convenience around the house. As soon as Dad gets his hands on something, it becomes hopelessly flummoxed. Goodbye, toaster oven. Farewell, pumpkin waffles. Hello, microwaved oatmeal and boxed cereal.

I'm not sure why, but ever since the school year ended

and Dad's been on break—he's an earth science teacher at the high school—he spends most of his days fixing stuff around the house. It started with the bathroom faucets (now we have to remember the blue one is hot and the red one is cold), continued with the lamps in the foyer (those don't work at all anymore, just click-click-click and no light ever comes on), and has kept going all throughout the house.

You have to hold down the lever on the upstairs toilet for at least five seconds to get it to flush right. Can't shut the hallway closet all the way anymore. And for some reason I need to remember to flip on the dining room light switch if I'm planning to use the kitchen blender to make myself a smoothie.

"Have a bowl of your wheat things," Mom suggests absently, somehow recognizing my disappointed expression without ever lifting her eyes from Dad's work. I hate that, how I think I'm keeping stuff to myself and she's still able to read me like a book. "Or I can make you eggs. Give you more energy for your big day."

I head toward the pantry. "It's not a big day, Mom."

"I'm just happy you're spending time with Frankie again. It's great that you're hanging out like you used to."

She means before Ms. Opal. Before Trevor. Before everything changed. Sometimes when I hear Brewster and all our other neighbors complaining that the Red Devil is altering their lives, turning Townsend Heights into a place they claim not to recognize, part of me thinks, "No kidding. Welcome to the club."

Because my life has been changing and changing and changing for months now.

The most important people to me, besides my parents of course, are gone. And those parents? They've been treating me like I've been body-snatched by a Martian.

For a second, I forget what I'm doing, standing at the pantry with my hand on the doorknob. It's been happening more and more lately—these freeze-ups—whenever I start to dwell on how different everything got when Ms. Opal left, how unrecognizable my life became when Trevor's leash slipped through my fingers—

"Mortimer?"

I turn toward Mom. After the incidents at the end of the school year—the multiple freeze-ups in front of class, to be exact—she knows about this . . . paralysis thing I have going on lately. She always keeps an eye out for moments like this, when I get so lost in my thoughts, I forget what I'm doing. Forget to even move.

I snap out of this one just in time, tugging the pantry door open. Throwing her off the scent.

"I said it's nice to see you—" Mom stops herself. "Well, it's just nice, that's all."

I hold her gaze for an extra second, but don't respond. We've had this discussion. It never ends well. All summer long she's been urging me to get on with things, to get back to the way life was before. But what happened with Trevor happened. It can't be changed.

Life can't un-change. Neither can I.

I can't go back in time and pretend to not notice that bit of crumbling sidewalk. I can't rewind, force my old self to avoid thinking about which ordinance might've helped get it repaired. I can't go back and warn myself to keep a tight grip on Trevor's leash, or stop that squirrel from darting into the street at that exact second.

A loud clang rings out. Dad straightens briefly, takes his glasses from his mouth, puts them back on his face. He peers closer at the guts of the toaster oven. Any hope I had of this being the summer's very first quick (and successful) fix fades away.

I drag out my box of Frosted Mini-Wheats from behind the oyster crackers on the middle shelf. Mom keeps most cereals up on the top shelf, but mine live two shelves lower—yet another reminder of my height challenges. Mom's always doing her best to make sure I never have to reach too far for anything I might need.

She trades out which hand is holding her mug and decides against delving deeper. "What time is Frankie supposed to get here again?"

"Seven." I grab a bowl. "First walk is scheduled for seven fifteen."

We glance at the clock together. Not even 6:00 a.m. "Oh, you've got plenty of time."

She's right, but suddenly I feel like the minutes are counting down and my opportunity to back out is running away from me. A familiar cold sweat, as common lately as those freeze-ups, breaks out on the back of my neck.

Why did I agree to this? Why did Frankie ask? I handed over my dog-walking business to him months ago because I couldn't do it anymore. Not after Trevor. So why start pestering me nearly every day to join him on one of his early morning routes? And now I'm doing it, which is . . . insane. What if something goes wr—

An urgent zap splits the air in the kitchen. The box of Mini-Wheats falls right out of my hand. Dad kicks it with his heel as he bursts backward. His glasses skitter to the floor. He cries out in pain.

"Nick!" Mom yells. She rushes over to him, unplugging the toaster oven after she slides to a sock-footed stop.

"I'm okay," Dad says, clutching his hand and wincing.

Mom tugs at his fingers, trying to locate his injury. "Let me look."

"I said I'm fine, Liv," he snaps. Snapping is not a normal Dad thing. Never has been, anyway. Lately, though, with each new job around the house he tries to take on without quite succeeding, he seems more and more agitated. Lately, snapping has *become* a Dad thing.

And I don't like it much. Neither does Mom.

He finally lets go of his own hand and shakes it out. As far as I can tell, everything looks normal. No burns or cuts. Not a single mark. All his fingers seem to be working. He's moving them, at least.

It takes a split second for Mom's worried expression to turn angry. "I've told you to unplug these things before you decide to mess with—"

"Are you seriously going to lecture me right now?" Dad shouts as he stomps toward the stairs. "I'm just trying to help."

Mom chases after him, huffing out her own frustration.

After a few seconds of distant yelling, I pick up the box of cereal from the floor and make my way to the table. Fill my bowl. No milk today. Better to let the crunching fill up my ears. Helps keep out all the other sounds.

At 6:45 a.m., I'm just pulling on a fresh T-shirt when the doorbell rings. Even with the Red Devil around, I didn't think there was any chance Frankie would be here early. My neighbor's crowing volume is about 50 percent quieter on Frankie's end of the neighborhood and my old friend is about 75 percent lazier than most of the kids I know. When we used to do sleepovers, I'd be up with his parents for almost an hour before he finally staggered down and joined us for breakfast.

"Our boy is not a morning person," Mr. Petillo used to say as we waited, struggling through small talk.

I really didn't expect to feel excitement, but I kinda do. I hurry downstairs, my feet running along the top edge of each step. I reach our front door and pull it open in a single motion, and there he is. Frankie Petillo. Taller and broader than me. Darker than me, too. Instead of smiling or grinning, though—anything to show he's as happy as I am that the day he's been bugging me about for weeks has finally arrived—my friend's eyes and mouth are wide open and panicked.

"Have you seen these?" he cries, holding a piece of paper so close to my face I can smell the ink. "They're all over the neighborhood."

The page is too close for me to read, so I grab it from his hands. Steady it at arm's length until the words come into focus. My pulse pounds in my ears as each sentence registers in my brain.

I'm looking at some kind of advertisement. Like, a flyer thing.

It's for a dog-walking business.

A dog-walking business that isn't Frankie's dog-walking business.

Run by someone named Will Cortez. Right here in Townsend Heights.

With cheaper prices than ours. Check that, cheaper prices than *Frankie's*.

"Did you pull this off a telephone pole?"

Frankie's mouth flattens into a grim line. "Don't you dare quote me some dumb rule about taking down signs.

This is important." He taps the back of the page I'm holding, hard enough for his finger to stab straight through the center. I let it go, and the sheet travels with his hand as he pulls it back.

The ordinances are important, too, I think to myself. To me, anyway. But I already know that Frankie Petillo doesn't care if Section 16-8 of the Townsend Heights neighborhood code doesn't allow for the improper removal of properly posted signs without cause or permission. So I urge code-enforcement Mortimer to bite down hard on his lip. The thing about being friends with Frankie is everything goes a lot better when you let him have his way.

"Who is *Will* Cortez?" I ask when, reading the sheet he's pushed back toward me again, I see the name of the new dog walker for the second time.

It's confusing, because our new neighbors, the rooster owners, are named Cortez. But old Mr. Cortez's name isn't Will. Is it? Suddenly I'm not so sure. What I am sure of is a guy his age couldn't possibly start a dog-walking business here in Townsend Heights. Our streets are so ridiculously steep, most people dread walking their *own* dogs. A business to walk everyone else's, like the one I started almost two years ago now, the one Frankie inherited from me, could only be run by a young person. I mean, I *guess* an adult could do it. If they were some kind of triathlete—an Olympian or something.

"Well, that must be the granddaughter, then," Mom says over my shoulder, and I jump. I didn't even hear her come up behind me. "I remember thinking her name was a little unique. I had no idea she was starting a dog-walking service, though. Sorry, guys. Guess you have some competition."

At first, I'm nodding like everything she's saying makes perfect sense. Like, "Oh, yeah, sure. Must be the granddaughter." But then my head spins around to Mom, all herky-jerky. *The Walking Dead*–zombie style.

And Frankie and I shout the same words at the exact same time.

"Granddaughter? What granddaughter?!"

CODE OF ORDINANCES—TOWNSEND HEIGHTS

Sec. 16-1—Sign restrictions / Advertising; posting or painting in certain places prohibited

It shall be unlawful for any person or persons to post or paint advertisements of any kind whatsoever on any of the streets or curbing of the gutters, flagging, gutter stones, or wooden or iron railings of any public buildings. Signage on public utility poles is only permitted at allowable limits.

Sec. 16-8—Signs / Sign removal

Excepting the existence of special council-granted permission, it shall be unlawful for any person or persons to remove properly placed bills, posters, or dodgers from any public telephone or electrical lampposts or poles.

Sec. 16-#!@*&%—No fair stealing my PlayStation fund

It shall be totally annoying to try to open another Townsend Heights dog-walking business and steal my customers so that I

can't save enough to pay for the PlayStation
I want!

Signed, Frankie J. Petillo

As we walk, Frankie keeps muttering the same thing over and over. "This can't be happening. This can't be happening. This can't. . ."

The thick air that always weighs down the Heights this time of summer seems extra heavy this morning. Maybe it's the tons of Will Cortez, Dog-walker Extraordinaire signs we pass, stapled to just about every telephone pole. I'm looking for a violation—some technicality to allow removal—but I can't find a single one. These kinds of ads are allowed at a specific height, to keep Townsend's utility poles from looking wallpapered, and all of Will's placements are exactly right. It's as if she actually bothered to spend a few minutes researching our ordinances.

Something Frankie would never do in a million years.

It's weird how he doesn't even care about so many of the things I love. The ordinances, for one. And the council meetings. Even Ms. Opal. He always wondered why I spent so much time with her, made me feel like I had to explain why I thought it was cool to hang out with a neighbor as old as our grandparents.

Not that I didn't sometimes question it myself. Ms. Opal had lived next door to us my whole life. The day Mom and Dad moved to the Heights, of course she'd been the first one to greet them. For my part, her face was the first one I could ever remember seeing—besides Mom's and Dad's, of course. She was a constant in all our lives, but especially mine. I spent as much time with her as possible. Sometimes it felt like I actually lived at her house, not ours.

But if it had been just that, Opal would've only been a close neighbor, a good friend. But she wasn't. Not by a long mile. Ms. Opal was the definition of inspiration to me. I think I liked hanging out with her so much because of all the things she did for the Heights—big things, small things, exciting projects, kinda boring stuff, too—not just for our streets, not just for our houses, but for all the people here. How she never forgot to check in with our neighbors, new and old. All the settling of disagreements and the creative solutions to problems that seemed impossible—at least to me.

Ms. Opal was the one who got our whole family involved in the Townsend Heights Council. Funny to think back now that it all started with Mom, not me. I still remember the morning the two of them had that three-hour coffee meeting at our kitchen table. Opal telling us about how she used to head up the council herself. Years and years ago. How, after she stepped aside, the Heights had stopped growing in the directions she'd once hoped it would. How she'd been secretly hoping for the right successor to come along, and had finally worked up the courage to ask Mom to run.

I swear I could see it in Mom's eyes—maybe sometimes I can read her as well as she reads me. She was agreeing to put in her name for head of the council before Opal had hardly finished her sentence.

It's funny, sometimes I think Mom forgets how close they were during that time, how inspired she'd also once been by Opal. What I remember is Mom got as wrapped up in our neighbor's enthusiasm and commitment as I ever was.

But that all seems like a lifetime ago now.

Seeing the way Opal made sure the people of the Heights felt important and heard made me look at our neighborhood way different from the way Frankie ever did. Different from any of the kids I caught the bus with down on Townsend Avenue every morning.

I was the only one of us who cared so much about all

the little details that made the Heights different, all the stuff I loved about this neighborhood. Mom said it made me unique. Frankie said it made me weird.

But Opal? She said it made me special.

I loved sitting with both of them—Mom and Opal, her place or ours—talking about the Heights. They had so many plans. They were ready to tackle them all together.

Slowly, though, things started to change. It turned out Mom and Opal were a lot more different than they'd realized. Ms. Opal never once cared about how many feathers she might ruffle, as long as she knew she was doing the right thing—but it soon became clear Mom was a lot more worried about finding compromises and keeping everyone happy than about charging ahead toward a goal.

For Opal, the ordinances were never about spending a bunch of time making sure people followed rules. They were always about making sure the rules followed the people. That every person in Townsend Heights had what they needed, felt free to be who they were.

My lawyer mom, on the other hand, grew more and more focused on understanding what the rules were and working within them. They started drifting apart, each one trying to help Townsend Heights in ways too different to let them stand together for much longer.

And somehow I got caught smack dab in the middle of it all.

This morning, walking with his face pointed skyward, gawking at each poster as we trudge up Townsend's steepest street, Liberty, Frankie struggles to hide how upset he is. I should be trying to help him somehow, maybe run home and grab Dad's precious Mr. Fixit home-maintenance stepladder, use it to rip these ads off the poles they're fixed to. But that would be violating Ordinance 16-8.

"I mean, is this even legal?" he asks, pointing at the latest poster.

I have to admit, this constant whining is getting on my nerves. "What, visiting grandparents? Yes, I'm pretty sure that's legal, Frankie."

After the big reveal that Will Cortez was my elderly neighbors' granddaughter, Mom told us the rest of what she knew. Which wasn't all that much. Only that she had heard through the grapevine—one benefit of having a mother who heads up the local council is she gets all the good gossip—that Will Cortez is about the same age as Frankie and me, and that she's visiting her grandparents for the last few weeks of the summer.

The rest Frankie and I pieced together on our own during a quick strategy session up in my room. One: for some reason, this Will decided to open a competing dog-walking business barely a day after arriving. Two: she had already stolen some of my friend's clients—Frankie had received a bunch of last-minute cancellations off this morning's schedule, and now he understood why. This led to three: it wasn't fair.

And also four: Will is a dumb name for a girl.

I should've called Frankie out when he shouted that last one into the air. I guess I hesitated because I didn't want to get him any more worked up than he already was. But if it isn't right to call a rooster a mean nickname, why should it be okay to say an actual person's name is dumb? Or wrong. Or anything other than what it is: their name.

Frankie shoots back his most annoyed Captain Obvious glower, chasing my sarcastic comment down the nearest gutter. "Hi-larious, dude. Visiting grandparents is legal, yeah, but it's also a waste of a good summer."

He gasps a little as he finishes his comeback. I've been noticing he's started to breathe more and more heavily as we've climbed higher up Liberty hill, heading deeper into the heights part of Townsend Heights. I wonder how he's been managing the intense dog-walking schedule our clients demand. Virtually every house in this neighborhood owns a dog. Like me before him, Frankie's been the lone Townsend service for months. He should be in great shape.

But he's panting like it's his first day on the job. "Anyway, that's not what I'm asking, Mr. Junior Council," he continues. Long, breathless pauses between every couple of words now. "I'm asking if it's legal to have two businesses that do the same thing in one neighborhood. There must be some kind of rule—"

"There isn't. And they're ordinances, not rules. Plus, I thought you didn't care about them."

"So you're saying there's nothing we can do?"

All the advice Ms. Opal gave me when I started the dog-walking business flashes into my brain. Her voice tends to do that, whether I like it or not. Especially in the past several months.

"Sure there is. You offer a great service. The best you can. No one will want to use someone else if you're doing an awesome job, even if your prices are a little higher." I reach out a hand. "Here, let me see your schedule."

Frankie frowns as he digs into his back pocket. He had mentioned making a list of today's appointments, but he'd been so worked up about Will Cortez, pacing while giving a speech about how close he was to banking enough for the latest PlayStation, I hadn't seen it yet.

His hand finally emerges with a crumpled piece of paper. Frankie tries to smooth it out on his thigh, but the page only grows more hopeless. He gives up and hands it over. It's totally unreadable, but not just because it's so wrinkled. It's also filled with tons of cross-outs, and double names in the same slot. Some entries are circled, others underlined. I can't even pull out the simplest information. Like who's first.

"Stay organized," I hear Ms. Opal's voice say again. "It goes a long way."

"What is this mess?" I ask Frankie, shoving his list back at him.

He snatches the sheet back, squints at it, and turns it upside down. But I guess it doesn't get any clearer to him, either, because he's forced to flip it around again. His eyes finally grow wide with recognition. He points near the top. "Look. The DiNuccis are first. What's so confusing?"

My turn again to focus on the spot where his finger is pointing. There's a line there, sure, and some letters, but they've clearly been erased at least once, written over, crossed out, and . . . more. Much more. Like, possibly he laid the sheet down in his driveway and let his dad run it over a few times. Or left it in his pocket when his shorts went through the wash.

But, yeah, sure. I see them now, at the very end of the first row of writing. Three slanted, not-crossed-out letters like the ones you have to squint at online to prove you're not a robot: *DiN*.

"How would anyone know what that means? And what about all these other times and letters? I can't figure out—"

"That's where I grouped some walks together. You know, so we could take advantage of having two of us. Get more done at once." Frankie waves his hand down the left side of the list. "My list of walks." Now, the right. "And yours." He points at some time slots with only a single column. "These we can do together. Trade off the leash. Give each other a little break."

I stop in my tracks. "Frankie, you know I can't walk any dogs. I said I'd help like, next to you, not . . ."

I open and close both fists. I think a freeze-up might be coming on. I fight it back the same way I always do. Picturing before in my head.

Months ago. Late afternoon, not early morning. But I still feel it, the burning sensation across my palm as Trevor's old, weathered leash slid from my grip. I still hear it, my retriever's barking as he streaked down the sidewalk and then into the road. I still see it, the bushy tail of that squirrel as it scampered up the tree on the other side of Prince Street. The wide eyes of the woman driving the car. I still smell it, the smoke coming from her squealing tires as she tried to stop in time.

And the worst part. Trevor, who always seemed to know what to do and when to run, standing frozen in the middle of the road. Like he was paralyzed there.

Frankie spins around to face me. The street's so steep here, even though he only got a few steps ahead of me, I'm already looking up at him. "I thought you were over that. I thought that's why you said yes."

Over it?

How do you get over something like that?

If he knows, I wish he'd tell me. I wish *anyone* would tell me.

"Come on, Mortimer. This is a *dog-walking* business. You said you'd help me today. What kind of help did you think I needed? An accountant? A receptionist? I mean . . . how many times did I have to ask you? And you finally say yes, and now what? You're backing out?"

As soon as he utters those words, I know that's what I really want to do. Back out. Because I never wanted to be out here in the first place. But when I said yes, he was so thrilled. Mom was beyond happy, too.

So I couldn't take it back. I'm starting to understand you can't ever really take anything back. Not all the way.

But, sure, now . . . I just want to go home. I don't even know what I was thinking, saying yes to him finally. I don't want to see a leash or a dog or owners of dogs . . .

Yes, I *want* to go home, but I can't. The look on my friend's face tells me that much for sure. His shock. His disappointment. He was totally counting on me today.

"No," I say, resignation in my voice. "I'm not backing out. I just . . . let's start by starting." Another Ms. Opal saying. Her words are the usually the ones I find when my own are lost. "You said the DiNuccis, right?"

I used to love stopping by the DiNuccis' house. Not only was their dog, King, a gorgeous husky with piercing eyes, one of the easiest walks in all of Townsend Heights, but they would also insist I stop in for the sweetest iced tea when I dropped King off again. On special days, the tea came with a big dish of Oreos. Mom never understood how I didn't work up an appetite walking so many dogs up and down so many hills. I blame the DiNuccis and their Oreos. Well, them and dozens of other customers offering thousands of other treats.

But now those Oreos and that iced tea seem like ancient history. Because as we walk up their driveway, all my mind conjures up is Mr. DiNucci's red face from the last council meeting, when he stood shoulder to shoulder with Mr. Brewster, complaining about "that Red Devil."

When he urged the council to *take steps.*

When he shouted that *something had to be done.*

That *this isn't that kind of neighborhood.*

I've lived here all my life. I've stepped inside more of these tightly packed, shotgun-style houses than almost anyone this side of Ms. Opal. Memorized the regal names of our steep streets. Liberty. Prince. Crown.

I thought I knew every inch of Townsend Heights. I thought I understood exactly what kind of neighborhood I lived in.

But I'm not so sure anymore. Not after months of constant rooster debate. I don't know how to make the Heights go back to the way it was. Maybe worse, as much as I try, I can't figure out what Townsend Heights is becoming, either.

This morning, everything about Mrs. DiNucci is gold—her hair and her fingernails and her necklace and her jangling bracelets and her giant sweatshirt, too. "Go Golden Lions" screams across the front of it. In the background, even though it's early summer and definitely not football season, a game is on at max volume. We can't see him, but we hear Mr. DiNucci reacting to some big play. "Oh, come on!"

"Did they just score?" Mrs. DiNucci shouts over her

shoulder. She seems alarmed.

There's a bunch of stomping. Mr. DiNucci appears at the far end of the hallway, still looking over his shoulder at the game on his big seventy-inch flat-screen. He's bald, and his old Golden Lions T-shirt looks like it might've fit him two sizes ago.

King paces alongside Mr. DiNucci, his bright eyes flashing in our direction. The dark circles of fur surrounding them always make him look like an evil plan is forming right in the center of his scheming dog brain. The truth is, he's probably just thinking about food.

Honestly, there's no such thing as an evil dog. Not in my book, anyway.

Mr. DiNucci's hand swims through a bowl of pretzels. "Not yet. About to, though." He half squints toward us. We're standing just outside their front door. "Frankie, my boy!"

Frankie waves back at him. "Hey, Mr. DiNucci."

"And Mortimer," Mr. DiNucci adds with quite a bit less enthusiasm. "Good to see you boys. Did we schedule a walk?" He snatches up a handful of the pretzels so fast the bowl teeters.

King, whose ears had perked up at the sound of Frankie's name, seems about to charge at us. More like, charge at the open door. But he senses the shaking bowl and decides to stay put. Clearly hoping for a mistake, one fallen snack to drop straight into his mouth.

"No," Mr. DiNucci, pointing down at King, orders his dog firmly. King obediently drops his butt to the floor. His tail thumps once, then stops.

"In or out, guys," Mr. DiNucci says to us almost as sternly. "Can't leave that door open too long. We'll be chasing this guy around all day long."

"Yes, sir," Frankie calls in. He holds up his wrinkled schedule. "And, yeah, I have King down for this morning. Is everything . . . are you still needing the service?"

"Why shouldn't we?" Mr. DiNucci calls back. "If we scheduled, we scheduled."

"You're worried about that other dog walker, aren't you?" Mrs. DiNucci, still standing beside us with one hand on the open door, realizes out loud. Her golden bracelets jingle and jangle as she gestures in the direction of my house. Or, rather, the one next door to it.

Mrs. DiNucci heads toward her husband, leaving the door open for us to walk in. "That's the one who . . . you know," she tells Mr. DiNucci with a lowered voice.

"Ah, gotcha." He thrusts a hand filled with pretzels in our direction. "Better watch out, buckoes. Got some girl trying to steal your business."

"And what about all that litter she's added to our telephone poles?" Mrs. DiNucci clucks.

"That's right," Mr. DiNucci agrees. "What's the council

doing about them, Morty?"

Here's the thing. Two things, actually. One, I have a name, and it's Mortimer. Not Mort, not Morty, definitely not Morticia. That's the nickname Chester Brewster—Mr. Brewster's son, who, of course, is in our grade—tried to stick on me back in fourth grade.

None of those. Just Mortimer, Mortimer Bray.

I walked Mr. DiNucci's dog for more than a year. He knows this about my name. And yet he still stands there calling me Morty.

The second thing? As much as I wish I could be on the council, I can't. I'm too young. And besides, Mom would never allow it. Mr. DiNucci knows *this*, too. But he's not the only one in the Heights who tends to ask *me* if some rule is going to change. Or be enforced. Or made up on the spot. Maybe because Mom's head of the council, and they think I have some kind of influence over her. If they only knew the truth is almost completely the opposite. Come to think of it, people probably keep asking because, even though I know I shouldn't, I usually can't help answering. At least that's how I was before all my freeze-ups started.

"Actually, they're all lawfully placed—"

"Well, it's just disgraceful," Mrs. DiNucci interrupts. "Such an awful look."

Her husband nods. "All I'll say is it warms the heart to see you boys out here protecting your business this way.

Out here keeping your customers."

Cheering erupts from the game, as if a big group of unseen people are encouraging Mr. DiNucci to continue this particular line of thinking. So he does.

"You boys have roots here, you know. Don't underestimate that." Even more cheering bursts from his television speakers and he turns his head fast, eyes focusing on the action. His shoulders droop with disappointment. "Now they scored."

"Are the Golden Lions playing today?" Frankie asks.

Mr. DiNucci laughs. "No, no. That's recorded from last year. I'm getting ready for the new season."

"You boys want a drink or something?" Mrs. DiNucci offers. "Got some fresh iced tea." Her golden bracelets clang and sing all over again as this time she points toward their kitchen.

"I think we'd better take King," Frankie says. Hearing his name, the dog rushes down the hall toward us. "If you're sure you'll be staying on as a client, that is," my friend finishes with a hesitant tone. I can tell he's a little shook now that he understands the reason behind all the other cancellations. The Robinsons and their corgi, Zelda. The Scott family and their terrier, Cocoa. The Dwyers and their dachshund, Relish.

I was hoping to see each and every one of them today. It was the part of helping Frankie I was looking forward to the most. Scratching the ears of old dog friends, doing my best to let them know how much I miss them. Trying to help them understand me going away wasn't any of their faults.

Frankie does his best to hide the fact he's on pins and needles as he waits for Mr. DiNucci's answer. He kneels and scratches at King's neck and collar, focusing his full attention on the husky so he doesn't have to meet Mr. DiNucci's eyes.

"Hundred percent," Mr. DiNucci says quickly, but Mrs. DiNucci steps in.

"It's, um, you walking the dog, though, Frankie. Is that right?"

From his kneeling position, my friend twists to check on me. Maybe it would've felt better if she had reached straight into my chest and grabbed hold of my actual heart. Still, Mrs. DiNucci isn't wrong to worry. She knows exactly what happened to Trevor. She knows who was holding his leash when it happened. Or who was *supposed* to be holding it.

"That's right," I gulp. "I'm not . . . this isn't . . . we're just hanging out."

A relieved expression passes over her face. She nods at me, staring directly into my eyes. Does she think I'm lying or something?

"A couple of months, boys, you'll see," Mr. DiNucci

says. "Everything'll get back to normal around here by then. You have my word. More importantly . . ." He nods at us seriously before he finishes, like if we only hear some of his words, it should be the ones he's about to say. "More importantly, you have Mr. Brewster's word."

We turn Frankie's crazy, unreadable schedule over three times before figuring out Mrs. Edwards and her bulldog, Monty, are next. We haven't finished walking King yet, but Frankie will be able to handle both leashes. There were times I would walk as many as five dogs at once.

The front door opens before we finish mounting the steps. "Hello, Frankie," Mrs. Edwards says, but she's actually staring at me, not him. Not just staring, the eyes behind her dark-rimmed glasses positively grin my way. The tufts of tight gray curls that fall down the sides of her forehead bounce. "And Mortimer." She lets out a huge, relieved sigh. "How long has it been?"

Ms. Opal had a ton of friends in Townsend Heights. We could hardly take five steps without her stopping and talking to someone, or petting a dog, or pulling some toy out of a hidden pocket for a toddler. But if I had to pick one person who was probably her best friend, I would say it was Mrs. Edwards. The woman she called Queenie.

The three of us used to sit and talk for an hour. Longer, even. But since Ms. Opal left, I've hardly said more than three words in a row to Queenie.

"A long time now," I say, breaking my record, trying for a smile even as Queenie's fades.

"Okay. Inside." She vacates her doorway and waves us in.

Frankie points at King. "Actually, we have to keep go—"

"Did that sound like a request, young man?"

Frankie glances at his feet. "No."

"All right, then. Get your skinny butts in here."

"Fresh out of the oven," Queenie says a few minutes later. The tray she's carrying—two perfect muffins, two tall glasses of milk—clatters in her shaky hands before she manages to set it down safely on the coffee table.

The sticky sweet scent of the muffins reminds me of the last time I sat here eating one. Months ago now, with Ms. Opal sitting next to me on this couch instead of Frankie.

"It's *so* good to see you again, Mortimer," Queenie says now. She gingerly lowers herself into a chair across from us. No muffin for her, just a cup of tea perched on a delicate saucer. "Mr. Frankie here *never* stops in when he picks up Monty."

Queenie glances to her left, where her slobbering bulldog, Monty, is on the wingback chair that, as far as I know, no one ever sits on but him. He's going to town on one of his legs, chewing at it so hard I'm afraid he might be trying to remove the thing. He hears his name, though, and looks up with an expression that seems to ask, "What? Am I missing something?"

I nod back at her, eye the muffin in front of me, but resist reaching for it. "I've, um, been kinda busy."

Queenie cocks an eyebrow at me. "Busy getting lots of folks worried about you, much as I can tell. You here to hand out one of them flyers again?"

She's talking about the notices I sometimes distribute for Mom, the ones that announce to the older Townsend residents an emergency council meeting is coming up. The last time I came by and got away with my three words, it was probably for that. Council business is the one thing I've kept up with since Trevor. That and taking care of Cinnamon every day.

I don't know why I feel like I can manage those, when everything else seems like it's way too much for me.

"Not this time." I decide to take the muffin. Partly out of politeness, but also because it occurs to me that filling up my mouth with hot blueberries has an outside chance of stopping her from asking me all these questions.

"My stars, I cannot listen to a single minute more of that man shouting nonsense about that little rooster. Never seen nobody so scared of a two-foot-high bird. I wish he would just leave those people alone."

"Well, yeah," Frankie interrupts. He's trying to chew muffin, swallow milk, and make some kind of urgent point all at the same time. "But those people are really making things much more difficult for their own neighbors, don't you think? Same goes for their granddaughter."

"How's that now?"

"Well . . . ever since they got here, everyone's arguing about that rooster, and . . . and . . . things aren't the same. There hasn't even been a block party."

"That's not their fault," I say quickly.

Frankie and Queenie both turn to stare at me. I stuff more muffin into my mouth. Another strategy, this time to stop my mouth from vomiting out the rest of what's in my head.

It's not their fault there hasn't been a block party. It's mine.

"You're not going to let her walk Monty, are you?" Frankie asks, suddenly cutting straight to the point. "He's one of my favorites. Always has been."

Favorite? All Frankie's ever done is complain about Monty. The bulldog doesn't even really walk. He lumbers. So. Slowly. Sure, at least he doesn't try to drag you down the middle of the street like some of the bigger, more excitable dogs, but that's only because he doesn't do much of anything else, either. All Monty is, I have to admit, is a giant pain in the rear. If he smells something interesting, he digs in with that low-center-of-gravity body of his and those heavy legs, and you could tug all day without budging him.

Mrs. Edwards frowns. "I guess that depends. Your new competition did stop by here. I've seen her ads, too. Have either of you met Will? Lovely young lady. Very sweet. Clearly conscientious. Did you know she had a dog-walking business back in California?"

I didn't even know she came from California. I guess I don't know anything about her, come to think of it. Except that she's in my friend's way. And that, according to him, she has a dumb name for a girl.

Slowly, I shake my head no. Frankie does the same.

Queenie purses her lips. "Well, I do like her. But no, that doesn't mean I hired her. Not yet." She leans toward Frankie, locking eyes with him. "Here's the best way I can answer your question, son. I really don't think I ask for that much. Just a little reliability. Do you think you can promise to start showing up on time? No shortcuts or hurry-up walks? No bringing back dogs who haven't done their business yet? Because . . . I have to say, this Will, she had all sorts of references, mostly people—according to the sheet she passed out—who said she was never late. Not once. Because, you know, when you don't show up when you're supposed to, it puts me in a real bind."

I can't believe what I'm hearing. Hurry-up walks? Shortcuts? Not showing up? The whole reason I gave Frankie the business was because I knew I wasn't responsible enough to be running it anymore. Not after what happened to Trevor. Not after the freeze-ups that started that very week and haven't let up ever since.

Even though I knew it was more about the money for him than it had ever been for me, his PlayStation and the games for his PlayStation plus maybe, if he was lucky, a new phone and accessories for the new phone . . . I still thought he would at least work hard. Feel the need to do the right thing.

I guess I thought what he inherited would matter as much to him as it had to me.

As I listen to Queenie, though, the truth slowly dawns on me. Frankie wasn't begging me for help these past few weeks because he missed hanging out with me. He thought I might be able to save his business. The one it sounded like he's been gradually ruining.

Do I think he needs an accountant or a receptionist? Is

that what he asked me outside? Yeah, matter of fact, I do. Maybe one of each.

No wonder he was so tired on Liberty. He's not in shape because he hasn't been walking like he should be. Exactly how many walks has he cut short? Or not shown up for at all?

Now I understand why so many clients canceled his service so quickly after Will posted her signs. It wasn't lower prices. His clients—my old clients—would probably pay double just to get someone to actually show up and give their dog a complete walk.

Frankie feels me staring at the side of his face. I know he does, because he's staying so intent on looking straight ahead at Queenie, who at that moment spreads her arms out to her sides. "I don't know. All I know, boys, is I'm too old to have to be worrying about having to walk my own dog. Especially when I've already hired someone else to do the job. These days, I just want to settle in with a cup of tea and watch my *Price Is Right.*"

Monty's back to trying to chew his own limb off. Really going to town, chuffing and panting, totally intent on his project. All of a sudden, he senses the room staring at him and freezes, mouth still on his leg but eyes cutting toward us.

Frankie tears his gaze away from the dog, his head nodding unnecessarily fast now. "Yes. Totally. Absolutely.

Reliable. I can do reliable. Maybe . . ." He bites his lip but doesn't meet my eyes when his next words come out. "Maybe Mortimer will be able to help me out some."

Queenie sits up straighter. "Oh, Mortimer! You're coming back?" Frankie looks at me and nods, like he's trying to silently let me know what my response should be. I ignore him as hard as he ignored me a few seconds ago. "Are you letting your mother get you that dog finally, too?"

I feel the color drain out of my face.

I can't believe Mom would talk to Queenie about the dog that we've agreed over and over isn't getting gotten, because I can't . . . I can't . . . I won't . . .

Oh no. Not another freeze-up. Not here. Not now.

I stand up before it can take hold. "I think I should . . . we have to go."

I watch as Queenie's face falls, and somewhere deep inside me, near my heart or my gut or maybe both, I feel bad that I've made *her* feel bad. But that can't be helped right now. This is all too much. I've been so careful to stay away from situations like this, from people who might force me to talk about Trevor, about what happened, about how I—

"We really should finish walking King," I explain. "And Monty seems ready to go, too."

Monty drops his chin flat on the chair cushion, huffing out drool.

Frankie stands with me. "Right, right. We should keep moving," he agrees. "Gotta stay on schedule. Part of being reliable, right? You won't be sorry, Mrs. Edwards. You're making the right choice. That Will person doesn't do half the things she promises anyway."

Queenie's disappointed gaze at me morphs into surprise. "Hold on a minute. We are talking about the same girl, aren't we? From the posters? Will Cortez?"

"Yeah, she says she's cheaper, but my parents . . . you know . . . it's not really, um, true." Frankie's voice falters and then fades as he reaches the end of his sentence.

"Well, now. That is interesting," Queenie says. But her tone doesn't sound interested at all. It sounds . . . confused. Doubtful.

"Who knows if those references are even real?" Frankie hurries to add. "She could've just typed them up herself."

"Can't say I asked for any phone numbers." Queenie looks between us. "Not that it matters much, honestly. I've worked with you boys for a long time. Monty likes you both." This time, at the sound of his name, Monty rises to all fours, sneezes loudly, and jumps off his chair, nearly face-planting onto the rug. He ambles toward Queenie, who reaches down to stroke the top of his head.

I hear a rustling to one side as Frankie grabs Monty's leash. He crouches in front of both Queenie and Monty, attaches it to Monty's collar, stands up again. The entire time, Queenie continues to stare at me. Neither of us speaks.

"Okay," Frankie says. "We got him. Full walks. Promise. All the business he wants to do, until there's completely no more business left in his—"

Queenie holds up a hand to stop him before he goes too far. "That's enough, dear."

"Right," Frankie agrees. "Right. Okay, be back in a jiff. I mean, not a jiff! As long as it takes. We'll be back after that."

He yells for King, whose collar jangles as he returns from whichever corner of the house his investigation brought him to.

I will my feet to move, to follow Frankie toward the door, out of the house. Out of this conversation.

As I pass Queenie's chair, though, she reaches out her small hand and grips my wrist. "Monty likes you *both*," she says. "And so do I." Her hold tightens, forcing me to stop trying to escape. "Mortimer, please. Listen to me. I like you, and I *trust* you, too. You know that, don't you?"

I nod at her, but the truth is nobody should trust me with anything.

Not ever again.

Outside Queenie's gray house, Frankie does a little hop-skip around a curbside garbage bin before stumbling toward the other side of the street. As his head whips around to check both ways for traffic, I notice how huge his grin is.

"Better than I thought!" he cries with glee. "Two clients, both staying. If this keeps up, I'll still be able to snag the new *Call of Duty* bundle."

I follow him across the street, but my stomach grumbles harder with each step. Eventually, I feel myself stopping in the middle of the road, even though I'm pretty sure my brain is continuing to submit orders to my feet. They're supposed to be moving.

The back of my neck heats up.

I avoided freezing up a minute ago, inside Queenie's house, but this time I'm powerless against it.

As soon as Frankie reaches the opposite side, he spins around, excited. "Are you going to get the same—" He stops talking when he notices my expression.

I force my mouth, at least, to move. "You didn't tell me Will is walking Einstein. Your own dog? Why?"

Despite not being the brightest animal I've ever met, I've always liked Einstein, Frankie's pet Weimaraner. If for no other reason than she and Trevor used to be such good friends. They had some tip-top wrestling matches, and raced each other constantly—in circles in both our yards—to be the first to leap into Frankie's pool. One time our parents even let us take them to a minor league baseball game on Bark in the Park night.

"Well, she's not, technically," he starts slowly. "Not yet, anyway. But they threatened me with it this morning. That's how I knew to look for her signs." He points at the nearest pole, and there's one of Will Cortez, Dog-walker Extraordinaire's perfectly positioned posters again. Then, in an imitation of his mother's voice, he says, wagging his finger at me: "If you forget to walk that dog of yours one more time—"

"You aren't even remembering to walk your *own* dog?"

He loses the grin and slaps his hands on both thighs,

frustrated all over again. "I might've forgotten once, okay?" He pinches his fingers together like he was *this close* to remembering. Then he shows me his wrinkled schedule. "It's just there are so many appointments to keep straight. You didn't warn me this job would be such a—"

"Such a what? Such a job?"

A car turns the corner, blaring music. It's headed straight for me. Not that it's driving fast or anything, but I'm definitely in the way. And despite what happened to Trevor . . . or maybe because of it . . . despite absolutely seeing this Prius coming right at me, somehow I still don't move. My legs remain locked in place. I start breathing really heavily.

The heat in my neck turns into full-out sweat. Even before it's officially started, I can already tell this is going to be the worst freeze-up I've ever had. It's almost like I'm not in my body anymore. Like I'm watching myself from above. I know what I have to do, what my legs and feet have to do. They're just refusing. Totally on strike.

It's as bad as those presentations at the end of the school year. When I would get in front of the room and suddenly be unable to speak. Unable to move.

Even when Bryan Landry threw that eraser hard at my head, I just stood there, blossoming black eye and everything. Mrs. Cronenworth grabbed my shoulders and snapped her fingers in front of my eyes. And Bryan mumbled, "I figured he'd dodge it," as he headed out the door, marching to the principal's office, while I ended up at the other end of the school with the nurse.

"Get out of the road," Frankie says in a tone that makes it sound like he believes I'm pranking him or something.

I'm not. Not at all. But he's right. I should move.

But I can't.

I can't. I can't. I can't.

Frankie repeats that thigh-slapping motion more emphatically this time, twisting his head, angling his neck. He screams my name.

"Mortimer!" His voice sounds way different. Is that . . . is he actually worried about me?

My feet are *so* heavy. My face is flushed and hot. The sweat building on my neck feels like someone stuffed a sponge down my collar.

I gulp and find my voice. "You *lied* to Queenie. How could you tell her I was going to be helping you? We already talked about—"

"I'm not even kidding right now, Mortimer! Move!" Frankie lifts his hands, a frustrated, desperate motion. The leashes in each one swing with them. King and Monty both look back at the wild gestures, the flopping chains, the panicked shouting.

When he sees I'm still not moving, his tone grows defensive. "Come on. I had to say something, didn't I? I needed to keep her as a customer. You want me to save your business, don't you? I mean, whose side are you on here?"

"It's not my business, Frankie. Not anymore. And I told you, the way to save it is by working hard. How many other people have you 'maybe' forgotten?" I ask. I make the question worse by imitating his "close call" motion, my fingers pinching theatrically.

"I don't know," he says, his head bobbing as his frustration turns to anger. "Do you want a quarterly report or something?"

"What I want is for you to take care of the business I gave you. I want you to not lie to our customers."

"The business you dumped on me, more like. And I thought they were *my* customers now, not *yours*."

The approaching car, completely stopped now, music turned down to a whisper, issues a polite toot of its horn.

"Seriously, dude." Frankie steps into the street and, doubling the leashes into one of his hands, grabs my arm with the other. He pulls me the rest of the way across. The force of his tugging finally loosens whatever glue was keeping my feet fixed to the pavement.

The way finally clear, the car zips past us. As soon as it's gone, my neck starts to cool down. My flushed face feels like it's shrinking back to normal. Despite our argument, I almost thank Frankie for helping me when I couldn't help myself for a second there. I half smile at him. He grins back.

It's hard to stay mad at Frankie, even in moments like this one, so I focus on taking a deep breath to quiet my nerves. We walk to the next customer on the list.

Our truce doesn't last long, though, because the next several houses turn out to be a string of clients who have already decided to switch to Will Cortez's new service. The bad news hits Frankie harder with each stop. We keep hearing the same reasons for the change. Reliability. References. Responsibility.

After a while, we stop asking why. I don't think Frankie wants to hear it anymore.

A few clients, most of them friends of the Brewsters or the DiNuccis, stick with us. Er, with Frankie. Usually after forcing us to endure strange speeches about how proud they are to see us fighting for our rights and jobs.

The final four houses of the morning route, however,

make up a string of nonstop letdowns, ending with the Hamadas and their Pomeranian, Lucy. The little puffball doesn't even make an appearance as Mrs. Hamada gives us the bad news. I feel another pang in my gut over not getting to see another old friend.

The Hamadas live at the top of Liberty, where it meets Prince Street. The end of this morning's route. No more dogs to walk, no more customers to lose. We find ourselves standing at the corner of Liberty and Prince, the only spot in all of Townsend Heights that makes me shiver.

Where the vacant lot is.

And no, not *a* vacant lot. *The* vacant lot.

The rough patch of dirt that's been on this corner my whole life and, I'm pretty sure, much longer than that. It never changes. Always surrounded by a heavy chain-link fence with foreboding barbed wire. Always sporting the big white signs with blue and red lettering reading No Trespassing and City Property, the ones that remind us the city owns it. The lettering on those signs is so big and bold, it practically shouts at us to stay away, even as the rest of the lot whispers the opposite temptation: come closer, we have dark secrets hiding in here.

It's a Townsend Heights bus stop tradition to come up with newer and more interesting rumors about the vacant lot every school year. The fence is electrified. A mob boss is buried in the center. It's pirate loot. Nuh-uh, it used to be a graveyard.

"I'm telling you, if they ever build on that thing, we're talking a total poltergeist situation," Tommy Tatum said one day. "You heard it here first."

I used to like being the one everyone looked to when rumors about the Heights like those would start to spread. Kind of hard to believe now, with the way I feel panicked if someone so much as glances my way, never mind expects me to actually talk.

Back then, though, everyone would wait for me to chime in to dispel Tommy's latest made-up story. I mean, all I used to have to do was ask Ms. Opal for the truth. She knew everything about every inch of grass and concrete along these streets. But she would never answer questions about this lot. She didn't want to talk about it at all, even got angry when I pressed her on the subject. That was the only time I remember her getting truly mad at me, and believe me, I paid attention. I never asked her about the vacant lot again.

Ms. Opal hated this corner. If we walked by it, she would either avert her eyes entirely, or stop and stare between the links of the fence, as if some tractor beam had locked onto her and pulled her toward it.

Two completely different reactions that seemed to say

the same thing—something did haunt this spot, our vacant lot. Or at least, something here haunted Ms. Opal.

Usually, whenever I come close to this corner, I keep moving as fast as my short-for-a-twelve-year-old legs will carry me. Frankie knows I feel this way. Always has. But right now, he either doesn't remember or doesn't care, because he's stopped right in front of the fence.

I'm forced to stop with him. I try to calm my skipping heart and steady my breathing. Avoid any more freeze-ups.

"You all right?" I ask, hoping the question will remind him we're supposed to keep moving.

"Am I all right?" Frankie kicks at a rock near his foot. It doesn't budge, and he cries out in frustrated pain. "We just lost half our clients!"

I'm not sure what to say. Before I can come up with something, my friend looks away from the rock he's abusing, taking aim at me instead.

"This is your fault, Mortimer."

"My fault?!"

"I thought you'd come back and help me out, not just disappear on me like you did."

I take a step back, almost can't believe what I'm hearing. "You thought . . ." I'm having a hard time speaking the words my brain has converted his into. "You figured what I was going through, what I'm still—" I'm panting now. I have to gulp to finish. "What? That it was temporary?"

"Dude, you have to get over it eventually."

"Who says? You think I'm—that this is all some kind of choice for me?" I stop, waiting for him to respond, but he just stares back at me, like I've hit the nail right on the head. "I can't believe—"

I swallow again. Can't believe what? The way he's coming at me right now? That I didn't know this is clearly what he's been thinking, not just now, but probably for a long time?

Can't believe what happened before, with Trevor? Or before that, with Ms. Opal?

Can't believe my friend seems to care more about a PlayStation than me?

Can't believe I thought I'd done something brave this morning? That I was actually proud of myself. And why? Because Mom seemed happy I was doing it?

Agreeing to help Frankie wasn't brave. It wasn't "turning a corner" like Mom kept suggesting. It was just me being dumb. Dumb for thinking I could be around my old business without everything falling apart. Dumb for hoping I could somehow change what happened before, or make a difference with whatever's going to happen next.

"Stupid," I mutter at myself.

"What'd you call me?" Frankie spits back.

And I guess I should tell him that I wasn't calling *him* that, that I was talking to myself, but by the time I pull myself together and look up, Frankie's not in front of me anymore. My eyes find him almost a block away already, heading down Prince toward his house.

"From now on, I don't need your help, Mortimer," he yells over his shoulder at me. "Just leave me alone."

CODE OF ORDINANCES—TOWNSEND HEIGHTS

Animal Control Section, Definitions

Attack

An approach to a person or persons by an unrestrained animal in a vicious, terrorizing, or threatening manner or apparent attitude of attack, without the animal having been teased, molested, provoked, beaten, tortured, or otherwise harmed.

Restraint

An animal is under restraint under the meaning of this ordinance if it is (1) controlled by means of a chain, leash, or other like device; (2) on or within a vehicle being driven or parked; (3) within a secure enclosure; or (4) within the dwelling house of the owner.

Friendly Fire (FF)

When Frankie and I used to play *Call of Duty* in Team Deathmatch Mode, he'd always scream, "No FF!" into my ear when I almost hit him accidentally.

No Friendly Fire.

I did it more than I want to admit. Truth

is, I kind of suck at *Call of Duty*. But I never meant for it to happen. You're not supposed to hurt your teammates. You're not supposed to injure your friends.

But maybe that's only true in *Call of Duty*. I guess in real life people sometimes do it on purpose. And they don't even care how it makes the other person feel.

—From the secret files of Mortimer Bray

It takes me a lot longer than usual to get back down Liberty hill. My shouting match with Frankie bounces around my head the whole way home. We've never been so angry with each other before.

Almost there, I keep telling myself, willing my legs to keep moving. By the time I make it to the front of the Cortez house, these little inner chants have changed to *One more house* and *Just a few feet more*.

But then I stop completely.

Because . . . the Cortez house. I'm right in front of the bluish-gray two-story with its parallel driveway and front walk, the garage set way, way back. And this is the first time I've called it that in my head.

The Cortezes live here now. Ms. Opal is long gone.

Sometimes I gaze at it out of my window, reminding myself of that. Now I stop directly in front and face it, doing the exact same thing.

When my rooster neighbor cock-a-doodled me out of bed this morning, I'd never even heard of their granddaughter, Will Cortez. Now it's barely lunchtime, and I just spent a big chunk of my day trying to stop her from . . . what? And why?

It's like Ms. Opal's standing right next to me, looking back at her old house, wondering why we're outside it, rather than inside. "Because I never welcomed the people who replaced you," I whisper to her. "Because . . . I think I thought the fact they replaced you made them my enemies."

A copper-colored Hummer charges past me, racing up my street. It moves so fast, wind blows through my hair. The big SUV comes to a sudden, fishtailing stop a few feet beyond me.

Everyone in Townsend Heights knows this Hummer. Even as fast as it passes me by, I make out the owner inside. Mr. Brewster. Next to him in the passenger seat sits his son, Chester. Standing up in the back seat, his head out the window and his joyous tongue wagging in the wind, is their big boxer, Teddy. He's the only one who notices me. I can tell by the way he pants happily in my direction. I can see the only thing he's thinking about written plainly on his face.

Car ride!

Dogs are so much simpler than people. They just love what they love. They don't overthink it.

Teddy's probably not thinking of yesterday. He's not wondering what tomorrow will bring, either. Heck, forget tomorrow, he probably hasn't thought about *later today* in all the hours since he woke up this morning. He's only worried about right here, right now. Making the most of this moment.

Sure, dogs are simpler than we are. Or maybe the better way to say it is that dogs are *smarter* than people.

Up front, in the driver's seat, Mr. Brewster's expression is serious. He's a man on a mission.

Chester just looks bored. Then again, the Brewster family could be going over Niagara Falls in a barrel together instead of pulling up to our curb and Chester would still have that same flat expression on his face, like he was letting everyone know to clue him in when something actually exciting finally happens.

The truck shuts off and the door springs open. Mr. Brewster levers his giant frame out. Swipes his huge, meaty hands over the top of his hood as he rounds the front. Rubs a shoulder over his full, dark beard. Firms his grip on the big rolls of paper tucked under his other arm.

I stare at him, shocked. Feel another freeze-up coming on. Clench my teeth against it. My eyes move to Brewster's rolls of paper. What are those? Plans of some kind? Blueprints, maybe?

It takes him a second to notice me. His determined expression breaks into a warm smile as he takes me in. It's like he physically puts the smile on his face, the same way Dad pushes his glasses up his nose first thing every morning, or the way an actor glues a fake mustache onto his upper lip to play a role. "Mortimer! Your mother home?"

"I think so."

"Fantastic." He starts ahead, then abruptly stops. "I hear you're back in the dog-walking business."

His Red Devil nickname apparently isn't the only thing to spread through Townsend's streets like wildfire. We saw the DiNuccis, what? Less than three hours ago? And already Brewster's heard that Frankie and I did the rounds together this morning. Nothing wrong with the Townsend Heights gossip machine, that's for sure.

The towering man lowers his voice, which, as deep as it normally is, doesn't quite work like I think he means it to. "Proud of you and that friend of yours. Freddie, right?"

"Frankie."

"Sure. Listen, keep up the good fight." He seems about to turn away, but his expression changes again. His eyes turn up, like he just got an idea. "Actually . . . tell you what. Lord knows convincing that one to walk the dog he begged us to get him is like pulling teeth." Brewster points over at the Hummer and I inspect Chester more closely. He's sitting in front with his Beats over his ears and his Switch in his hands, same posture he always assumes on the bus. Somehow conveying intent and disinterest at the same time. "You boys should give me a call. The least we can do—*should* do—is support a community business." Brewster reaches into his pocket, extracts a business card, and extends it toward me.

I asked him if he needed someone to walk Teddy two years ago, when the boxer was still a puppy. Back then Brewster had given me the flattest no I'd ever received from a Townsend neighbor.

Now? He pushes the card toward me a little more, tempting me with it.

I'll have to cross the ten feet between us to accept it. If I refuse, would he come toward me? Doubt it. He'd probably just stuff it in his pocket again and shake his head with disappointment. But if I do cross the space between us, what am I agreeing to besides promising to—maybe—call him?

In the end, the part of me that was trained by both Mom and Dad to be polite to adults wins out. I hurry forward, grab the card from his fingers, and step back again.

"Make sure you reach out soon, now, you hear?"

I nod, but don't respond.

Brewster seems about to say something more, but his phone buzzes. He takes it out of another pocket to check the screen. "Is that the time?" He doesn't wait for an answer. He hurries up our front steps, parking himself to wait under the light Dad changed two days ago before I even knew it was out. Light bulb swap-outs are one of the few projects he seems able to pull off without breaking anything.

Brewster rings our bell.

I stay where I am. I don't want it to seem like I came home with him or he brought me here or . . . I don't know what. That we're here together. I look down at the card. It reads *Reginald Brewster, CEO, BrewsterTech*. There are two addresses—the one here in the Heights, and one in Los Angeles.

Mom opens our front door, all beveled glass, the one she had to have when we moved in. She smiles up at Brewster, and I wonder if I smiled at him just like that a minute ago. I shudder a tiny bit.

Mr. Reginald Brewster of BrewsterTech crosses our threshold, and I swear it takes his shadow longer than it should to follow him inside. Like it's not his shadow at all, but some other dark creature that just happens to follow him around all day long.

When I walk through our front door a minute or so later, Dad's backing out of Mom's office. He's already in full snapping mode. "Well, it doesn't have to happen here, Liv."

"Are you asking me to leave, Nick?" Brewster's unseen but still booming voice comes from deep inside the office.

"As a matter of fact, yes, Reggie. I'd rather you two take your—"

All I see at first is Mom's hand. It bursts out of the office and lands on Dad's chest. The rest of her marches out soon after, her hand still flat against Dad's shirt, pushing him backward with each forward step she takes.

"No, he is *not* asking you to leave," she says. Her glowering eyes remain focused on Dad's face. "Because that wouldn't be up to him, would it, Nick?"

Mom's cheekbones clench as she waits for Dad to respond. He takes a quick step to back away faster than she's coming forward, and her hand falls away from him, back to her side. Mom closes the door behind her.

"Excuse us one second, Reg."

The door shut now, Dad tilts his head in shock and disappointment. "Reg? Seriously, Liv? What, you two are best buds now?"

Both my parents are so focused on each other, I don't think either one of them has noticed me standing in the foyer. I'm not about to alert them to my presence, either. The shouting has put me in a near freeze-up as it is.

"Don't be a child. You know what I'm trying to do here. This is my business, Nick. I'm responsible for—"

"It's all our business, Liv. Everyone in Townsend."

I almost pump my fist, because even though I'm not sure what's going on yet, it's exactly what Ms. Opal would've said.

"I'm handling it, Nick," Mom repeats, clenching her teeth even harder.

"Tell me how, Liv. What, exactly, are you doing to handle it?"

"Whatever I can, okay?" Mom swipes at the lock of hair

that tends to swim over her forehead when she gets worked up. "Whatever it takes."

"That's exactly what I'm afraid of. So help me, if you make some kind of half-baked deal—"

"Last time I checked, only one of us is on the council."

"So only council members are allowed to care? Only council members can have ideas or thoughts about what's happening in this neighborhood?"

I finally move, crossing into our front room quietly, sinking toward the window to stay out of sight. When I lean against the radiator, though, it creaks, and both my parents' heads dart in my direction.

"Oh, that's just great," Mom says, gesturing toward me.

Dad seems just as dismayed as she is. He stares at me a long moment before his shoulders slump. He shakes his head over and over. Slaps one hand onto his forehead.

"I can't be here." Dad starts to wander off, heading toward the basement door.

Watching him go, Mom matches my father's head shaking. She turns to me, her expression softening. "Mortimer, I—never mind right now. Just go upstairs, please. We'll talk later."

I nod. There's so much I want to say, but it is definitely *not* the right time.

Mom sighs heavily. She turns back to her office, taking a moment to straighten herself up. She takes a deep breath, flattens her wrinkled sleeves, and slaps on her own fake smile before reaching for the knob. Soon, the door clicks shut behind her, and she's gone.

I catch "Sorry about all that," before the voices fade. After that, all I pick up is rising and falling tones.

I stand there shocked. Neither of my parents even asked me how it went with Frankie.

As I push away from the radiator, taking a first step toward the stairs heading in the direction of my room, I catch quick movement out of the corner of my eye. Outside, in our front yard, Chester and Teddy have left the Hummer. No leash on Teddy, a clear violation of Townsend Heights Ordinance 45-7. Then Teddy squats and starts dropping his business on our grass. Chester notices, crinkles his nose, and steps away from his dog. He turns his attention back to his Switch.

His fingers fly wildly across the controls. I don't see a poop bag anywhere in them. Of course, he *might* have one in his pocket, but this is Chester Brewster we're talking about. It's highly doubtful.

Good thing I have a ton of poop bags from my dog-walking days. A whole box in the front hall closet. I know they're there, at least they should be, even though I haven't looked for them since I gave up dog walking.

And I'm not sure I can look at a poop bag now, either, but the flagrant ordinance violations going on right outside my door push me past that worry. I head up front, find the box, and grab a few bags. I hesitate one second, wondering if I should just leave it alone, but a high-pitched noise from inside Mom's office chases me outside.

No idea what all that's about, but the raised voices are stressing me out. I need to escape.

I'm not freaked out by Teddy dropping a bomb in my front yard. I was a professional dog walker. Trust me, I've seen it in all shapes and sizes. But picking it up's the right thing to do. The ordinances couldn't be clearer—the dog's owner is the responsible party.

When I reach Chester, I extend a blue poop bag out to him. "Here. On the house."

He crunches up his nose again before reaching up to push his Beats off his ears. They drop onto his shoulders. "What's this?"

"For Teddy's . . . you know." I point my chin toward the pile. Teddy's in the middle of kicking grass back on it. "You looked like you were missing one," I say when Chester only continues to stare at me with a bewildered expression on his face. I twist my head, pointing it in the direction of our front door. "I got a ton in there."

"Congratulations," he says. Then he gestures at the steaming pile. "If it's bothering you, be my guest."

I shake my head. My words come out weird, all halting-like. "N-No . . . Ordinance 45-9. You're the owner. You're responsible." I point at Teddy and his pile again, as if he didn't see me do it the first time. "Also, he's supposed to be on a leash. That's 45-7."

"Ordi-what now?" Chester reaches for his Beats again, like he's about to lift them back over his ears so I'll know for sure this discussion is over. "Dude, it's your yard. He's a dog. Whattaya want me to do? Make him use a toilet?"

"No, that's—"

Two doors burst open at the same time, almost like the movements were choreographed. Ours draws my attention first. Chester's father steps out of it, seeming in a huge rush. "We'll see what the rest of the council thinks," he says at full volume, looking back at Mom, who's coming out close behind him, brushing that same misplaced lock of hair off her forehead.

The other door that opens is the dark one next door. Mr. Cortez leans out, reaching low to pick something up. I squint in that direction. Looks like some kind of cage.

What happens next happens in slow motion. At least, for me it does.

From behind Mr. Cortez, the Red Devil himself, the little bird causing all the trouble this summer, struts onto the porch. His chest is out and his head bobs and pecks, eyes searching his surroundings. Mr. Cortez, focused on picking feathers from the wires of the cage, doesn't seem to notice.

But Teddy does. A few feet away from me, I catch the boxer's eyes going wide. His tail wags. In an instant, I read his intent. He's about to storm across the yards. To do what, I'm not quite sure. Nothing good, I'm guessing.

There's no time to think or plan or evaluate if I'm doing the right thing. I just move. Only with my first big step forward, my foot sinks straight into Teddy's fresh pile. My sneaker slides through the slick poop, painting the grass with what I know must be a long brown smear. Not that I see it. More like I feel it. Kinda smell it, too.

Like a distant echo, I hear Chester snort out, "Oh, nasty!"

Ignoring him and the stench, too, I stretch out one arm, searching for Teddy's collar. Just as the dog starts to dart away, my fingers find a spot inside the nylon. I close them tight.

Teddy bursts forward. I end up airborne, my body stretched out, completely parallel to the ground. Suspended in midair, no idea how I'll land, a poop smear on one sneaker.

I probably should've thought this whole thing through a little better. The dog I'm clinging to, the one much too big for me to have any business trying to stop on my own, doesn't seem to realize I'm attached to him at all. But when my arm straightens out and I offer the slightest resistance, he finally looks over his shoulder at me. A giant, surprised blob of saliva flings into the air from the tip of his tongue.

I hear Mom talking to Brewster behind me, but it sounds farther away than it should. "Reg, come on, be reasonable . . ."

"You have the plans," Brewster replies. "That's all I'm required to supply until the hearing." He sounds so calm, but that must be the moment Mom finally sees me, because when I hear her again, her voice is about as far away from calm as it can get.

"Mortimer!"

Teddy yanks me forward. My arm is pulled straight, fast and hard. Pain flashes a shade of red across my vision, like a paint brush just slapped me in the face.

I can't let go. As my body starts to descend toward grass again, as my shoulder flames up like it's actually on fire, I concentrate on exactly that: Not letting go. Stopping Teddy. Preventing disaster.

Because disaster's happening. Right now, it's happening. It's not something from before, a thing I can't do anything about because it's already done. It's not something that maybe might happen later, that I feel powerless to stop because I don't know its whens, its wheres, its hows.

Disaster's here—right here, right now.

Which means I *can't* let go, no matter how much holding on hurts.

I manage to stab my non-pooped foot downward,

spiking its pointed toe into the soft ground like an anchor. The boxer's head jerks backward. All at once, he stops. With my free hand, I clutch dirt and grass, coming up with a fistful of loose blades. I crash down roughly, and all the air goes out of my body with a *Whoomph!* The blob of saliva misses my face, thankfully, but still manages to land on my fingers, right across the knuckles.

Yuck.

Teddy checks behind him again, looking for what— or who—stopped him. When he sees me lying on the ground, he seems to forget about the rooster. He turns and his big, wet tongue slashes across my forehead. I end up with dog saliva on my face anyway.

Great.

I still don't let go of his collar. I can't—not until someone gets here.

Anybody. *Please.* Because this shoulder . . .

Mom screams my name again, but her voice is closer this time. She's on her way. "Mortimer!"

I look toward Ms. Opal's—the Cortezes'—porch and see Will out there now. She's cradling the rooster in her arms. Her eyes are wide. Pretty sure she guessed what might've been about to happen, too.

It might *feel* like slow motion, but actually Mom and Dad are on me in moments. Dad takes hold of Teddy's collar, helping to free my fingers from it, and I finally get the break I need. Mom's checking me all over, trying to figure out what I did to myself.

"I can't believe . . . what were you thinking?" Mom tries to meet my eyes, but I'm still kinda facedown. "Honey, are you okay?"

I'm fine, I'm about to say. But then I realize that I'm not fine at all, and I say a different thing entirely.

"I can't move my arm."

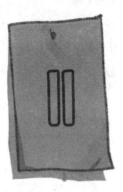

I spit out grass and try to lift myself off the ground. The stabbing pain in my shoulder stops me. I mumble a word, I think. I hope it's not something wimpy like, "Ow!" But that's probably exactly what I say.

Mom rubs my back. "Easy, Mortimer. Take it slow."

"Let's go," I hear Brewster saying. I manage to turn my head far enough to catch sight of him grabbing Teddy by the collar, ripping the dog away from Dad's grasp. Brewster waves at his son to follow him as he drags Teddy toward their Hummer. The boxer's goofy smile disappears, and he ducks his head in fear and shame.

"Now, hold on, Reggie, you can see my son is hurt here—" Dad starts to say, but Brewster cuts him off.

"Talk to them. It's their rooster that caused this mess." Brewster points vaguely at the Cortez family, all three of them on the porch now, looking across the yards with concern. It's my first proper view of Will, but lying on the ground like I am, all I really see is brownish hair and skinny arms and legs. It occurs to me this is probably her first look at me, too. The boy next door whose friend's business she's stealing. Flat on the ground, one shoe poop-smeared, my mother fawning all over me.

Awesome.

"And actually . . ." Brewster turns and waves at Dad. "Who gave your kid permission to restrain my dog like that? Could've hurt him." He yanks Teddy's collar way harder than I ever could've as he continues toward the Hummer. Teddy tucks his tail between his legs. He whimpers.

I'm still squirming, trying to sit up without putting any stress on my shoulder. Turns out it's not that easy. A desperate thought crosses my mind. That I'll never be able to use my arm again.

That what just happened is somehow permanent.

And, like clockwork, here it comes. The worry I've done another thing I can't take back. That there's no way to fix my mistake. It brings the panic, and the panic brings everything else. First the sweat, forming on my temple. Next my mouth, gone completely dry. A carbon copy of my last freeze up. Of all my freeze-ups.

After those first few happened in school, whenever I was the focus of attention, it seemed, they kept coming. Pretty much every time I tried to get back to my before-Trevor life—whenever I walked a dog, every time I had any sort of job to do, really—until I realized I couldn't handle responsibility anymore. I had to give it all up, starting with the dog-walking business. I was too afraid of messing up again. Worried someone else might get hurt.

And then came the arguments between my parents. After that, Mom's nonstop ideas, floated to Dad in whispers she thought I couldn't hear.

"He needs a new dog, that's what he needs," in hushed voices behind their closed bedroom door.

"I think Mortimer might benefit from a vacation, Nick. Let's go to Disney," thrown out at the breakfast table just as I started down the stairs.

"Just talk to him. He's obviously not listening to me," when they thought stepping into the frame of Mom's office doorway would keep me from hearing them.

The whispers brought more panic and the panic brought more sweat, more dry mouth. The feeling that I couldn't talk. Like I was *allergic* to talking, to standing in front of anyone, to being the focus of attention. Those times in class especially. I'd never felt anything like it. Heck, in fifth grade I'd been voted class clown. Mrs. Bagmore couldn't get me to shut up half the time.

Lately, all I wanted to do was stay quiet. Disappear, be invisible.

I can't breathe. It happens without any warning at all. My eyes go wide. Mom hears me gasping for air and launches into action, slapping me on the back, like I've gone back to infant days and she's burping me.

Smack! Smack! Sma—

Air swooshes out of me in a huge rush. I fight to pull it back in, catching my breath in heaves.

"Okay. All right," Mom says, calming down and going back to rubbing my back after hitting me so hard a second ago you'd think she was trying to send my spine through my chest. "You're okay. You're all right. Just breathe. Are you breathing?"

"I need to get up," I manage to hoarsely tell her. I try to stand on my own. With pain shooting through one arm like it is, though, the struggle is 100 percent real.

Mom fumbles, stuck between stopping me and helping me. She decides on helping, placing both her hands under the armpit of my uninjured shoulder. "Slow. Take it real slow."

Turns out I'm not quite ready to get all the way up yet. But, working together, we manage to spin me into a new position, with one of my knees on the ground. I'm able to use it to flip over and plop down again, end up sitting face forward with my knees bent toward my chest. Better than lying flat on my stomach.

I can see the scene playing out on our lawn better now. The whole Brewster clan's back inside their copper-colored Hummer. Doors slam. The SUV roars to life. It makes a three-point turn in the middle of Cromwell, then heads back out the same way it came in. Dad watches it go from the sidewalk.

"He's just leaving?" he asks, hands on his hips. "I can't believe that."

"I can," Mom says with a frown. She rests a hand on my chest and seems to be measuring its rises and falls. "Do you have air?"

I nod back slowly. Between deep inhales and slow exhales, I add, "I'm okay."

"You're definitely not okay, Mortimer," Mom assures me. She nods toward my shoulder. "What does it feel like?"

I glance at my dangling arm. "Like . . . it isn't there."

"Totally numb, or does this hurt?" She pokes at it.

I bite my lip and wince in response, and she has her answer.

"Nick," Mom calls. Dad's still staring down the street, even though the Hummer's long gone. As if gazing after it hard enough will force the Brewster family to come back and apologize. Take responsibility.

Yeah, right. Townsend Heights would probably freeze over first.

"Nick!" Mom repeats, louder and harsher this time.

Dad spins around.

"Get the car," she orders him, using her head-of-the-council voice. She might as well bang her gavel, call our family to order. Huh. I bet she really wishes she could do that sometimes.

This time, she succeeds in helping me to my feet, supporting my bad arm the whole way. "We're going to the hospital."

It's midnight by the time we pull back into our driveway. "Are you sure you can walk?" Mom asks me, concern etched in her expression.

"It's my arm, Mom, not my legs," I say, raising my wing, tucked into a sling now. "The only thing is my shoes." I step up onto our porch in my socks and glance backward.

"Your father'll get those." Mom gestures at Dad, making sure he heard her. He nods back. "Leave them on the porch, Nick. We'll see about rinsing them off in the morning."

It had taken a few minutes of silence on the way to the hospital for my parents to mention the smell, and another several confused seconds for me to remember that one of my shoes was covered in Teddy's poop. It was good, though, because Mom and Dad laughed together about it for a long while. They almost couldn't stop. It's been ages since I've heard that kind of laughter coming from both of them at the same time.

In the parking lot outside the emergency room, things got serious again. Mom carefully removed my sneaker from my foot, using only the tips of her fingers, as if she were defusing a bomb. She tossed it away, to the other side of the back seat. By then, Dad was in view again. He had run inside the hospital. He came back pushing a wheel-chair.

I started to protest, but Mom silenced me with, "I won't have you walking across this parking lot in your socks. What if there's glass?"

I felt kind of silly getting wheeled in when I could walk perfectly well on my own. At the same time, the throbbing in my shoulder had steadily increased during the fifteen-minute drive up Townsend Ave. Even the quick bounce over a speed bump made me feel like my right arm was about to completely detach from my body. So maybe getting pushed in wasn't the worst thing in the world. Besides, the waiting room was crawling with people. The wheelchair made my injuries look official and serious. The other patients, even the nurses, were forced to make a path for us.

I couldn't stop thinking about Ms. Opal. The day she left Townsend Heights in that ambulance. The last time I ever saw her. Almost the same thing, except she must've been on a gurney, not in a wheelchair.

It took hours for us to get called back to a room, and another hour for the doctor to come in. By then I was getting super tired. All I remember about the doctor is that she was really tall, and her skin was dark. She reminded me a little of Ms. Opal, which only made all those Ms. Opal– shaped memory pinpricks this hospital had already dotted in my brain that much worse.

"We should get a scan," the doctor told my parents after Mom described what happened.

It took yet another hour for my turn in the X-ray room to arrive. Then we waited some more for the scans to come back and the doctor to have a look. I could hear Mom's exhalation of relief when the doctor told us that I'd only sprained my shoulder really badly. My rotator cuff, actually. Which, honestly, I didn't know what a rotator cuff was or where it was located until we all looked at the films together.

It was kind of neat seeing my insides all lit up on the wall. Like maybe that picture could help me figure out what else was wrong with me deep down.

The doctor assured us that, as long as I kept my arm in this sling for a few days, avoided lifting anything heavy, and iced my shoulder three times a day, I should be fine in a week or two.

"Everybody heals differently," she warned when Dad, rubbing his eyes under his glasses, pressed her on which one it was—one week or two.

"But after that, it'll be fixed, right?" he asked, sounding super worried. Mom and I exchanged a look at that word. *Fixed.* It reminded us of swapped out faucets, constantly running toilets, and light-switched blenders. All Dad's obsessions. I really hoped my shoulder wasn't going to become his latest.

Now, back home, a much more normal-sounding Dad snaps his fingers in the midnight air. "Got 'em," he responds, following Mom's instructions to retrieve my sneakers. I watch as he lifts my fallen shoe with two fingers on one end of the unraveled shoelace, holding it away from him at full arm's length. His frown makes me think he probably wishes he was born with longer arms.

Inside the house, Mom flips on the lights. "Straight upstairs," she orders. I'm way too tired to argue.

In my room, she helps me into my pajamas and bed, warning me the same way the nurses did not to roll onto my arm. I've never slept flat on my back before, but worries that I won't be able to fade into dreams when I drift off in about five seconds flat.

★ ★ ★

The Cortez rooster crows at 5:00 a.m., same as always, and I jolt awake with Teddy's poop on my brain. I mean, I'm *thinking* about it, not that it's actually *on* . . . never mind. Pain or no pain, I can't rest with such a clear violation of Townsend Ordinance 45-9 left sitting smack dab in the middle of my front lawn.

Thing is, lately Mom and I butt heads a lot, but every once in a while, I try to remember to do something nice for her, especially when I'm feeling guilty. So my first thought this morning is that neither she nor Dad should have to keep paying for my mistake by having to clean the disgusting poop off my sneaker. Seems like an extra insult. I should be able to take care of it myself. Even one-armed.

My sling slipped a little overnight. I shrug it back on the way the nurse showed me. Downstairs, I ease the front door open, as quietly as possible, and tiptoe toward the spot on our front porch where I saw Dad leave my sneakers to air out. I lift the right one up, expecting another whiff of regret, but all I smell is a strong cleaning odor. Not the brand Dad normally uses in the bathrooms on toilet day, either. I turn my shoe over, and there's not a single remnant of Teddy's gift left. In fact, my sneakers look sparkling new. Very wet and very new and very . . . clean.

I glance over at our garden hose, but it's wrapped tight

around that new, crooked holder Dad installed last week. There's no puddle that would indicate evidence of recent use.

My mind kicks into mystery mode. Who rinsed off my sneakers? I can't believe, as tired as they were after our long night, that Mom or Dad—

That's when I notice the footprints on our lawn. The early morning dew makes them super easy to see. They march from our porch to the spot where I dove for Teddy. Back to the porch again. Then from there to Ms. Opal's— argh! *The Cortezes'*—front walk, where they disappear when whoever made them reached the concrete.

Quickly, I slip my mysteriously clean sneakers on, not bothering to lace them up. Heading down the steps, I follow the prints to Teddy's pile. Also gone. I retrace the prints toward our house again, puzzled. Unlike our dark windows, lights blaze out of nearly all the front windows at the Cortez place. I guess Mr. or Mrs. Cortez could've been the ones to come over and pick up Teddy's poop, then clean my sneakers, but I kind of know it wasn't them.

No, now that I'm walking in the echoes of these footsteps, I can see that they were definitely made by feet smaller than even mine.

It had to be Will. What I don't know is . . . why?

I check the Cortez porch again, half expecting to see her standing there, waiting for me to figure things out and cross the yards. But it's empty. There's no movement next door at all.

My feet start stepping into the path, heading over there almost involuntarily, until I realize I'm still wearing pajamas. And that it's not even 6:00 a.m. yet.

I should probably wait—and be wearing actual pants—before ringing the Cortezes' bell and asking Will why she would wake up so early to clean up Teddy's poop off my lawn and sneakers.

I mean . . . until *six thirty*, at the very least.

CODE OF ORDINANCES—TOWNSEND HEIGHTS

Sec. 45-7—Dog Control / Regulations and Restrictions

It shall be unlawful for any owner of a dog in Townsend Heights to permit or allow such dog to:

1. Run at Large
2. Be off the owner's property unless leashed
3. Engage in habitual loud howling

Sec. 45-9—Dog Control / Removal of Animal Feces

The owner/guardian of any animal, when such animal is off the owner/guardian's property, shall be responsible for the removal of any feces deposited by such animal on public walks, streets, recreation areas, or private property.

My opinion? Sometimes the best way to make a friend is showing them you're willing to get your hands dirty to help them out. And sometimes that means dealing with their . . . feces. Or at least whatever feces might be lying around in their yard.

(Okay, seriously, though. Why is poop a less gross word than feces? Doesn't even make sense.)

—Will Cortez, Dog-walker Extraordinaire

Everything is wrong.

Or, at least, none of it is exactly . . . right.

This is the first time I've seen the changes to Ms. Opal's house up close. All the work the Cortez family has done over the past couple of months, their efforts to turn her old house into their new one. I was aware of them doing the projects, but only kind of, and only from a distance. Now, standing here on this porch makes every little difference so . . . real. Real and . . . well, *wrong*.

The creaky white porch swing is missing. Opal used to sit right here, rocking slowly, looking out over our little corner of the Heights, waving to each and every neighbor who wandered by.

And where's her cranberry-red front door? They've painted it black. Don't they know red means welcome?

Don't they understand why Ms. Opal gave her door a fresh coat of the same color red every spring? So that the people of Townsend Heights would always feel welcome to stop by, ring the bell, ask for some advice or a favor. Anything.

Was it really necessary to erase her so fast? What was the big hurry to make her disappear like this?

My foot tap-tap-taps on the welcome mat that isn't Ms. Opal's either. I'm thinking maybe I should leave. I'm just starting to turn around when the dark door pops open and the hallway light streams into my eyes.

Will's a little taller than me, but then almost everyone is at least a little bit taller than me. She has light-brown hair and brown eyes to match. The tiniest of smiles crosses her face, and I realize for the first time she wears braces. They disappear really quickly, though, as soon as she notices my sling.

"Oh no. Is that from yesterday?"

I had a plan when I stomped over here. Start by interrogating her about cleaning my sneakers, like I was catching her in the act or something. The act of what, though? Being nice?

"Oh. Oh, yeah, but it's nothing, just a sprain." I try to play it cool, end up wincing anyway.

Will bites her lip. "Ouch. Doesn't look like nothing."

"Not . . . well, okay, yeah. It does hurt. A little."

She glances past me, toward the spot of my poop-sliding heroics. "I'm so sorry all that happened."

"Thanks, but there's no reason for you to be. . . . Hey, so did you clean it up? And my sneakers, too?"

It still comes out like an accusation. I'd punch myself if I weren't already one-armed.

"I didn't know how else to thank you." She glances away, but only for a second. "Guess that dog was pretty strong, huh? I'm sure he's a good boy and all, but I can't imagine what might've happened to Gustavo if you hadn't done what you did."

"That's your rooster's name? Gustavo?"

"No! I mean, yes, that's his name. But no, he's not my rooster. He's my grandfather's. I'm . . . I'm just . . ." She looks down, almost like she's ashamed of something. But then her head pops up again, and her smile returns, wide this time, braces in full view. "I'm just visiting. Hey, do you want to meet him?"

"Your grandfather?"

"Sure, if he's around, but honestly Papa C. doesn't speak much English. I meant Gustavo."

"*He* speaks English?"

That earns me a chuckle. "Come on."

Will turns and starts retreating down the hall, leaving

the front door wide open for me. I catch the sounds of cooking. Pans clattering, something sizzling. Something that smells amazing.

I hurry after her, shutting the door behind me, rushing toward the kitchen. I know it's straight ahead because I've been in this house a thousand times before.

Back when it belonged to someone else.

The sizzling is a strange sound to hear in this place, because I don't think I've ever witnessed any sort of frying happening here before. Ms. Opal wasn't much of a cook. She never had the time.

In the kitchen, I find Will's grandmother swaying in front of the stove. Her feet shuffle along the tiles in flat brown slippers. Behind her, through the window, I glimpse Mr. Cortez, puttering around their backyard in the big safari hat I've seen him wear a bunch before. Gardening was another thing Ms. Opal was usually too busy for. Her yard ran tall and wild, but the Cortez version is trimmed and cared for, with flowers everywhere.

The pan on the front burner has a couple of inches of bubbling yellow oil in it. Sitting in the middle of the crackling pool, slowly browning, are several crescent-shaped things, pinched closed along their curved tops. The smell filling the kitchen is salty and rich—definitely some kind of meat. Not even Mack's block-party, charred-to-perfection hot dogs have ever smelled this good.

I could hear Will's grandmother humming as I hurried down the hall, but now she glances up and notices it's not just Will in the room with her. Mrs. Cortez quickly finishes flipping over the last of the three pies in her pan, reaches out for a lid, and covers them. A memory of Ms. Opal, here in this same kitchen, making us ham sandwiches before another exhausting day going door-to-door flashes in front of my eyes. Packing lunches so we wouldn't have to break for too long between asking neighbors for favors. Suggesting they pitch a hand on one of Opal's pet projects. Or sitting at her table, strategizing over a map, maybe her notebook of ordinances, or some petition she was readying for signatures.

I squeeze my eyes shut, pushing the ghostly images away. They might have happened in this house, but those memories belong in a different time, with a different person.

"Grandma, this is Mortimer." Will says my name loudest, like when you're talking to someone who you think might not hear you so well.

"Ah, Mortimer," Mrs. Cortez says, smiling at me. Now that we're standing so close for the first time, I hear her accent more clearly. She says my name slowly, like she's trying it out, but she still somehow manages to roll both the r's. She glances at my sling but quickly averts her eyes, gesturing at the pan instead. "Sit. Almost ready."

Will shakes her head. "It's a little early for pastelillos, Grandma. Maybe later. I'm taking him downstairs. He wants to meet Gustavo."

"Gustavo," Mrs. Cortez says with a little cluck of disapproval. "Cuidado."

"Oh, he's fine," Will says. She's already in front of the basement door. Man, she moves fast. She opens it and zips down the steps, waving at me to follow. "This way."

"Nice meeting you," I say to Mrs. Cortez before speeding to catch up with Will. I get to the top of the stairs just as she's about to reach the bottom.

"What's a . . . a pastelillo?" I call out as I rush down the steps after her. "Like empanadas?"

She turns around at the base of the steps and watches me nearly stumble down them. "Almost. They're different, though. . . . Like a pork pie, I guess? Grandma makes them all the time. They have olives and stuff in them. They're really good. But I'm telling you, she's making them, like, constantly. That and fried chicken." She shakes her head. "We eat a *lot* of fried chicken in this house. I've already told my mom—*no chicken* when I get home. I could murder a slice of pizza right now. Or—ohhh—sushi." She collapses against the nearest wall and groans. "Hey, you're from around here. Is there any way for you to finesse us a spicy tuna crunch roll somehow?"

I rub the back of my neck while racking my brain for

the nearest sushi place. My mind is blank, but not in a freeze-up way. "Maybe. Honestly, I'm not really big on sushi. It's a texture thing."

"Doesn't. Like. Sushi." She says each word slowly as she mimes pulling an imaginary pencil from behind her ear and making an imaginary note on an imaginary pad. "And yet she lets him live, doesn't kick him out of her grandparents' house," she finishes, sounding proud of her own generosity and restraint.

I laugh. "Well, thanks."

Will peps up again. "De nada. Anyway, pastellilos are from Puerto Rico. I don't actually know how to make them." She sounds a little embarrassed, though I don't know why. I change the subject.

"So how'd you get a name like Will? Is that Puerto Rican, too?"

She steps to one side as I join her on the concrete floor of the basement. Turns and puts her hands on her hips. Crinkles her nose, loses the grin. "That's a weird question."

Frankie calling her name dumb. I feel my cheeks burn, like she somehow overheard him say it, but she couldn't have.

"It's just, I never met a girl named Will before. Will is usually . . ."

She presses her fists into her hips harder, and it seems

like a good idea to stop talking. "A boy's name. Nice. Stereotype much?"

"No! I mean, it's different, so I figured it comes from somewhere else. That's all I meant."

If I'm reading her annoyed expression right, that's a hard no. I've overstepped big-time.

"Oh, so it's unusual, so it must be Puerto Rican? Is that what you're saying? Being Puerto Rican is weird? As in, what? Wrong? Being Puerto Rican is wrong? Is that what you're saying?"

My whole face is burning now. "No, I—"

Will smirks at the way I'm shifting on my feet. I get it now—she's winding me up. "It's German, actually. My mom's side is from there. Her name's Willene, and so's my grandmother's. So I got Willene, too. Family tradition. I just shortened it. Speaking of, do you like Mort or Morty—"

"Mortimer," I snap back, a little too quickly. "Just . . . Mortimer. No abbreviations."

"Okay," she says with a tiny flick of her eyebrows. Same as she did upstairs, she turns abruptly to head deeper into the basement, continuing to talk over her shoulder. "Should I ask the origin? Because . . . that's also a weird name, if you don't mind me saying so. Let me guess, Slovenian? Wakandan?"

For a quick second, I'm left standing by myself, and I

realize I don't know this *whole* house like I thought I did. Because, somehow, in all that time spent upstairs with Ms. Opal, we never came down here. These are my very first moments in this basement.

I mutter a distracted reply. "I don't actually know the whole story. Some old black-and-white movie my mom likes, I think. She watches it every Halloween."

I catch up with her just as we emerge into a second room. She pulls the chain on a light dangling from the ceiling. The bulb stays dark. She tries twice more super-fast. Nothing. I almost step to one side, figuring Dad will be right behind us, maintenance stepladder in hand. But this isn't our house, and he's not here to swap the bulbs out like some NASCAR pit crew worker.

Even in the dim light cast down on us by the rectangle-shaped basement window, I'm able to take in most of the room. The built-in shelves along one wall filled with stacks of *National Geographic* issues, the washer and dryer straight ahead, the little yellow table in one corner. How much of this did Ms. Opal leave behind? Like, are those *her* magazines? Did she do laundry in *these* machines? Use *that* table to fold her clothes?

I have no idea. It's weird, thinking you knew every-thing about a person for years and then realizing you were completely wrong.

We take a quick right. Step up into yet another room,

the tiniest one yet. The light here works. As soon as Will yanks it on, the dark corners rise to life. A hot water heater in one. Some kind of pantry or closet in another. She heads in that direction. Instead of a door, there's a dingy plastic curtain covering the opening. Heavier than a shower curtain, with thick, vertical, translucent slats.

Will reaches up and grabs the farthest edge of plastic with one hand. "Ready?" she asks, and before I can consider what I need to be ready for, she pulls the slats across the opening. They slap together as they fold into one another.

At first, nothing happens. Will frowns and blinks. She bends her neck down, gazing into the opening with a clearly befuddled expression.

That's when the biggest rooster I've ever seen storms out. He even surprises Will. She hops back, hugging the wall behind her to make way.

I'd spotted Gustavo yesterday—at the start of the poop incident—but only from a distance. I didn't appreciate how massive he is from that quick, faraway glimpse.

Now, up close, the bird looks top heavy, so much so that it leans forward as it runs. At first, I think he's going to stop, but he doesn't. The rooster keeps on coming straight for me. I take a step back, my good hand reaching out for the table behind me. It sweeps across the top of it clumsily, sending tools skittering.

With one hand on the table and the other in a sling, I've got none left to defend myself with. More panic seizes my throat, making the yelp I release come out way high-pitched.

Will's eyes bug out of her head. She releases the curtain and starts toward me, chasing after the rooster. She'll never catch it before it gets to me. Not even if she dives. Which, honestly? I don't recommend. Not if you prefer your rotator cuffs to continue to . . . well, *rotate*.

"Gustavo!" Will screams.

I close my eyes, turn my body to protect my bad side. Clench my teeth, and hope for survival.

A million things happen at once.

Wings flap. Claws scrape. A shrill squawk bounces off the basement walls.

Gustavo slams into my legs. My knees buckle. I'm knocked backward a step. My hip crashes into the table. Tools fly off it, clanging to the floor. I fight for balance, wrap my good arm across my face. If Gustavo's going to claw at me, he's not getting my eyes.

Which, honestly, I don't even know how I think of that. I'm possibly getting too good at animal entanglements. Maybe I should move to the middle of the ocean, where there are no dogs, no roosters, no—but hold on, I'd probably just get eaten by a shark.

Nature, man. The stuff is everywhere.

As quickly as it began, everything stops. The fluttering (Gustavo's), the stomping feet (Will's), and the whimpering (mine). Which, honestly, was pretty darn justified, if you ask me. Only a few seconds passed in the real world, but in my head, I was under siege for hours.

Will's voice rings out, directly in front of me. Her tone is calm, soothing. "It's okay. I've got him now."

I lower my arm. She must've picked Gustavo up, because she's holding him and stroking his feathers. The rooster seems relaxed now, completely different from the crazed maniac of a few seconds ago.

"I'm sooo sorry," Will says. "That doesn't usually happen." She ducks her head and whispers softly to Gustavo. I can't hear the words until she rears back her head and says, louder, "What got into you, huh?"

I straighten up. Step away from the worktable. Shrug my sling back into order.

"You okay?" she asks.

"Totally fine." I mean, as soon as my heart stops yammering. Yeah, sure. Fine. The totally kind.

"Can I set him down? He'll be good."

I want to say no, but my brain autocorrects it to . . .

"Of course. No biggie."

Will gently lowers the rooster to the floor. As soon as his feet hit concrete and he's free, he immediately starts

hunting and pecking around, like absolutely nothing happened a few seconds ago.

I watch him closely. In case—I don't know—I need to
run or stop, drop, and roll into the fetal position or something. I can't get over how big he is. Huge, actually. His
head would be over my knees if I let him get that close
again. Gustavo's pretty hefty, too. Definitely the biggest
rooster I've ever seen, though I guess I haven't seen an
actual rooster this close since . . . when? That petting zoo
in second grade?

"You *sure* you're okay?" Will asks me, one eyebrow
raised.

"I'm good. Seriously."

She smirks and gives me a side-eye, but drops the subject. Instead, she watches Gustavo cock his head to and fro.
"He's cool, isn't he?"

I glance at the shower-curtained opening. That weird
pantry-closet space. "I don't get it. Why is he down here?"

Will shrugs. "Papa C. doesn't like to leave him outside,
at least not overnight. It's . . . he's special to him, that's all.
Came all the way from Puerto Rico with them."

The bird looks up at me, as if noticing I'm standing
there for the first time. Or realizing I'm asking questions
about him. Gustavo holds my gaze for a few moments
before deciding I'm not that interesting after all. He doesn't
seem fazed by losing our staring contest. He continues to

wander around his surroundings, still occasionally checking out the floor with a quick peck.

"How'd that go down?" I ask, my attention turning back to Will.

"What?"

"I mean . . . what made your grandparents come here all the way from Puerto Rico?"

"What does it matter? They're here now."

She seems eager to change the subject. "What's wild to me is this whole neighborhood is filled with pet people, right? Dogs galore. And they treat them so great. I've never seen anything like it. I didn't have half this many customers back in California. But bring a rooster in, and it's mass hysteria." She gestures at Gustavo, who's ignoring us entirely now, staring at the water heater. He's cocking his head this way and that. I realize I can see my feet reflected back by the shiny metal of the heater. The curvature's making them appear huge. Which means Gustavo's looking at . . . a giant version of himself?

"Does he see?"

"Yeah," Will says, shaking her head but grinning at the same time. "He likes his own reflection. Loves it, actually." She starts talking in baby voice. "Because he's just the handsomest rooster, isn't he?"

The big white cylinder suddenly hisses, and we all jump

back. Gustavo scampers to the other side of the room.

"Gustavo's just a different kind of pet. That's all," Will continues. "Maybe he came out hot just now, but so did that dog yesterday. They're animals. It happens."

"Did your grandparents ever think about explaining exactly that, maybe? Come to a council meeting and talk to everyone?"

Will snorts. "Unlikely."

"Why not? Defending himself would help your grandfather. I mean . . . Papa C."

"Let's just say I already know it wouldn't go well."

"But how can you be so sure if you don't try?"

Will reels on me. The movement is so sudden, I take an involuntary step back. "Why should he have to defend himself to *anyone*? And how, exactly, would you suggest he do that anyway? I told you already they don't speak much English. There'd be no way for them to keep up with all the . . ." She waves her hand, searching for the right words. "Community yelling."

"Human crowing," I suggest.

"Yeah, human crowing. I like that." She picks up a few of the tools I knocked to the floor. I bend to help her. "It's just . . . I think my grandparents have gotten pretty used to being ignored around here."

Just then, Gustavo clucks past my feet. Before I have

the chance to step back, he stops to peck the top of my clean sneaker. I feel the point of his beak on my toe, but it doesn't hurt.

"What do you mean?"

"I mean," Will continues, setting a wrench on the table while looking off in the distance. "They're Puerto Rican. Think about it. Did anyone listen when Puerto Rico needed help after Hurricane Maria? No. Can they vote for president? No. Do they get senators and stuff to represent them, like a normal state does?"

"I'm guessing . . . no?"

She tilts her head, making a face that says *You're catching on.* "So, yeah, like I said. They're pretty used to being ignored."

After that, there's a quick, awkward silence. It lasts long enough for me to get a little uncomfortable, make me feel like I have to fill it.

"Did you, like, do a paper on all this or something?"

"No, I just—" Will starts, but right then the ceiling creaks with movement above us. She glances up at it. "Never mind."

She seems to be in a hurry all of a sudden. Will makes a clucking sound, urging Gustavo to strut back into his enclosure. She pulls the heavy plastic curtain shut behind him.

"He'll stay in there?"

She nods. "As long as we keep this closed."

"That stinks about Puerto Rico," I say. "I guess I understand why your grand . . . why Papa C. wouldn't want to . . ." I bite my lip, switch gears. "But we've done a lot of good work on that council. Really. We always try to be fair, or we did before anyway. With all kinds of different people. If you live in Townsend Heights, you're a part of this community."

Will looks doubtful. "Doesn't always seem like it. Who do you mean by 'we' anyway?"

"Me and—" I shrug. I'm not getting into the subject of Ms. Opal right now, especially not while I'm standing in this basement that isn't *her* basement anymore. "Just . . . everybody. My mom's the head councilwoman, you know." I say it to move on from her question, but also because maybe I think she'll be impressed.

Will raises both eyebrows this time. "Yeah, I heard about that," she says, in a tone that's clearly the opposite of impressed. She shakes her head, glances at the ceiling, where another noisy creak rings out. "It's just not happening. Trust me."

"So what about you, then?"

"What about me?"

"Come to the next meeting with me. Maybe people will . . ." I trail off.

"You want me to come represent my grandparents at

your council meeting?" She scoffs as she interrupts me. "And say what, exactly?"

"You don't have to *say* anything. Maybe just listen. But if you did want to speak, especially since you're doing all that dog-walking, since lots of people here seem to respect you already, you could explain how Gustavo's just another kind of pet." I raise my index finger, barreling along, getting new ideas with each word. "That he's not, like, dangerous—"

Will eyes the curtain, almost like she's not so sure about that. She lifts her head and inhales. "No, just annoying sometimes, I guess."

I shrug. "So he crows early. They're animals. It happens, right? People should see it as a help. Everybody gets an early start to their day."

A smile tugs at the corners of Will's mouth. I'm making headway. I go in for the kill, raising my sling up as high as it will go without pain, drawing her attention to it.

"Besides, I think you owe me, don't you?"

I don't get it," Will whispers. Two days later, we're in her grandparents' basement again, standing on the yellow table in the laundry room. Spying on my own house from this tiny window. "Your mom knows you come to the meetings, right?"

I stand on my toes to peek out again. "Let's just say she's not exactly a fan of my council work lately."

I've been waiting twenty minutes to see Mom's car back out of the driveway and head down the hill, across Townsend Ave. toward the auditorium in the community center, where the council meetings are always held. "So we have this kind of truce. Mom knows she can't stop me from attending." I raise my eyebrows at Will. "Not that she hasn't tried. On the other hand, I don't make her drive me. That way she doesn't feel like she's supporting me being there."

And besides, I used to have someone else to go with, I think but don't say.

Finally, Mom steps out of our house with a big stack of papers cradled in her arms. "There she is," I announce.

A wind whips up just as she reaches our driveway. It causes a loose page to fly off the top of the stack. The page flutters up over her shoulder, turning over once before landing in the grass behind her, a few feet in front of our porch.

Dad walks out of the house just as the page lands. At first, he only stands on the porch, glancing at the lone sheet, shaking his head slightly. But it doesn't take long for him to descend the three steps to the front lawn. He picks up the piece of paper attempting an escape and walks it over to Mom. She re-adds it to her pile. Dad even gives her a peck on the cheek.

It's so weird, the way they've been with each other. Arguing one minute, being polite to each other the next.

As soon as Dad backs away to give her room, Mom reverses her Nissan out of the driveway. She turns up Cromwell and disappears around the corner.

"Ready?" Will asks once she's gone.

"One second."

I can't stop watching Dad, because he hasn't moved. Mom's well out of sight now, but my father's still standing there in our driveway, staring after her car like there's a chance she might turn around and come back. After almost a minute where he seems deep in thought, his phone must ring, because he jumps slightly before looking toward his pocket. He fishes out his cell, stares at the screen for a long second. Before he answers, he glances all around, even behind him, like he's worried someone might be watching. Or overhearing.

But I can't hear anything, not from all the way next door. I do catch a whole lot of nodding, though. Dad waves his hands around. He seems really animated, excited, like he's fighting with the person on the other end of the line. Or agreeing really hard with them, maybe.

Is it Mom, calling on her way to the meeting? Are they talking about me? Is this a repeat of all those whispered discussions they thought I couldn't hear?

We have to do something about Mortimer.

"Mortimer?" Will says, her voice urgent. I wonder how long she's been staring at me, waiting for a response. If I was in the middle of another freeze-up without realizing it.

I can move now, though, so I do, backing away from the window. "Okay, let's go."

★ ★ ★

Will's quiet as I point out the row I usually sit in, way in the back of the auditorium. Personally, I'd sit right up front if I could, but it's definitely easier if Mom and I aren't staring straight at each other the whole meeting. About a minute after we settle in, though, Will finally asks her first question. "Where's this Brewster guy?"

There are so many people milling around, it's hard to single anyone out, even Brewster's hulking figure. Hindered by my sling, I fidget to sit up straight and search the crowd. "I don't think I see h—"

Just then, Brewster storms in loudly, marching down the center aisle to the front row. His voice bellows as he makes his way through the throng of neighbors, picking and choosing the most loyal of his followers to greet. He's got those same rolled-up plans under one arm again, but this time he's carrying something else, too—stiff, laminated cards almost as big as me. I crane my neck, but the cards are covered with a white film. I can't read them.

"Never mind," Will says, rolling her eyes. "I see him."

Technically, scheduled speakers have to ask for preapproved time to present. Unless, of course, an open forum is declared; only then are neighbors allowed to step up to the podium and microphone on demand.

But ever since Gustavo arrived, Brewster's always kicked off these emergency sessions. He seems to assume he'll be granted the same permission tonight, because right away he starts setting up those card-things on an empty easel.

I'm staring up front so intently I don't see Queenie until her leaning face fills up my vision. "These seats taken?" she asks with a smile.

I smile back, knowing she doesn't need an answer. When I used to come here with Opal, these were our seats. Right behind Queenie and Mack, every single meeting. The four of us used to chat up a storm while the room settled in, but the last several sessions I've stayed quiet behind them, concentrating on my notes from the last meeting, and though every once in a while they seemed like they might be thinking about it, they haven't talked to me, either. Hardly look at me, like they don't want to bother me. Tonight, though, Queenie casts a longer-than-usual glance in my new council companion's direction as she balances one hand on her chair back. Noticing her eyes, Mack checks us out, too, as he sidesteps along the row right behind her, waiting patiently for Queenie to land in her chair.

"*Mister* Bray." He always says my name the same way. This time, he follows it up with a gesture at my sling. "How's that shoulder doing?"

I glance down, like I need to make sure I still *have* a shoulder. "It's okay."

"Quite the hero, our boy here." Queenie meets Will's eyes. She seems to have forgotten I acted like the biggest chicken ever the other day, basically sprinting out of her house with Frankie and Monty. She also seems to assume we're back to chatting at these meetings. Apparently, someone's found the cure to the worrying about the "give Mortimer some space" virus that seems to have infected the Heights the past couple of months. Ever since . . . well, after Trevor.

Will nods seriously at Mack. "Oh, yeah, we've been trying to decide his superhero name. *Dog Man* is taken, so I've been leaning toward *Poop Boy* myself."

The laugh Mack barks out is so sharp and loud, several heads turn our way. He wags a finger in Will's direction. "I might switch Cantaloupe's walks over to you after all," he says to her. "On the basis of that joke alone."

Mack, who has a huge, very orange-furred Saint Bernard named Cantaloupe, sends me a knowing smile. He's old-school Townsend, one of the ones, like Queenie, who stuck with Frankie, though I detected a lot of hesitation in his eyes the other day. I'm guessing Frankie's been avoiding Cantaloupe. The ginormous dog isn't the easiest walk, that's for sure.

Will perks up. "I would *love* to walk Cantaloupe. She's so adorable. No pressure, though. I might have more than I can handle already."

Queenie just shakes her head in Mack's direction. "That thing you call a pet is more mutant than dog. You oughtta get some real superhero, with superstrength, to walk her—quit bothering these kids about it."

"A real superhero, huh?" Mack continues facing forward, but stretches his neck so his next words feel headed in my direction. "What about it, Poop Boy?"

Will has to cover her mouth to quell her giggle.

I hide my eyes, not sure if he's being serious or not. Is he pushing me to get back to things like Mom's been doing all summer?

Queenie saves me. "Finally got some friends to join you at the meetings, did ya?"

"Well. One friend, anyway," I say, nodding toward Will and wincing a little, hoping it isn't too early to call her a friend. I lift my hand up to my bad shoulder to make it seem like that's where the wince came from. "Frankie would never—"

"You sure about that?" Queenie waves toward the side of the auditorium. I follow her gaze. Frankie and Chester Brewster are just picking out some seats. Together. My surprised intake of breath is so quick, I start coughing.

Does he hear me? I swear Frankie's head almost turns our way, but I probably imagine it.

We haven't spoken since the vacant lot. He didn't even call to ask about my shoulder. I mean, I'm sure by now he must've heard about it. After all, it happened in front of Chester, who Frankie's sitting next to at this very moment.

There's no time to dwell on it, though, because from her

spot up onstage, in the center of the long table where the five-person council sits, Mom bangs her gavel. The room settles down; people who were standing sit. Neighbors who were talking stop. Satisfied, Head Councilwoman Bray sets the gavel down and arranges the papers in front of her, making the already neat stacks even more precise.

"Please be seated," she requests in a raised voice. "This emergency session of the Townsend Heights Council will now come to order."

Tonight's agenda has only one topic." Mom sighs, like she doesn't want to have to utter her next sentence. "You have the floor, Mr. Brewster."

Mr. DiNucci stands to begin a lone clap. A few others soon join in. At the same time, from other corners of the auditorium, I hear groans. Everyone's here to talk about the rooster problem but also no one really *wants* to have to talk about the rooster problem. Adults are so confusing sometimes.

"Get ready," I whisper to Will. I'd already recounted all the ways Brewster had criticized Gustavo during these meetings, if only so she wouldn't be shocked when she heard it with her own ears.

I peek at the laminated cards up front, wondering if he has something new lined up for tonight, but they're still covered. I'm guessing some fresh, hot-off-the-press complaints are hiding underneath.

Rooster. Loud! Waking up. Early!

Only this time . . . with charts!

"Thank you, Councilwoman," Brewster says. He approaches the first card. I narrow my eyes. Not sure I've ever heard him *thank* anybody on the council before starting to speak. Definitely not Mom. "Esteemed members of the Townsend Heights Council and preliminary planning commission."

He nods toward some people in business suits, a man and a woman. I hadn't noticed them before now. The man is bald. The woman has an angled face—her nose, glasses, and cheekbones, everything on her seems sharp, like she spent time filing it all to a point before arriving here today.

They're both seated in the front row. Brewster turns and gestures to the scattered Townsend residents. He finishes his introduction. "Good people of our fine neighborhood."

More weirdness. His voice is normal volume, not yelling level. He's being almost . . . pleasant. Will elbows me in the ribs, sends me a confused look. Nothing that's happening matches what I told her. I shake my head. I have no idea what's going on, either.

"Ours is such a beautiful part of the city, isn't it?" Several of the people behind us murmur agreement with him. Someone shouts out, "The best!" and a few people laugh.

Even Brewster smiles. "We have just one blight on our streets. I'm sure you know the spot, vacant for so long. An eyesore in our community."

Brewster walks over to the easel. He yanks the film off his top card with a flourish. "Presenting . . . the corner of Liberty and Prince."

What the heck? Why does he have a blown-up aerial photo of Ms. Opal's vacant lot?

"Not only a blemish on our otherwise pristine streets, but a danger to our young people as well. Fenced off by the city, allowed to fester like an open wound for years upon years. Barbed wire, twisted metal, dangerous concrete rubble."

In front of us, Queenie shifts uncomfortably.

Next to me, Will whispers, "What does this have to do with Gustavo?"

I shake my head again, surge forward in my chair. There's always a screen set up for these meetings, but it's hardly ever used. Today, though, it broadcasts Brewster's photo to the entire room from behind Mom's head. I don't know if it was taken by a drone or a satellite or what, but the whole neighborhood is displayed from high above, with the vacant lot outlined in red. I'd know that angled shape anywhere, because I've seen it a hundred times, whenever Ms. Opal brought out her Townsend Heights maps. Six-sided, closest to the ridge-riding railroad tracks, not far from Frankie's house.

I glance over at my old friend. He's watching, but with his chin in one hand, almost like he might fall asleep any second.

"Not only a danger," Brewster continues, raising up a finger. "But an *opportunity* for the wrong sort of development to one day worm its way onto our very streets. Subpar development," he emphasizes. Then he gestures behind him again. "I've heard from many a resident on this matter. Each and every one of us wants to make sure, if anything is ever built on this corner, that at minimum it be fair and comparable to what's already here. Especially considering other . . . *recent events* . . . well, that's all the good people of Townsend can ask for, is it not?"

The rest of the auditorium issues low murmurs and whispers. Lots of heads nod along.

Even *I* feel the budding excitement. Who wouldn't want something cool built on the only vacant lot in the Heights? Maybe even Ms. Opal wanted that. Maybe she was so concerned with that corner because she hated to see it wasted, sitting there empty. Isn't it possible that it just bothered her that every inch of her neighborhood wasn't being put to good use?

"But I say 'fair and comparable' is the *least* we can do,"

Brewster says, the volume in his voice increasing steadily. "I say we can do *much* better than fair! Far surpass comparable!"

Finally, he's raised his voice like I expected him to be doing from the beginning. The whispering all about the room increases to a constant hiss. Brewster's biggest supporters applaud; a few even emit soft, encouraging cheers.

Brewster turns back to the council and moves to his next laminated card. "With that in mind, I want to introduce you to—" He peels more of the white film off this one. A gleaming artist's rendition of a tall office building surrounded by shorter structures comes into view. It's drawn from a lowered perspective, so that it appears massive, with a courtyard filled with faceless people milling about, fresh from work or shopping, heading out to dinner, sharing ice cream cones.

"Brewster Station."

The entire room erupts. The people of the Heights exchange confused looks. They nudge each other and point, shake their heads. My throat drops into my stomach as I realize this meeting was *never* a rooster meeting. Frustrated, Will slides back in her seat and folds her arms across her chest. She jostles my slinged arm, sending a fresh jolt of pain straight toward my forehead. I pull my elbow in tighter to my body, but that only makes the throbbing worse.

Brewster attempts to continue, pointing at the artist's rendering. But even through Mom's constant gavel pounding, the residents of the Heights won't fall silent again. I've never seen my mother so aggressive with that tiny mallet of hers.

I can't make out any of the individual comments at first; the voices and words jumble together with my own shock. It seems Brewster has surprised even his most ardent supporters with this proposal. We haven't heard the full details yet, and it's already the most upheaval I've ever seen at a council meeting.

"Where will people park?" I overhear Mack whisper at Queenie.

He's right. All those visitors coming to work in such a big building? Every day? Plus, the shopping? I've already heard Mom complaining about the parking outside the grocery store enough to last me a lifetime—matter of fact, we've had to change the way we shop to account for it. We have it down to a science now: She waits, double-parked, while I run to grab the essentials at superspeed. We're like two gears in a well-oiled machine.

"The man named it after himself," Queenie replies. "You think he cares about parking?" She leans over and continues hissing at Mack, pointing toward Brewster and his easel. "This is going to be just like that spot on Prospect. You know the one? Where they put that office building?

After the construction finished and it opened up, people flowed into that area like the tide in the morning. Then they ebbed back out in the evening. All they left behind was a giant void."

"Right," Mack whispers back. "I had a buddy lived over there when that thing went up—what was the name again?"

"Darvish Plaza."

"That's right, the Plaza. I remember he got all excited about the stuff coming along with it. Coffee shops and restaurants that would be so close by he could walk to them. Thing he didn't understand was they'd all close up as soon as the workers left for home. Place was dead after about six o'clock, and worse on the weekend. Big empty building and shops without enough business to warrant being open and staffed on Saturdays and Sundays."

"Did it ever come around?" Queenie asks, interested.

Mack shrugs. "Don't know. My buddy ended up moving out to the city center. At least there's something like a community out that way still."

Listening to them while staring ahead at Brewster's smug expression, his fancy maps and professional drawings behind him, a kind of terror hits me. The Heights has already been falling apart. Half this room looks super upset. What if people start moving away, like Mack's Prospect Street buddy? Worse, what if they—we—don't move away, and after Brewster Station is built, our neighborhood becomes just what Mack and Queenie are describing? Big crowds of strangers flowing in during the morning hours and flowing back out every night.

Dad taught me how waves work once, a lesson he'd been noodling while we stood barefoot on the sand of the beach in Destin, Florida. He showed me how, when the water comes in, it drops shells and rocks and sea life onto the sand.

"Wait for it," I remember him saying as we watched the water flow back out again. The quiet moment between waves. I watched closely as the salt water pulled almost all the stuff it had dropped off only seconds before back away again. It was kind of neat how smooth and empty the receding ocean made the sand look.

Sure, neat for the sand in Florida, but definitely not something I want to see happen here.

Townsend Heights isn't a place that should ever be smooth and empty. Our neighborhood should stay the way it's always been—messy and filled with life. Steep and disorganized in its own beautiful way. I didn't want any daily tide or wave of office workers or any other kind of temporary people changing that.

Mack grunts. The gruff sound brings me back to the moment. "Tell ya what. Good thing Opal ain't here."

Instead of answering again, Queenie spins around to

look at me. Her expression is drawn with concern. As soon as she sees I've been listening, she shoots Mack an annoyed look. He shrinks back in his chair.

Mom continues to bang her gavel, still trying to call the room into order. She keeps shouting, "Nothing can be decided until we present this to the city! To the *entire* planning commission. I hear everyone's concerns about traffic and zoning." Mom huffs out exasperation when the room only gets noisier. "But nothing can be decided until the next hearing—"

The two people in front, the bald man and the pointy woman, both in their business suits, straighten proudly, and I realize who they are. When he started speaking, Brewster said something about a preliminary planning commission. Right after, he looked straight at them.

The city. Those people are the people from the city. They're the ones who really get to approve this plan.

Mom can't seem to regain control. Some neighbors are already leaving, storming up the aisles, shaking their heads. A few arguments have erupted between others, people pointing and shouting at each other as they debate. Some, like the DiNuccis, remain standing, applauding their enthusiasm for Brewster's plan. Yet more Townsend residents sit back in their chairs, just like Will, stunned into silence. In their seats on the far side, Chester Brewster is talking fast into Frankie's ear, pointing and explaining everything.

Frankie's eyes go wide. His own house is way closer to that corner than any of ours. So he doesn't look the way he always did whenever I would try to get him involved— bored to tears. He seems almost thrilled.

And, in the middle of it all, still right up front, Brewster's facing the crowd, huge grin on his face, hands on his hips, like some kind of Superman who's just struck the first blow in an epic battle. He's watching all the panic he's just created, clearly loving every second of it.

Superman. Yeah, right. The only superpower that dude seems to have is the uncanny ability to rip this neighborhood clean in half just about every time he opens his mouth.

17

"**Y**ou're going to wear a hole in that floor," Dad warns me. He glances back down at his phone, sends another text to Mom.

"Is she answering?" I ask.

"No, she's not," he says slowly. "But I'm sure she's on her way."

Mom shouldn't just be on her way. She should be home already. Sometimes she has wrap-up work after a council meeting, but never an hour's worth. It's been even longer than that since the emergency session adjourned, since I walked home listening to Will rant about how the whole meeting was a "big waste of her time." That it had nothing to do with Gustavo or her grandparents.

Didn't it, though? When Brewster mentioned he wanted to build his project on the vacant lot in order to prevent some other *subpar development* from popping up there, when he talked about everyone agreeing with him because of *recent events*, wasn't he referring to Gustavo? To the Cortezes bringing their rooster to Townsend Heights?

I tried to apologize, even though it wasn't really my fault. All it made her do, though, was walk faster. She bobbed up and down on her toes waiting to cross Townsend Ave., pressing the button requesting the walk sign about a hundred times. As soon as the walk light flashed white, she practically sprinted to the other side of the street.

Will hardly said good night when we split off in front of our houses in the dark, the evening finally letting go of some its constant humidity. I'd been waiting in the entry hall for Mom to get home ever since, pacing this hole Dad was so worried about. He kept eyeing my feet with his Mr. Fixit X-ray vision, like he could see the damage to his precious hardwood growing worse with each step I took.

Maybe he's right, but it doesn't matter because I can't stop. I shift my sling back up on my shoulder and turn on my heel to make another pass. I *need* to be here when Mom gets home. I need to talk with her right away because . . . well, the truth is, I'm kinda furious with her. Brewster was here—inside the very walls of our own house, *three days ago*—with those plans tucked under his arm. Mom saw them. Right there in her office.

And she didn't say a single word to me. Not the slightest warning about what was coming. I was totally blindsided. The whole neighborhood was.

"Tell me what happened again," Dad says.

I stop and turn. Maybe if I explained it slower than the rapid-fire shouting I'd sent his way when I first got home—

The door swings open and Mom comes through with a bunch of papers she's trying to balance. I turn to her and open my mouth, but she holds up a hand and stops me before a single word escapes my lips.

"Please don't start with me, Mortimer. I've had a tough enough night as it is."

"Mom, you can't let him do this!" I yell.

"I've been hearing that for hours. I can only tell you the same thing I've been telling everyone else in this neighborhood. You're right, I can't let him do this. Or stop him, either. Because it's not up to me. Mr. Brewster's proposal is in the city's hands now."

"What does that mean?" I demand.

Mom sighs. She wrestles her papers, finally managing to set them down on the entryway table. As soon as she lifts her hands away, the pages all slide to one side. She stares at them a moment, like their refusal to stay in a tidy pile is a personal betrayal. Or like she's waiting to see if the fall will get worse and they'll end up toppling all over the floor. They remain in their lopsided position, a leaning tower. She breathes out a relieved sigh. It's the one thing from tonight that didn't end up a complete disaster.

"No, Nick. No, Mortimer," she says in a high-pitched voice, her face shading pink. "I don't need a hand. Thank you, though. Thank you *so much* for offering."

Mom lets her purse slide off her shoulder and takes an even deeper breath to calm down. To my side, Dad fidgets, like he wants to come forward and do something, but there's nothing left to do. He missed his chance. We both did.

Dad mumbles the word *vacuum* incoherently. Abruptly, he heads for the basement door. That was today's project, one he never finished. The vacuum cleaner is still in pieces on the floor down there.

Mom throws her empty hands into the air. "Fantastic. That's just great, Nick!" she cries after him. "Go fix something. Or break it, whatever. That'll really help the situation."

I try to level my voice. Blowing up at her clearly wasn't the right approach. "Mom."

She brushes her annoying bangs to one side again. "What, Mortimer? What?"

"What do you mean it's up to the city?"

She steadies her voice. Mom's at her best when she's explaining things, especially legal or council stuff. "I mean that from here, he'll file the papers with the city and the city development manager approves them. There's a committee review, after one more community hearing. All he was obligated to do was notify the council at an official meeting, supply some documentation. Those plans from tonight."

I almost start another protest, but Mom interrupts.

"Mortimer. He doesn't need our approval. That land belongs to the city. If they want to sell it to him, if they want to give him permission to build that . . . monstrosity, there's nothing I or anybody else on the council can do about it."

It doesn't seem right. My mind searches through the ordinances I have memorized. There has to be one we can invoke to stop Brewster's project. But my head swims. I can't think of a single clause or bylaw that applies to this situation.

"Okay," I say slowly, my brain following a new path. "But they'll say no, won't they?"

She shakes her head and half smiles. "I don't see how. Or why. I researched it after he was here the other day. Called the city, found the one person who would actually listen and answer my questions." She holds that same hand up again, to stop what she knows I'm about to say. "Yes, I knew this was coming. But I thought I could reason with Mr. Brewster. And you hurt your shoulder, and your father's been too angry all the time to add anything constructive . . ." Her voice trails off.

"You still should've told me."

"Maybe." She sighs again, fights with that same stray hair. "Maybe I should've." Big exhale. "Anyway, I've researched it, and the only time the city ever stops this kind of project is if there's a historical landmark on the site. Something the community wants to protect."

"So let's find one of those then."

Mom cocks her head at me the same way Frankie sometimes does, when he thinks I'm being naive about something. "Mortimer, you've walked past that lot quite a few more times than I have. There's nothing there but a big fence, lots of dirt, and crabgrass. Whatever's left of whatever was there is just . . . gone. There's nothing historical to protect."

Ms. Opal, just staring through that big fence, straight at all that nothing. As if she were remembering . . . something. There *had* to be a reason for the way she acted around the vacant lot.

It can't be nothing.

"There must've been something there before."

"Probably there was. But what does that matter now? Whatever it was, it's gone. I'm sorry, Mortimer." Her eyes close. She's thinking.

When nothing new comes out after half a minute, I start again. "Can't we—"

She steps toward me and wraps her arm around my head, pulling me in for a tight hug. "I need to lie down a minute, okay?" We separate. She leans back so her eyes can meet with mine. "Listen, stop worrying about this so much. This is not your fight. You're twelve years old. And . . . you've already had a tough go of it these past few months. You'd be so much happier if . . ." I'm pretty sure she's going to suggest getting a new dog again, but my eyes tell her not to and maybe sometimes the way Mom reads me like a book is actually useful. "You should get some rest, too. Okay?"

She trudges upstairs. She only gets halfway up when there's a popping noise, and our whole house goes black. Dad must've flipped another circuit breaker.

Mom stops in her tracks. "Not tonight," she mutters, sounding truly exhausted. "I can't do this tonight." She continues up the stairs, feeling her way in the dark step-by-step, lacking the energy to turn the other way to start another argument.

I'm still near the front door, standing in the now-black hallway, waiting for my eyes to adjust to the light before I move so I don't bang another knee. I use the moment to think some about adjusting my eyes in another way. I need a way to see into the past, find out the vacant lot's old secrets. But how can I do that if I wasn't there when whatever happened, happened?

The answer seems simple once I give it some thought. Maybe I wasn't there, but other people must've been. All I have to do is figure out who knows the truth. Then I just have to get them to talk.

PROTECTING HISTORIC PLACES, DEFINITIONS

National Register of Historic Places

The National Register is the nation's official list of buildings, structures, objects, sites, and districts worthy of preservation for their significance in American history, architecture, archaeology, or culture.

Why Preserve?

Historic landmarks and districts provide a tangible link with the past, with people, and with events that have made significant contributions to our history and thus have helped shape our present. They help give our communities individual character and ourselves a sense of place and connection.

You can't protect a place if you don't know its secrets. And you can't know its secrets until you find out its history. It's impossible to bring back the past—and you probably shouldn't even try—but finding out about what happened back then might help you save the future. And that seems like a thing worth trying for.

—From the secret files of Mortimer Bray

The next morning, standing on Queenie's porch and watching Monty bark at me through her front door's sidelight window, I tell myself this is the only way. With Ms. Opal gone, Queenie has lived in the Heights the longest. Not even Mack's been here as many years. If anyone knows about the vacant lot—what used to be there, why it's been sitting empty for so many years—it'll be her.

Monty barks again, backing away with each low gruff, as if he's determined to do it even if he's not so sure it's a good idea at the same time. I smile straight at him, hoping it will calm him down. There's been no sign of Queenie. I wonder if *The Price Is Right* is on, and she doesn't want to be bothered. But then I hear footsteps. And, moments later, the front door opens. She squints at me from behind those dark-rimmed glasses of hers.

"Mortimer," she says, clearly surprised. "What can I do for you?" She glances down at her dog. Her voice lifts a little. "You're not here to take—"

"No!" I don't know why I shouted that. "No, I'm not," I repeat more calmly. "I have some questions I'm hoping you can answer."

I heave a breath. "They're about the vacant lot."

Minutes later, I take a seat across from her on the couch. She balances another cup of tea, bringing it to her lips. I stare at another piping hot blueberry muffin. She seems to extract them from some hidden endless supply.

Queenie purses her lips. "I guess I should've expected this after that meeting." She takes a quick sip of her tea, but doesn't say more. She waits for me.

I nod. No choice left but to get into it. "Usually when we passed by there—the vacant lot, I mean—Ms. Opal would act real strange. Like she was afraid of it. Other times, it was more like she was . . . I don't know . . . fascinated by it? I asked her a few times why, but she never wanted to explain. So . . . do you know what it was about it that bothered her?"

A silence falls between us. The only sound in the room is Monty chewing at one of his paws again, a front one this time, stopping every once in a while to sneeze drool onto his own personal chair.

Queenie takes another sip of tea, peering at me over the rim. When she nods, her gray curls bounce on either side of her head like miniature slinkies. "As a matter of fact, I think I probably do."

I lean forward until the stretch of my sling stops me.

"But, Mortimer, this isn't my story to tell. I'm not even sure I know all the details."

I slowly drift back, letting the couch swallow me again, trying to mask my disappointment. "But you can tell me what you do know, right?"

She seems to contemplate this before answering. "I don't think so, no. At least, I don't think I should." Queenie takes another sip of tea. Her eyes grow distant. "I'm just going to say it, son, because it seems like nobody else has. You don't know how much you hurt her, pretending she doesn't exist anymore."

I clutch my slinged elbow with my good hand. The closest I can get to folding my arms across my chest. This isn't the time for lessons or lectures. Doesn't she understand how much trouble our neighborhood is in right now?

The movement frustrates Queenie. She bites her lip and gives me a slight shake of her head. "You think I don't miss her, too? I know you were probably just going to stay angry for a little while. I thought you would've understood eventually, but then . . ." Her eyes glisten, and her voice changes, cracking a little as she fights to continue. "But then Trevor had that awful accident." She inhales sharply. "We haven't talked about that, just you and me. Mortimer, I can't tell you how sorry—"

I shake my head and interrupt her. "It wasn't an accident," I whisper.

She cocks her head. I can tell she isn't sure she heard me right.

"It wasn't an accident," I repeat, raising my voice. "What happened to Trevor wasn't an accident."

Her face falls again. "Yes, it was. Nobody wanted it to happen, Mortimer. Opal didn't want to take that fall, either. She didn't want to break her hip. She didn't want her children to decide she'd be better off in a home, where she could avoid steep hills and falls with no one around to help her."

"I was around!" I shout.

"It's not the same thing, son. You didn't live with her. You're not old enough to . . . you couldn't always help her with everything she needs help with. She was all alone in that house." Queenie lowers her voice. "Getting old is no picnic, Mortimer. Opal never wanted to have to leave the Heights. She certainly didn't want to leave you, either. You must know that."

"But she did leave," I say, fighting the urge to stand and

run out like I did the last time I was here. Our voices are raised high enough, Monty has stopped chewing his paw. He releases a low growl that turns into a bark.

Stop fighting, that bark says.

I didn't come here for this. I just wanted to know about the vacant lot. Instead, she's lecturing me about Ms. Opal, about Trevor, trying to tell me what happened, as if I somehow don't already know. Doesn't she get that I wake up thinking about what happened to Trevor every single day?

I know exactly how my dog died. And I know exactly whose fault it was.

"She did leave," I repeat, more quietly this time, looking down at my hands. "And then Trevor—" I can't finish. I stretch out my neck, breathe in deeply.

"Okay. It's all right." Queenie takes a deep breath with me. "Opal did leave," she agrees, nodding, her voice soft. "She did leave, but only because she had to. Sometimes you only have one choice. You either make it, or you don't. Opal only had one choice back then. Her daughters only let her have one choice. And you know what? It was probably the right one.

"Now it's your turn, Mortimer. If you want to know about that vacant lot, you have one choice."

She stares at me a long moment before finishing.

"You're going to have to go see Opal and ask her these questions yourself."

★ ★ ★

"You'll watch over the Heights?" Opal asked me. "For a little while, anyway? Until I get back on my feet?"

Five months ago. Late at night on a Thursday. A school night. I remember because the next day I was supposed to do a presentation in class about the Aztecs, and I was kinda nervous about it. If I think about it, that was the start of my freeze-ups. The very first one. I remember thinking how horrible it was. I had no idea how much worse they would get.

Maybe if I'd had Ms. Opal to talk to that night, she would've told me there was no reason to be nervous. But I didn't have her, because she fell coming down her own stairs. Carrying too much at once, they said. It made sense. She was always trying to carry as much as she could. Sometimes it seemed like she was carrying all of us on her back, the whole neighborhood.

That night, Thursday, the paramedics were wheeling her out of her house on a gurney. I watched from our front yard scared, glued to Mom's side. Trevor, like always, was attached to mine. The three of us stood there, Mom and I shivering a little, but Trevor rigid, ready to snap into action. As if he knew something bad was happening, and he might need to save someone, be a hero.

I can't even tell you how long we stood there. Ten minutes? Twenty? All I remember for sure is how everything looked surreal. The swirling red lights spinning from the ambulance parked at the curb made the whole scene seem like some kind of planned-out stage play. A half-lit dream.

Nearing the sidewalk, Ms. Opal seemed to think of something. Or remember it. She twisted on the gurney, causing one of the paramedics to say, "Relax, ma'am." But she didn't stop. She didn't relax. She stretched out her hand toward me. I hesitated, but when I felt Mom's hold on me loosen, I rushed forward. Trevor trotted along beside me.

Wherever I went, Trevor always followed.

Ms. Opal's fingers were freezing, but I held tight to them. Like when you're eating a tasty popsicle and it's too cold to hold but you don't want to stop, can't let go.

Her grip had no power at all. I remember that part for sure.

That was when she asked me to watch over the Heights— "for a little while"—and, like a fool, I nodded agreement. As if I knew what having that kind of responsibility really meant. But she said it so calmly, like she was only asking me to water her plants or pick up her mail. She said it like she knew it was something I was already capable of doing.

She wasn't wrong very often, Ms. Opal, but on the rare times she was, it was by miles and miles and miles.

The paramedics kept wheeling. Before I knew it, we'd reached the ambulance. They collapsed the gurney into a kind of a bed-thing, and one of them gently walled me away from the scene while the other two lifted Ms. Opal into the back of the still-rumbling hospital van.

I got only a quick glimpse of tubes hanging and lights flashing before Mom took over from the stranger, guiding me back to our yard, her firm hands gripping my shoulders, steering me.

"She'll be just fine," she assured me. Sometimes Mom is wrong by miles, too.

The ambulance's double doors slammed shut and the sirens started up. Two of Opal's adult daughters, wearing worried expressions, hopped into their cars and followed the departing lights down toward Townsend Avenue.

For the first time, Trevor didn't stay by my side. He rushed up to the sidewalk, stopped, and watched the ambulance lights fade into the distance. I was upset my friend and neighbor had gotten hurt, but now that I think of it, Trevor was the one who saw what was truly happening. He stared after that ambulance like he knew it was the start of a permanent change. It seemed like he understood that something was happening that couldn't be undone.

He was right, too.

Because after the swirling lights disappeared around the corner, Ms. Opal was gone forever.

And then, not even a week later, so was Trevor.

Papa C. passes a long-handled duster-brush over the hood of his bright-yellow pickup truck. He flicks it around each headlight, humming as he works. His eyes are shadowed beneath the wide brim of his big gardening hat. I know, because I keep trying to meet them to figure out if he's close to being ready to leave or not.

It's hard to tell how old the man is. My grandparents are in their seventies. Grandpa uses a cane and Grandma wants to sit down as soon as she gets anywhere. But Papa C. practically dances around his truck.

I back down the driveway a few steps, coming even with Will. "He does know this place is only ten minutes away, right?"

She frowns at me. "He's seen the address. We GPS'd it together. Do you want the ride or not?"

For a second, I'm in that uncomfortable place again. Wondering if asking her for this favor was the right decision. Knowing I can't go back and change it any more than I can fast-forward to see if it ends up working out or not.

I'm stuck right here, in the middle. Waiting.

The whole reason I showed up on Will's doorstep twenty minutes ago was because I couldn't talk to Mom, not in the state she's been in since the council meeting. Two days of being continuously frazzled, no time for anything but a quick cup of coffee before heading out to work. Then, when she gets home, straight into her office. Poring over council documents or some such thing, she keeps telling us.

Dad probably would've given me a ride, but then if Mom found out he did . . . well, that would likely end in an explosion louder than any of Gustavo's early morning crowing.

It's just . . . Mom and Ms. Opal . . . well, the thing is, they used to be such good friends. But once Mom started running the council her way, something changed. I think maybe Ms. Opal was disappointed Mom didn't approach things the way she always had. Ms. Opal would shake a tree all day, even if there was only a 1 percent chance of the coconut she was hoping might drop actually falling.

Mom just isn't like that. Not at all. She's always trying to keep everyone happy, the great compromiser, so willing to relax the original plan if it means getting more people to be okay with the result.

They never really argued about it. Not that I saw, anyway, but I was with them both often enough to pick up on the growing tension. And I definitely noticed when the coffee dates stopped, those long chats at our kitchen table. Soon after that, communication between them halted almost entirely.

I felt stuck in the middle. And even though, after Ms. Opal's accident, Mom tried to get me to go see my old friend, to stop ignoring her phone calls from the nursing home, her emails and texts and all those handwritten letters, too. I knew Mom never stopped feeling a little betrayed by Ms. Opal. After all, she was the one who had convinced Mom to become involved in the council and had then started opposing some of the things Mom was trying to do once she got there.

Mom would want me to see my friend. But she's also definitely made it clear that she doesn't want me to get riled up about council stuff. She's ordered me to stay far away from Brewster's project. Council business in general, for that matter. In fact, just this morning she asked me again if I wanted to look at photos of some puppy up for adoption across town.

For all that Mom says she doesn't want me living in the past, she's been the one who always seems to want me to go back to how I was.

As if that's even possible, anyway. I'm not a switch. I can't be flipped with the flick of a single finger. I can't just snap my fingers and go from Mortimer now to Mortimer then, from Mortimer is to Mortimer will be. On. Off. Off. On.

"Sorry." I breathe out. I need to get out of my head. "It's just . . . does he always wipe down his truck like this before a trip? How long does it take him?"

"I've never timed him," Will answers flatly. "He doesn't take the truck out that often, so when he does, he likes to make sure it's in the best shape it can be. I think it's because my dad bought it for him. He wants to take good care of it."

"Cool," I say calmly. But inside, I'm fighting back my impatience like I'm guarding the only hole in the fence surrounding a dystopian compound. Hundreds of zombies are fighting to squeeze through, and I don't know how much longer I can hold the line.

For some reason I feel like a clock is ticking down. Like the bulldozers could be rolling up Liberty hill this very moment to start Brewster's project. When the truth is that it's not even fully approved by the city yet.

Will smiles at a memory. "Papa C. kept saying, 'No,

no, too much!' to Dad when we all went to that huge Ford dealership in Grandview to pick it out. I think Dad was mostly feeling guilty about moving away. He wanted to leave Papa C. with something special. He already had a pet he loved, so . . .'"

"Big yellow truck was the next best thing," I finish for her. "But why would you go all the way up to Grandview to buy a car?" Grandview's a town at least forty minutes north of the city. Almost not the suburbs anymore, more like where the suburbs start to become country. Farms, mountains, the big lake even people from Townsend Heights sometimes drive up to on summer weekends so they can boat or Jet Ski across the choppy water.

Will looks at me like I have two heads. "We didn't *go* there. We were *already* there. That's where we lived. Why, you have something against Grandview?"

Papa C. rounds the front of the car, and for a second it looks like he might be finished. My heart leaps. But then he starts brushing down the passenger side, getting the door handles, the windows, half the windshield, even the spot where you step up to climb into the tall cab of the truck. The man doesn't miss a millimeter.

"No . . . of course not," I say. "I've never even been to Grandview. It's just . . . I thought my mom told me you were from California. No one ever said anything about Grandview."

"No one ever asked." Will lets the truth of that hang in the air a second. She's right, I've been so eager to drag her to council meetings, force her to help me with my life—well, most of it, anyway—I never asked her about hers.

"Anyway," she continues, softening her tone, "*now* I'm from California. But before that we lived in Grandview." She points at her grandfather, humming while he works. "All of us did. My parents even fixed up our basement into an apartment so my grandparents could move in with us after they left Puerto Rico. Before my mom got her new job out west and we had to go there."

"Couldn't your grandparents have gone to California with you?"

Will pauses a moment, like she's trying to decide if she should consider that question insulting or not. "I know my dad tried hard to convince them. I overheard them arguing about it a lot." She shrugs. "In the end, though, they stayed and we went."

I hate where my brain immediately goes. If Papa C. had moved to California instead of Townsend Heights, a chicken-shaped alarm clock wouldn't be ripping this neighborhood in two. Frankie and I could still be friends. Brewster might not have gotten so angry. Maybe he wouldn't have made his big move on the vacant lot.

But what good are maybes and might've beens now?

All those things did happen, along with a million others.

Whether I wanted them to or not.

"But you're back here," I say to Will. "For the summer."

She nods. "I liked living with them. I was even learning a little Spanish. Then, just like that, we move. California's all right, but when the school year was over, I told my parents I wanted to come back here, spend some more time with Papa C. and Grandma. They couldn't really argue against it."

She scratches her cheek, checks on her grandfather. He's coming back up the driver's side with his brush now. Same routine as the passenger side: door handles, windows, footrest. Will's gaze shifts from Papa C. to the houses around us.

"If they were set on staying, my father thought they'd at least have a better time down here in the Heights, where there are more people around. You know, tight-knit community and all that? They could make friends. Up in Grandview, everybody is so spread out. We couldn't see our next-door neighbors' houses without binoculars. Dad didn't want his parents to be all alone in what was still a new place to them."

Just then, Gustavo lets loose with one of his late morning crows. I didn't realize he was outside, in the backyard, and not in his basement hideaway. I've never been standing this close to Townsend Height's chicken-shaped alarm clock when it started ringing. Er . . . crowing. It's even louder than I thought it would be.

A bang rings out right after. The fence between the Cortezes' house and Brewster's place rattles. Will hears it, too. She starts to move toward the backyard. "I swear that dog has to be the dumbest—"

"Teddy! Get away from that fence!" Brewster's voice booms across the yards.

Will turns back to me. "Teddy's been going wild since the day you stopped him. Now, every time he hears Gustavo, he practically tries to knock down the fence. There's this hole in the middle, just big enough for him to stick his nose through. I swear Gustavo knows it's him, the way he struts back and forth right in front of it, just out of reach. Totally taunting that poor, dumb dog."

Brewster's voice screams out again. This time his rage isn't directed at Gustavo. "You're running out of chances to shut that Red Devil up!"

The corners of Will's mouth pinch down. Her tone drips with sarcasm. "That tight-knit neighborhood thing, by the way? It's going super great."

I get this desperate urge to defend the place I've loved and lived in all my life, to stand up for the Heights, but what would I say? She's 100 percent right.

Suddenly Papa C. is right in front of us, no longer holding his brush, but still wearing his hat low over his eyes. He pushes it up so we can see his grin better.

"Okay," he says, acting like he's totally unaware of

the epic back-and-forth commotion—rooster annoying human, human screaming back at rooster, goofy dog in the middle of it all—going on behind him. "Ready now."

Minutes later, Will points ahead, instructing her grandfather to take a left at an upcoming intersection. She's been doing that the whole way, reading the directions from her phone and guiding him in a broken mixture of body language and Spanglish.

So far, I think I've figured out *hacia la derecha* is right and *hacia la izquierda*, left. Beyond that, I'm pretty lost.

"Straight on this road for a few blocks," she finishes, pointing ahead with her whole hand.

Papa C. nods and agrees. "Sí, sí."

Will twists to look at me. "So this visit is some kind of secret, yeah?" She doesn't wait very long for my nonresponse. "It's just, I was thinking. Have you figured out how we're getting past the front desk?"

"What do you mean?"

"I mean, look at us. Two kids and the only adult with us doesn't really speak English? And it doesn't sound like this whoever-we're-visiting knows we're coming. Are they really going to let us through, you think?"

My lips separate. I fight the urge to look shocked. I hadn't thought of any of that.

She smiles and nods. "It's okay." Jabs a thumb into her

own chest. "Where there's a Will, there's a way."

I sigh with relief. "So you have an idea?"

"Not really. Well, one, but it's too late. I was thinking maybe we should've brought Gustavo and let him loose, caused a big distraction."

Hearing his rooster's name, Papa C. grins wide, looking first at Will, and then, using the rearview mirror, meeting my eyes. "Gustavo," he agrees.

Okay, so we might be in a slight amount of trouble here.

CODE OF ORDINANCES—TOWNSEND HEIGHTS

Sec. 77-1—Parking Near Mailboxes

No person or persons shall stop or park a vehicle within ten (10) feet of any public or private mailbox if the blocking of such mailbox leads to a) the inconvenience of either Townsend Heights residents or businesses or b) inhibits the United States Postal Service from delivering mail safely.

Sec. 77-2—Mail Collection and Delivery

The United States Postal Service will not collect nor deliver mail to a public or private mailbox unless a full approach and exit is clear of all obstructions, which includes parked vehicles.

Mail in boxes (under beds); Mortimer's definition of infinity

I wonder what all those letters from Ms. Opal say, the ones stashed in that box under my bed. Sometimes I take one of the sealed envelopes out and turn it over in my hand, hoping it might open accidentally. If one ever did . . . well, then it wouldn't have been my fault if I read just a few sentences, right?

Sometimes I wish Mom would stop giving them to me. Sometimes I think she probably did stop giving them to me, that there are a lot more of them than I've seen. Sometimes I wonder how many more.

That's when I think about how big a number infinity really is.

—From the secret files of Mortimer Bray

As soon as Papa C. starts to search for an open spot in Woodford Terrace Living Center's packed parking lot, Will dumps her phone into the cup holder. She begins peppering me with questions.

"Okay, schemes for getting in there," she starts, like we're all right there with her in the middle of this conversation she's apparently had going on in her head. "I've got a few ideas, but to figure out which one is smartest, I have to know more about who we're visiting. What did you say her name was again?"

I bite my lip. "Opal McKenzie."

She rubs her chin. "Why does that sound familiar?"

Because your new house is her old one?

I hold my breath, but she shakes her head. "Doesn't matter. Focus, Will." She heaves in a deep breath, as if she's hitting the reset button on whatever game she thinks we're playing. "So how do you know her?"

Before I can answer, Will switches subjects again. It's not the first time I've noticed her brain sometimes jumps from topic to topic as fast as her feet rush around her grandparents' house. Down the hall, into the basement, winding around the laundry to the rooster pantry. Random thought to disconnected idea back to random thought. "Man, though, I really do wish we would've brought Gustavo!"

"Gustavo," Papa C. agrees again with the same smile, his eyes glossy and wistful again, like he's recently swallowed a rooster-shaped love potion.

Right then, three things happen at once. Papa C. yells out, "¡Aquí!" as he finally scores a parking spot. I answer Will's question. And I realize we don't need any of her plans.

Because it doesn't matter if we're two kids chaperoned by an adult who doesn't speak a ton of English. Only one thing matters, and I wish I would've remembered it a long time ago. Months ago.

"She was my friend." No. Not was. Is. "Ms. Opal *is* my friend."

★ ★ ★

At the front desk, the receptionist's eyes go even wider than I'd expected when I announce my name and tell her who I'm there to see. She allows her gaze to float over the three of us: one (1) elderly Puerto Rican man in a giant gardening hat and two (2) sixth graders going on seventh, standing on tiptoes on the other side of her curved welcome kiosk.

Cautiously, the receptionist lifts her phone. She's so focused on us, she smacks herself on the cheek with the receiver before finding her ear.

I hear her whisper my name a few times, and Ms. Opal's several more. "Someone should be along at any moment," she tells me with a nervous smile after hanging up.

The receptionist gestures toward a waiting area with twin black-cushioned leather couches bracketing a low, white coffee table. A lime-green vase filled with tall flowers sits in the center of the table. Once we're away from the bustle of the reception desk, I hear faint music coming from speakers hidden in the corners. Sounds like the stuff they play in elevators.

I start to think we'll end up waiting here forever when not one but three nurses show up all at once. The one in the middle is smiling broadly, while the other two wear curious expressions, like they've stumbled upon a street performer with an act so entertaining they can't tear their eyes away.

"Mortimer?" the smiling nurse asks. I nod slowly. I'm not sure whether she's excited or I'm in trouble. "Oh, but it's so lovely to meet you. It's . . . it's just so . . ." She settles down and waves me toward her. "I'm Nurse Monica. Let's take you back."

I stand and Will rises with me. I feel her trying to meet my eyes, ask me telepathic questions, but I keep my attention fixed on the nurses.

Papa C. was already standing, inspecting some paintings on the far wall. He sees us moving to leave and falls in behind us. The six of us cross the lobby together, then pile into the waiting elevator. Nurse Monica presses the button for the fifth floor.

Halfway up, one of the other nurses leans over and says, "This is very exciting for us, you know. That you're here."

The third nurse leans into the conversation. "Finally," she adds with a reassuring smile.

Nurse Monica agrees. "I can't tell you how often Opal asks about you. After all those problems with her hip replacement . . ."

Will widens her eyes at me, and this time I can't look away fast enough. I try to read the message they're sending me. She's either impressed or surprised.

I feel more embarrassed than anything. Or . . . maybe it's not even embarrassment. Perhaps this emotion I'm experiencing is a bit closer to horror.

Hip . . . *replacement?*

Problems?

The elevator bumps to a stop on the fifth floor and our six-person band troops off. Right in front of us is a big desk, another reception area just for this floor. More nurses stand there. They were talking, but as soon as they notice us, they fall silent.

There are some patients in the hallway, and they all stop whatever they were doing and gawk as well. It's like we're rock stars or something. Will's repeated glances at me shift from surprised and impressed to confused and almost worried. I'm not exactly sure what we're walking into, either. All I know is the confidence I felt entering this place has slowly evaporated, replaced by a growing dread.

The reality of what we're doing, of how little I've told Will or Papa C. about it, has been slowly creeping up my body this entire time, from my feet to my neck. Now it feels like it's about to slap me right in the face.

I haven't seen Ms. Opal in months.

But now here I am, feet away from her. Seconds away.

Nurse Monica and her support team hold a quick, hushed conference. When it's over, the other two nurses step to one side while Monica comes forward and gestures at all the onlookers. "I guess you might gather Opal's told a few folks about you."

My face burns red, and Nurse Monica's smile widens.

She gestures down the hall. "Last room on the left, dear. She's waiting."

I hesitate. Is she suggesting I walk down there on my own? Cut straight down the middle of all these strangers?

"Go on."

Guess that's a yes.

The hallway's probably only fifty feet long, but I might as well be on the starting line of a marathon. The last room on the left is so far away, it seems to keep going in and out of focus the longer I stare at it.

For a second, I can't move. For a second, all I'm able to muster is a hard gulp as I watch our audience grow larger, more patients arriving in their doorways, peering my way. They're in robes; leaning on canes; running fingers through gray, thinning hair; tucking their hands into deep fleece pockets. One woman brings her wriggling fingers close to her chest, like she wants to clap quickly but has been warned not to.

"I don't know what's going on, but I don't think we can just stand here," Will whispers behind me.

I nod without looking back at her. She's right. It's like lifting my foot up out of cement, but I find a way to take the first step, even if it's super slow and deliberate. My sling might as well be a straitjacket. I know I keep shrugging against it, trying to get comfortable.

Usually, I freeze up when I make a mistake, when I let

myself get all wrapped up in what I could've done differently, what I should've done differently. But here, now, this almost-freeze-up feels like it's more about not knowing what's coming than regretting what's already gone.

Will follows me. Papa C., too. As we get closer and closer to the last room on the left, however, my dread increases. I almost stop walking, afraid of what's about to happen.

I let too much time pass before I finally came to visit Ms. Opal. She's going to be angry. She's going to kick me out. Another mistake. One more disaster.

Halfway down the hall, I hear raised voices coming from the room I'm heading toward. This time I do stop, but immediately feel Will's hand on my back, urging me to keep going. The voices come again, and this time one of them is familiar, though she sounds more tired than I ever remember her sounding.

"Hush now, leave me be," Ms. Opal says. "I can walk. Let me see him."

"If you would please just slow down, dear," the other voice cries. A strange thumping sounds out, its echo rebounding off the walls to my ears. The thumping continues, picking up speed the closer it gets.

And then . . . it's her. Opal, emerging from her room. She leans over a silver metal walker, bright ribbons tied near the handles like streamers on a bike, lifting and dropping it with each step. That was it—that strange thumping I heard. Clatter, clang goes the walker. Clatter, clang, the sound rising and falling with each of her labored steps.

Another nurse follows Ms. Opal out, her hands searching the air. She's hoping to be in the right position in case her patient falls backward, but my old friend is leaning forward the same way Gustavo was when he charged out from behind his plastic curtain—poised for a fight. In no time at all, Ms. Opal reaches the middle of the hall and turns toward us, squinting right at me.

I hold my breath. For months, I've thought about what I would say if I ever saw Ms. Opal again. How I'd demand to know how she could leave the Heights when she did. How she could leave me, how it made me feel like she left Trevor, too. How I'd tied her leaving together with what happened to him in my mind, like she could've prevented it if she'd stayed.

I was so sure I'd say so much.

But now that I'm here, now that she's right in front of me, all those words, all those plans and accusations, they just . . . float away. It's as if someone douses me with a hose.

Anger I didn't realize I was feeling washes away. Regret washes away.

This disoriented feeling that I should've been able to control something that was never in my control in the first place.

Whatever that feeling was, it's suddenly gone.

All that's left is me, the real me, the person Ms. Opal knew. Her friend.

The friend who should've written back, called back, texted back.

The friend who should've *had* her back.

That switch I thought didn't exist, the one Mom's been searching for, flips. I feel like old Mortimer again. Before-Trevor Mortimer. Before-Opal-left Mortimer.

I didn't need a new dog to find myself. I needed my old friend.

Even my shoulder feels better. My once-strangling sling, looser. For the first time since I was injured, I straighten up completely, thrust both shoulders back so I'm not slouching. I want Ms. Opal to see me standing tall.

She's right here in front of me. My friend, who, apparently, even though she was clearly told, didn't believe I was actually visiting until she saw me with her own eyes. Because when she sees I'm here—really, for sure here—her eyes go wide and her mouth opens into a big O shape.

Can I blame her? After not reading any of her letters, not answering a single one of her calls or texts or emails, I guess she had a right to figure I'd never show up.

But it's really me. And it's really her.

A bunch of time has passed. We're both different. We're both the same.

I've been holding my breath for too long. In this hallway, yes, but even longer than that. For months now, I've
been holding it. I have to let some air out. But as soon as
I do, it catches in my throat again. Because I'm so happy
to see her, but Ms. Opal must be so angry with me. She
should be angry. My fear and worry explode in a thousand
directions at once, and I can't stand here doing nothing.
Not for one more second, I can't.

I run toward Ms. Opal. She sets her feet, wincing a little
as she does. She moves the walker off to one side.

The nurse behind her starts to protest. "Opal, you need
to keep that—" she says, reaching out for her arm.

Ms. Opal swipes at the nurse's hand, slapping it away.
I reach her. She stumbles a little, still favoring the hip she
broke. In the back of my mind, I'm hearing those same
words again.

Hip replacement. Problems.

At the last second, I decide my hug will be a one-armed
one.

But Ms. Opal was ready for me. She snatches me up
with so much force my hesitation evaporates. She's crying
and shaking. I start to cry, too.

Behind us, nurses, patients, and even doctors burst into
applause. I twist in Opal's grasp, and I feel her grip tighten,
like she doesn't want me to escape. A few feet down the
hall, Will and Papa C. clap and nod along with everyone

else, though the expressions on their faces make me think they don't quite understand what's going on.

How could they?

But the thing is, even though I told them so little, they still got me here.

I need to let them in, tell them more. Remember to thank them both. But all that can come later. For now, I concentrate on hugging Ms. Opal.

"I missed you, kiddo," she whispers. And I'm pressed so close to her, I feel her words hitting me in my actual bones.

Eventually everyone in the hallway calms down and the nurses convince Ms. Opal to return to her room. The way she moves, so slowly, leaning on that walker, it's as if several long years have passed, and not just a few short months.

Ms. Opal settles into a chair at the foot of her neatly made bed. I feel this overwhelming responsibility to lend a hand at nearly every moment—as she slowly crosses the room, eases herself into her chair, pushes her walker off to one side. The Opal I knew, the one who existed before the paramedics wheeled her into that ambulance, did just about everything on her own. This one barely moves without showing signs of pain: winces, grimaces, groans, sharp intakes of breath.

Her chair has controls on the arm. After a painful-looking scoot back, she presses a button. A footrest lifts Opal's slippered feet into the air.

Just as the chair stops whirring, the footrest as high as it's going to go, Ms. Opal shifts awkwardly. The same nurse who followed her into the hallway carefully places a blanket across her legs. "Sore now, aren't you? I warned you to wait."

The nurse turns her back, bending to retrieve something from the other side of the bed. Opal takes the opportunity to stick her tongue out, straight at the nurse's behind. Then, grinning, she meets my eyes and winks.

I can't help myself. Despite all my worry and concern, I start to giggle. The suspicious nurse spins around but finds only an innocent expression plastered across Ms. Opal's sneaky face.

"So," Opal says, her tone very serious. The abrupt switch quiets me down.

Ms. Opal looks at me likes she's waiting for me to start. "I'm really sorr—"

"Tut," she says. "No apologies. You're here now. That's what matters."

"Let's get some heat on that hip," the nurse says, approaching the chair with a blue heating pad.

Ms. Opal opens her mouth to protest, but the nurse cuts her off before she gets a word out. "I had about enough of your hushing, ma'am. You're the one who decided it was a good idea to stress out that hip. So now you just let me do my job and then I can leave you alone with your friends." She looks toward me, sternly, like she's giving an order. "Y'all can have yourselves a nice, long talk."

As the nurse plugs in the heating pad and adjusts it under a wincing, fussing Ms. Opal, I glance at Will. She's still squinting and biting her lip. Another million thoughts are clearly running through her mind. She's trying to figure all this out.

I gulp again. I know I should've explained. At least told her *something*.

Opal continues to fidget, but eventually the nurse finishes. "There. Feel better, don't you?"

"Go away," Opal barks.

"Suit yourself," the nurse says, acting hurt, but she's smiling slightly and shaking her head as she exits the room.

It's just us and Ms. Opal now. For the first time, she turns her full attention to Will and, behind her, Papa C. "Where's Frankie?" she asks me while still giving Will and her grandfather the once-over.

"He's, uh—"

"Not here," she finishes for me. "I see that. So who's this?"

"This is Will." Before I'm able to finish the introductions, my old neighbor speaks up for herself.

"Hello, Will. I'm Opal. Happy to meet you. I hope you don't mind me saying so, but you look a little confused."

"Actually," Will says, "I'm *very* confused."

Ms. Opal's eyes flick in my direction. "He didn't tell you about me? Why you're here?"

Will shakes her head.

I feel like I should stop this back-and-forth, but I'm suddenly frozen again. It's like all my secrets are about to spill onto the floor in a big, messy pool, but it's too late to prevent whatever's about to overflow from . . . well, overflowing. I'm on the edge of change again. Seconds from falling into the abyss.

Ms. Opal glowers at me. "I should be angry with you, young man. You understand that, right?"

I start to hang my head again.

"And not just for not telling your new friends about me." Her injured expression looks a little fake, and soon it breaks, morphing into a smile. "I used to be his neighbor, dear. Right next door. I was in the brick house with the red door. Somebody else lives there now."

The way Ms. Opal glances at Papa C. right after finishing her sentence, it's as if she already knows who he is. Who they both are.

The side of my face is burning from the power of Will's intense gaze. "Yeah, somebody else does live there. And that door isn't red anymore." She jabs a thumb over her shoulder at Papa C. "It's his door now. He painted it black."

I glance at Ms. Opal, expecting a protest, but she's smiling. Doesn't she get what they're telling her? Her red door is gone.

"I see," she says. She meets Papa C.'s eyes. "¿Señor Cortez?"

"Yeah, that's right," Will answers through a sigh. "So now that we all know each other, can someone fill me in on what we're doing here?"

My mouth opens, but there's so much to explain. How do I even start?

But I don't have to, because Opal does. "If I'm guessing right," she tells Will. "I expect you've come here to save Townsend Heights."

"I never could keep up with that garden," Ms. Opal says to Will. She looks over her shoulder at Papa C. "¿Y a usted cómo le va con el jardín?"

Both Papa C. and Will nod enthusiastically. "Papa C. loves gardening. He and Gustavo are out there constantly."

Ms. Opal tilts her head. "And who's Gustavo?"

"A rooster," I hurry to say. For the past ten minutes I've been mostly quiet. Will and Ms. Opal have been talking about the house. I felt myself shrink into the chair when Will started openly telling my old friend about the rest of the changes they've made to it—removing the porch swing, swapping out the doormat . . . I thought it would make Ms. Opal feel even worse about leaving. I thought it might make her feel even more trapped in this place, her new home, while her old one is transformed into something else by someone she doesn't know.

Instead, she seems super interested. Not upset. In fact, Ms. Opal sounds almost happy. Like she not only expected change but actually *hoped* for it.

It should be me who explains the rift in Townsend Heights that Gustavo has caused, I decide. Will can't possibly know what our neighborhood was like before, how different things are now. But Ms. Opal knows more than I thought possible already.

"The infamous rooster. I've heard quite a lot about him."

I guess the shock must be plain on my face. "Come now, Mortimer, you may not visit or write me back, but Queenie does. Mack does. Lots of the old neighbors stop by or respond to my texts. I know pretty much everything that's been happening in the Heights." She gestures at my sling. "Including all your heroics, by the way."

Ms. Opal keeps eyeing Papa C., too, speaking to him and Will at the same time. "I'm truly sorry your grandfather hasn't received the welcome to our neighborhood that he should've gotten," she says seriously. "I tried to get out of this prison—prison!" she yells louder, casting her eyes and voice toward her open doorway. But if any of her nurses hear her, they don't respond.

She softens her tone. "I tried to get out of here to visit and give him a little tour of the old place, but they wouldn't give me my day pass. This damn hip."

"Did you really have to have it replaced?" I ask. "Did it hurt?"

"I did. And yes, it hurt. A bit more than it was supposed to, actually. Not so much the surgery, but later, when an infection set in. They've got some amazing technology nowadays, get yourself a new knee, a new hip, whatever you need. But every once in a while, one of 'em goes bad. Lucky me, I got the lemon." She chuckles and shifts, but immediately winces. It seems like the slightest movement causes her pain.

"Can they fix it?" I ask.

"They can try. Again. This infection has been pretty stubborn, so they keep having to postpone things. Latest promise is next week. I never know for certain, though. Promises, promises. Doctors are full of them."

Ms. Opal glances around the room. "Meanwhile, I don't get out much. *Real* familiar with these four walls. And that hallway out there." She nods at her walker, the streamers wavering because it's parked near an air vent. "My walking track."

"If we would've known, we could have brought you

anything you need," Will says, giving me the evil eye. Guess I hadn't even thought of it.

"I think our friend Mortimer may have been a little too focused on the vacant lot."

"Is *that* what this is about?" Will asks us both at the same time. "We're here because of Brewster's proposal? Is that what you meant by 'saving the Heights?'" She's back to rapid-fire mode, asking question after question. "But how could we do anything about that?"

"I think Mortimer believes I have some secrets to tell," Ms. Opal says. "I think he thinks uncovering them will help him figure out how to save the corner of Liberty and Prince from our friend Brewster. Your rooster hater."

When he hears Brewster's name, Papa C. huffs.

"That about right?" Ms. Opal asks me.

I nod and avert my eyes, as if I've been caught doing something selfish. Or stupid. When really what I want to do is something good. The right thing. Only I don't know how.

"So is he right?" Will asks, the budding intrigue pulling her voice down to almost a whisper. "Do you have secrets?"

"Perhaps a few." Wearing a sly smirk, Ms. Opal turns to Will's grandfather. "Papa C., en el cajón de arriba del mueble detrás de usted hay un archivo. Tráigamelo, por favor."

Will and I exchange bewildered shakes of our heads.

Neither one of us understood a word, but Papa C.'s face lights up when he hears the Spanish that I had no idea Ms. Opal could speak. In fact, that was her second long sentence since we walked into this room. And that one was even more complicated than the first.

Papa C. stands quickly, eager to follow Opal's request. He turns to pull open the top drawer of a small nightstand behind him. Extracts a blue expanding folder.

He raises the folder into the air, showing it to Ms. Opal with a question in his eyes. She nods. "That's the one." She pushes another button and her chair whirs, dropping her feet to the floor. She points to the nearest corner of her bed. "Set it here if you would. Aquí," she repeats in Spanish, indicating the end of her bed.

"You were kind enough to bring your grandfather to meet me," she says to Will. "I guess that means I should return the favor." Ms. Opal clutches at the file folder. "Allow me to introduce my grandfather to you."

Ms. Opal's hands tremble as she unwinds the red string tying the folder shut. Once she frees it entirely, it expands fully, flapping open. Pages and photos and folders within folders spill out onto her bed. Some slip off the edge, falling to the floor. I bend to pick one of the loose pictures up, angling awkwardly to keep my chicken wing in a sling from banging into any of the room's sharp edges.

The photo is old, with faded colors and rounded corners. In the center, there are two adults standing proudly in front of a store. The man sports an apron over his lower half, while the woman is wearing a dress with a white section over the front that almost looks like an apron, too. The sign over both their heads reads: Carter's General. At their feet, sitting on the curb, poking a stick at something in the street rather than looking up at the camera, is a little girl about our age. She's all skinny arms and legs, just like Will. The only difference is the girl in the picture is Black, like Ms. Opal. So are the two adults.

After some initial shuffling through the mess on her bed, Opal notices what I'm holding. Her face lights up. "That's it. That's what it looked like. From the front anyway. Along the side there was this long, concrete bench where everybody sat at night. You've seen what's left of it. It was so nice, being young, allowed to sit out there on summer nights because that's where all the adults—our parents, our grandparents, aunties and uncles, everybody— were gathered up. Drawn to the top of the hill like there was some kind of magnet up there pulling them together. Just 'bout same time, every night."

She turns toward the window before continuing. "At least, that's what I thought then. But now I wonder if it wasn't the top of the hill. Now, I think they pulled each other together. They would've gathered anywhere, because they came for each other. They were a community. A family. And that's what families do. They come together."

"Sorry," Will says, propping herself up to get a look at the photo in my hand. "I think I'm lost. That's what *what* looked like?"

Ms. Opal starts to lean forward excitedly, but she stops

short when pain takes over most of her face again. Her hand drops to her hip and she falls back. "Carter's General," she answers through slightly clenched teeth.

I glance at the picture again. "But . . . what's Carter's General?"

She laughs and it threatens to become a cough. She covers her mouth with the inside of her elbow, and isn't able to continue until the fit passes. "That's my grandparents' store. Their dream. Saved up all their money to open it," she says proudly. But then her face falls a little. "They had every last penny sunk into that place."

"Carter's?" I ask. "Not McKenzie's?"

This time her laughter does become coughing. "I'll have you know, young man, that I had a life before I married that husband of mine. Before I was Opal McKenzie, I was Opal Carter." She points at the picture again. "Granddaughter of George and Henrietta Carter. You're looking at the two of them right there. And that's me, too busy playing in the street to get a proper picture taken."

"That's you?" I look again. I see it now. Of course that's Opal. Always poking a stick at something. Urging the world to move, whether it wants to or not.

It's what I always admired about her. How many problems did I watch her poke sticks at all these years, always finding the answers by hitting just the right spot?

"I haven't been this old my whole life, Mortimer," she

protests. "Once upon a time, I was y'all's age. And back then, I spent practically every waking moment in that store."

Will smacks me on my good elbow. I turn to her, annoyed, noticing for the first time that, while I've been asking Ms. Opal about this photograph in my hands, Will's been riffling through the papers scattered across the bed. She shoves a stapled packet in my direction. Her eyes are wide as she releases it from her hands into mine.

The top page is some kind of land deed. Stapled behind it is an aerial map that, from the quick glance I give it before going back to reading the first page, looks familiar. The people Ms. Opal just introduced us to—her grandparents, George and Henrietta Carter—are listed at the top of the deed. This must be the property they bought, where they built their store. I skim the document, but it's all legal stuff I don't totally get. Mom would probably understand it, but that doesn't matter, because the way Will points past it, I know it's the map she really wants me to take in.

I flip the page to it.

The street names are faded and lopsided, but as I tilt it to read them, they become clearer. It's not quite the way I think of it in my head now, but after walking dogs through every inch of the Heights for so long, it doesn't take me long to recognize the way our neighborhood could've looked back then. A few of the lot lines are different, but there's Townsend Avenue at the very bottom, which means that other street is Liberty hill. I follow it up toward the marked lot, the spot the Carters bought, where they built their store. I gasp.

I mean, I *actually* gasp.

The outline of the building for Carter's General is already drawn in, showing whoever approved it exactly how it would lay on the lot.

The corner lot. Six-sided, high up on Townsend Heights' ridge.

Liberty Street on the far side, Prince along the front.

It all makes sense. Ms. Opal's grandparents owned a general store, a business they sunk their life savings into. It was called Carter's General, and it was built on a vacant lot at nearly the top of the Heights.

The vacant lot.

Ms. Opal's vacant lot.

But there's no store there anymore.

There's no anything there anymore.

And I still don't know why, but I have a feeling I'm about to find out.

They had these little jars," Ms. Opal says, showing us, with a small separation of her hands, the size she means. Tiny.

She glances at Papa C., trying to keep him involved in the conversation. "Frascos pequeñitos."

Papa C. nods and smiles.

"Of everything," Ms. Opal continues. She keeps switching languages like she's shifting gears in a car. "Heinz ketchup, Hellmann's mayonnaise, baking soda, and Borax soap—those last two were little boxes, actually, not jars—anyway, there was Maxwell House and . . ."

She pauses, lost in another memory. Ms. Opal's been doing that every few sentences since she started describing

Carter's General to us. "There was a stand of those individual potato chip bags, clipped by little metal clips, and—oh!—they had miniature peanut butter, miniature jelly, miniature everything, really. Small packaging helped people afford things, you know? The folks who lived in the Heights back then had a bit less money to live on compared with the people who live there today."

Ms. Opal's swimming in memories, little details hitting her constantly, like rolling waves. "Just about anyone could run a tab. My grandmother kept track of what people owed on index cards in a box under the counter, near the register. Folks came in when they were able, paid what they could manage." She inhales. "It wasn't just things they sold, either. The groceries and snacks, milk and bread and soda. Sure, people needed all that stuff. But the neighborhood needed other things, too. Like, if you came to town looking for work or you were needing an apartment, someplace to hang your hat for a while till you got back on your feet, folks sent you to Carter's General. My grandparents were the center of the community back then. They knew everybody. Including who had what available. Jobs, extra rooms, vacant apartments, you name it."

"I don't understand," Will says when Ms. Opal pauses. "There's nothing on that lot now. It's totally empty." She pauses, too, and her next words come out in a whisper. Like she really wants to know. Like at the same time she doesn't. "What happened to their store?"

When Opal doesn't answer right away, only shaking her head slightly, I chime in. "The foundations are still there, aren't they? Those random concrete piles on the side of the lot?"

I've never seen Ms. Opal smile quite like she does then, as if a bunch of people she hasn't seen for a long time just walked in the room. "That's right. The longest one—you know which piece I mean? That was the bench. What's left of it anyway. That bench was where the whole neighborhood would gather in the evenings. People brought folding chairs up the hill, too, in case the bench ran out of space. Which, with so many folks wanting to be around the store at night, around each other, it usually did."

Ms. Opal's still smiling as she sifts through her memories, but I keep thinking about how she looked on the days when she would stop and stare at the lot instead of hurrying past it. How she gazed so intently at the rubble inside the fence. Because that's all it was to me. Broken concrete. Scattered grass. Junk.

But I realize now that's not what Opal was seeing. It's not what she was drawn to, not what she was running away from, either.

Ghosts. That's what Ms. Opal was pulled toward and afraid of at the same time. Ghosts . . . and memories. They both come from the past, and they can both haunt you if you aren't careful.

Tommy Tatum making up his own ghost stories at the bus stop. Sure, that was all they were, just stories pulled from nothing. But sometimes, if you pay the right kind of attention, made-up stories have this funny way of pointing in the same direction the truth does.

The vacant lot *was* haunted. Maybe not like with a full-on ghost, exactly, but in its own way.

My old neighbor's eyes glisten. "Those foundations are all that's left of the place I loved. People I loved, a time I loved."

We still haven't heard what happened to Carter's General. I take another stab at asking, just in a different way from Will. "So was there an accident? Some kind of . . . like an explosion or something?"

Ms. Opal shakes her head and stares at her slightly trembling hands. She clenches her teeth. "What happened to that store was no accident."

For the first time today, she shows signs of real anger. "It was the city. The city is what happened to my grandparents' store."

Opal reaches down, sifting through more of the files and pages that fell out of her folder. "They wanted to build a train station, see? Maybe not Grand Central, exactly, but the same kind of idea. There used to be a trolley." She shows us the map again, but I already know where she's going to point. You step over the embedded tracks in the street every time you cross Townsend Ave. The ones that seem strange now, because that street's only for regular cars these days.

Guess I never thought about why those tracks are even there. What might've happened or been built or used before on that street. I just assumed the version I see today is the same as it's always been.

"What made them build houses there instead?" Will asks.

"Oh, those houses were already there, dear."

"But . . ." I start, "how were they going to build a train station then? Weren't there people living in the houses?"

"Yes, there were," Ms. Opal says. "The city was going to have to find a way to take the houses away from them to turn the Heights into what they wanted it to be."

Will gasps. "They can't do that." After a quick pause, she adds, "Can they?"

"You'd be surprised what people with power are willing to do to people without it."

Ms. Opal taps another page, a photocopy of an old news article. "All it takes is the wrong words at the right time. Words like *blight* and *slum. Eminent domain.*"

"What's that?" I ask.

"That"—she taps the page a final time, the hardest yet—"is how they take people's houses away so they can build a train station."

"Houses . . . and general stores, too?" Will asks. The catch in her voice makes it sound like she's recounting a plot of a horror movie.

"And general stores, too," Ms. Opal agrees. "The first step is offering to buy the houses at insulting prices. Of course, a few folks sell fast, take the quick buck and leave. They figure it's not worth the trouble when they can just buy another house a few blocks away. But where does that cycle end? You go from being shoved a few blocks away to being pushed right out of the whole city. Then maybe the state. And after that?

"Once you start running, it's really hard to stop. Grandpa George kept warning everyone about that. He wanted the neighborhood to stand strong."

"So people just . . . sold?" I cry, unable to hold myself back. "Gave up? Why wouldn't *everyone* fight?"

"I asked myself the same thing at your age. All I can tell you, Mortimer, is that not everyone starts off in the same position. Not everyone has all the same options." She sighs. "I don't know. Don't be too hard on them. Some folks held out as long as they could. Even after they left, they still protested with us and showed up at the meetings and in court. There's more than one way to go about something. Fighting in a different way from your neighbors is still fighting. It doesn't make a person wrong."

"What's this?" Will asks, holding up a news clipping.

A shadow passes across Ms. Opal's face. "That article," she says, her tone darkening too, "was the beginning of the end. *The Times* interviewed someone from the city about the station project. Made Grandpa George so mad. This city guy, he called the Heights a dangerous slum. Made the streets I loved, grew up on, sound like a threat. Made *us* sound like threats. Like something really bad was going to happen if we were allowed to stay where we were, on land we bought and built on and cared for. Suddenly there were urgent meetings, people gathering downtown and asking for something to be done."

"Making up names, I bet," Will mutters. "Like the Red Devil."

All those people in the council meetings, standing up and shaking their fists at my mom and the other council people. Over a *rooster*.

They kept saying something had to be done, too.

That someone should take steps.

That Townsend Heights wasn't that kind of neighborhood.

Ms. Opal nods and sighs. "Once the city put the fear of slums and the promise of revitalization in everyone's heads, they found more than enough support to ramp up their pressure campaign. Started sending take-it-or-leave-it letters to the people who refused to sell in the first round. My grandparents fought tooth and nail, but it didn't much matter. They didn't have enough money for good lawyers, and eventually the city scooped up the rest of the houses and even the store without having to pay hardly a dime. They used eminent domain."

"But that isn't fair," Will whispers. She glances up at her grandfather. He turns back from the window to meet her eyes. I can tell from the look on his face that, while he might not have understood all the words in our conversation, he could hear the tone of our voices. Feel the sadness of Ms. Opal's story.

Emotion has its own language. Everyone speaks it.

"There was a city manager. He sat on the city council, too. Kennedy was his name. Councilman Stuart Kennedy. He was so angry with my grandparents for leading the charge against his project, he decided to send the bulldozers to their store first. I remember the morning it happened. Grandpa George had just come back from convincing some new lawyers to help him for free. They were people who cared about the city and didn't think what was happening was right. He was so happy to find them. But when he got back to the Heights, the machines were just finishing up. His store was already gone. Kennedy's bulldozers had turned my grandparents' dream into rubble.

What took years to build up got torn down in barely an afternoon."

Ms. Opal has to take a second just to breathe. "They didn't even give them notice. No time to box up those little jars. I remember seeing all the Heinz ketchup jars, shattered. It made the lot look like a crime scene. And it was. It really was a crime what happened that day.

"It took another decade for my grandfather's body to quit. But I believe . . . I think his heart died the day those bulldozers drove straight up Liberty hill and plowed right through everything he had poured his entire being into. I know it did, because I was there. I saw it happen with my own eyes."

EMINENT DOMAIN, Definitions

Eminent Domain
The power of the government to take private property and convert it for public use.

The right of a government to **expropriate** private property for public use, with payment of compensation.

Expropriate
To take away property from its owner.

List of Townsend Heights things I didn't know (and some I still don't)

1. There was a trolley on Townsend Avenue once. That's why those tracks are still there. Go figure.

2. The city tried to build something called Townsend Station a long time ago. Now Brewster wants to build Brewster Station here. It seems weird the names are so close.

3. The vacant lot was where Opal's grandparents had a general store.

4. The city demolished Carter's General after using eminent domain to take everyone's houses.

So how did the houses end up with people like my family in them?

And how can I be as brave as Ms. Opal's Grandpa George was?

Because here's the thing: Bad stuff happens . . .

. . . and you can't change the past . . .

. . . but there *must* be some way to stop it from happening all over again. Right?

—From the secret files of Mortimer Bray

"I guess you probably thought I was obsessed with that lot, didn't you?" Ms. Opal asks me a few minutes later. "And you know what? Maybe I was. Sometimes memories got the better of me when I was near it, that's for sure."

"But you never told me why."

"No . . . no, I guess I just didn't like talking about my grandparents or their store. All the things we lost."

Opal inhales, like she needs to summon some extra energy to finish her story.

"Those free lawyers my grandfather found stopped the city's project eventually, but it took them years. By then, Townsend Heights was a ghost town, and the vacant lot was worse. Because not just the people had gone—the whole building had disappeared, too.

"Years later, once they gave up on the train station, the city resold the houses to new owners. When I found out about it, my heart broke all over again. I forced myself to go back to the Heights. Stood right there on the corner of Liberty and Prince, that empty, empty lot, and promised myself I would find some way to live in the Heights again. Those hills were my grandparents' hills. The streets were *their* streets. Mine, too. I loved every inch of that neighborhood just as much as George and Henrietta did. Still do."

She eyes me. Maybe she thinks I'm going to doubt her love—remind her that she *left* Townsend Heights. And you know what? Yesterday I probably would've. But today, in this room, standing close to her again, everything's different. I see now Ms. Opal must've done everything she could to stay.

But just because you like things the way they are doesn't mean you can force them to remain the same forever. Opal's grandfather taught her that lesson a long time ago. I guess now she's trying to teach it to me.

"I promised myself something else, too," Ms. Opal adds. "That I would buy back the vacant lot when I could afford it."

"But you didn't." I don't mean to, but I end up saying it in a way that sounds like I've caught her in some kind of lie. I guess I'm just . . . angry. Not at Ms. Opal, but at the fact that this happened at all. That I didn't know anything about it happening. That *no one* in Townsend Heights seems to know anything about it happening.

That's where I stop myself, though. Because I never bothered to investigate the history of the place I've always claimed to love. So why should I expect other people to?

It was never Ms. Opal's job to tell me all this. Not hers or Mom's or Dad's. If I really loved Townsend Heights as much as I always said I did, I should've found out more about it on my own, not waited for someone else to tell me their version. Because not all made-up stories point at the truth.

"Nope, you're right. I did not buy it back. City still owns it," Ms. Opal confirms. "Guess I spent too many years away. Had a life to live. Got married, had kids, tried to forget that patch of land existed, what happened to it. For a while, anyway."

A memory-filled sigh reaches my ears. "But when my Charles passed on and the girls were all grown up, first thing I did was make my way back. I scooped up the next house that went on sale. Didn't even care which one it was. Just wanted to get back to the Heights. Get down to work helping whatever the new community here had become. My way of honoring what had gone before. All the good it did me."

"How long did you live there before we moved in?" I suddenly realize I never asked anyone this question. Not Ms. Opal, not Mom, not Dad.

She gazes at the ceiling for a few seconds. "Was about five years, I think. Your mother was pregnant already the first time I saw her standing in the driveway, showing the movers where to put things. She was about to lift a box. Can you imagine? I rushed out there to take it from her hands. Took some convincing, but eventually I got her to spend the afternoon on my porch swing while your father and I finished helping the movers. They never told you?"

I shake my head.

"They bought that house so you'd have a better place to grow up in, you know."

"They never told me that, either," I say softly.

Will's been scrolling away on her phone. "It says here eminent domain's for public-use projects. I get the train station might fit that . . . maybe . . . but how does a giant, butt-ugly office building count as public use?"

"It doesn't," Ms. Opal agrees. "But I'm not sure that matters anymore. The city owns the lot now. They won't have to use eminent domain again. They can sell it to anybody they want."

"That's dumb," I say.

"One thing I've learned over the years," Ms. Opal replies with a resigned expression, "is that *that's dumb* isn't a very compelling legal argument."

She's probably right, but she's also starting to sound like my own lawyer-councilwoman mother. "So Mom—I mean the council—is telling the truth? There's no way to stop Brewster?"

"Probably not." Ms. Opal shifts and grimaces again. "But my Grandpa George would also tell you that it doesn't mean we shouldn't try. Remember, his mission was supposed to be impossible, too."

"Yeah," I say. "So impossible he lost."

Ms. Opal tilts her head. "That's what you got out of everything I just shared?"

"Well . . . his store *is* gone, right?"

"That's true. Carter's General is gone," Ms. Opal agrees. "But *did* he lose, though? Think about it. All the rest of those houses are still there to this day, aren't they? Every one of them was supposed to have been torn down. My grandparents' house." She points a bony finger at me. "Yours. You think they woulda been there for us if Grandpa George had quit? He made it so the *only* building knocked down was his store. Sad as it was, if he were standing here today, he would still tell you he *won* that fight."

"Okay," Will says, nodding, getting that million-thoughts-running-through-her-head look on her face again. "So what can we do? How do we stop Brewster Station?"

There's an empty silence at first. It seems to stretch on forever. But, eventually, the ideas start flowing. All over the place at first, a thousand different possibilities for the lot that aren't Brewster Station but also . . . don't really work, either. We toss most of them away almost as quickly as we come up with them.

One idea keeps coming back up. An idea with a love we all have in common at its heart. And that idea doesn't get rejected quite so fast. In fact, instead of growing small enough to be crumpled up and chucked to one side, it only seems to get bigger and bigger and bigger the longer we talk about it.

An hour later, I'm closing our front door quietly, bracing my slinged arm with my good hand so it doesn't bang into something noisy by accident. It's amazing how often that happens when your arm's always folded into a tight device that's not really a part of you.

I'm hoping I can sneak in without alerting anyone. Mom's car wasn't in the driveway, so I'm fairly sure I've beat her home. Not surprising, as late as she's been working lately, council stuff mixing in with her day job at Madison & Jennings Law Offices more and more, so that she has to work longer and longer to get everything done.

But Dad's been here the entire time. He knew I went over to Will's, but he's been so wrapped up in today's toilet flusher project (something about needing to rig up a metal chain of just the right length), I'm kinda hoping he didn't notice how long I was gone.

My back still turned, I'm just relocking the door when his bright voice makes me jump half a foot.

"Where'd you guys go?"

I spin around. My hands flatten against the door, as if maybe I can reverse-phase back through it and try coming in again, only quieter the second time around.

"Um . . . what?"

I thought I'd done so well making it back before dinner. But here's Dad asking about . . . wait, what *is* he asking about? He doesn't seem overly suspicious.

"Where'd Mr. Cortez take you guys? I saw you hop in his truck, figured you were safe with him and Will. How is the cab on that thing, anyway? Looks like a hot rod from far away. All that shiny yellow." Dad shields his eyes. "Like it was manufactured on the sun or something."

"Yeah, it's definitely awesome," I answer, wondering if ignoring the first part of his question will work. I describe the knobs and dials and fancy lights on the digital dash of Papa C.'s prized vehicle. Dad's not exactly a car guy, but he does like gizmos. "You should see how clean he keeps it, too. Spotless. Hey! Did you know they used to live in Grandview?"

"Grandview, really," Dad says. "I have a cousin up that

way. She says it's really pretty. Too far out for me, though."

We talk about Grandview some more, and Papa C.'s truck. I tell him how Will's father bought it for them before they moved to California. Dad never gets back to asking where we were, and even though I kind of feel like a big liar for dodging his question, I'm relieved. Will and I need to strategize before either of my parents figure out what we're up to.

Because Mom will reject our plan in two seconds flat if I don't get it exactly right first.

In the beginning, our meetings go great. We have to spend our time working at Will's place, away from my parents' prying eyes. I just know there would be a thousand questions from Dad, and a million more from Mom, if we tried to do any of our planning right under their noses.

Will's grandparents, on the other hand, don't really bother us at all, only popping their heads in now and then to bring steaming hot pastelillos (pork and olives and wonderfully greasy dough) or fried chicken (always extra crispy). Sometimes strange sodas I've never heard of before. We break to stand at the window and try to catch distant glimpses of the vacant lot while arguing about zoning laws and whether Coco Rico is better than pineapple Jarritos. For my money, not much beats pineapple, but Will leans toward Coco Rico.

"Not just because it's from Puerto Rico?"

"Of course not," she says, feigning offense and taking another swig.

Every few hours, we have to take a different kind of break, the ones Will needs so she can make good on her dog-walking appointments, which she never even considers missing. During the third one, Will stops to tie her shoe and hands me Cantaloupe's leash. If I think about anything as I take it, it's my sling. I angle myself in case the big Saint Bernard gets excited and tries to swing her big paws toward my bad side.

It isn't until Will hops back up to standing position that I realize I've actually been solely responsible for a dog's safety for probably thirty seconds straight.

And you know what? Nothing bad happened. The world didn't end.

Cantaloupe didn't get hurt. *No one* got hurt.

Will smiles strangely as she takes the leash out of my fingers. Before she leads Cantaloupe toward our next pit stop, I take another risk, doing something I haven't done in I don't know how long. I kneel down in front of the Saint Bernard and scratch her back hard. My fingers search for the neglected spots beneath her collar, digging in to the rolls of fur along her neck.

Cantaloupe doesn't run off. She doesn't back away. Instead, before I can avoid it, she laps her tongue across my lips and nose. Will starts to giggle when I pull back and use my entire sleeve to clear about a gallon of dog saliva off my face.

Her giggling quickly turns into laughter. Soon enough, I'm laughing with her. Cantaloupe's trying to join in, jumping up, paws searching the air like she wants to be let in on our joke.

"Well, come on, then," Will finally breaks in. She tightens the leash to calm Cantaloupe down. "We have a lot of work to do."

She's right. Our idea is starting to take shape, but there's a ton more to get right. And that moment with Cantaloupe reminded me of exactly who will benefit most, if we can pull off what we're thinking. But that's a big *if*.

Turns out dog parks don't just plan themselves.

About every five minutes, I decide we're barking up the wrong tree. Pun totally intended.

Because . . . a *dog park*? Way at the top of the Heights? How in the world could an idea like that ever compete with Brewster's?

"Don't forget what Ms. Opal told us," Will kept reminding me every time I let my doubts escape out loud. "Open. Space. Standard."

Once we'd started brainstorming back in Opal's room, we bounced through a dozen or more ideas. Dog park didn't bump up to the top of the list until she suddenly remembered that the city had passed something called an open space standard a couple of years ago. The new code, she explained, required that they add new park space in line with the city's population growth. And with more and more people moving here lately—people like Papa C.— there should've been a ton of new parks to match. But the government hadn't done a good job of keeping up.

"*They* don't know it yet, but they *need* this space to become some kind of park," Ms. Opal had said, tapping her finger on the stapled map, right where Carter's General once stood.

So, sure, maybe this plan could work, but we soon realized designing a dog park—any kind of park, probably—wasn't nearly as easy as Ms. Opal had made it sound. She had such confidence we could do it, but we only had a few days to create a proposal. Four, to be exact. Council meetings had become weekly events, and the next one was scheduled for Tuesday night.

I asked Opal to help. I was sure she'd say yes, which is why my heart sunk so low when she told us that the surgery to replace her already-replaced hip was happening Monday after all. She was dreading the rehab, set to start immediately after. There was something about the way her voice quavered that made the surgery sound scary.

There was no way she could make it to a meeting on Tuesday, not so soon after they put another new hip into her. She would still barely be getting around her room.

"But text me," Ms. Opal insisted, holding up her phone. "I'll be around. And listen, you can do this. I know you can."

Ms. Opal's confidence made it all feel possible. But now, barely a day later, the idea of two kids figuring out this proposal—formatting it properly, making sure it had all the right sections and clauses and all the rest of . . . well, everything—seemed completely impossible.

I never met him, but I could practically see Grandpa George shaking his head and scolding me.

Because he had done all he could to find a way to slow down that first project threatening this neighborhood. Because he didn't let anything stop him. Because he'd taught Ms. Opal the same attitude. The stick-to-it stubbornness she'd always tried to teach me, too, whether I understood it at the time or not.

So I couldn't stop now, either.

No way.

Two days after our visit to Ms. Opal, it seems like we've just about worn out Google. The best article we find is a long history on "Dog Parks in American Society," written by a guy named Frances Booldug. It's super complicated. At least, it strikes me that way. I keep getting turned around trying to make sense of it.

Will, on the other hand, seems to find it easy keeping the different points and instructions the article spells out organized in her head. It's almost like she wrote the thing. She figures out enough of it, anyway, to pull out the most important parts. She also keeps mispronouncing the author's name on purpose. Soon we're both calling it the Frenchie Bulldog article.

We keep hitting up Ms. Opal all weekend long. Calling, texting, emailing, asking her question after question. On the first morning, she answers fast, as if she'd been waiting next to her phone. By the time we get to Sunday, though, her texts get farther and farther apart. When we can't wait anymore, we try calling instead. Her line just rings and rings and rings.

Just before lunch, we try again. This time, one of Ms. Opal's daughters picks up. She tells us she's been taken downstairs for a bunch of tests. Tests needed to prep for the surgery, to make sure the infection's clear. And with her procedure planned for Monday, she's not sure when her mother will be able to get back to us.

All we have left is the Frenchie Bulldog article. It's not nearly enough.

Sunday evening, it's time for another one of Cantaloupe's weekend walks. I still think about my bad arm, constantly glancing at my sling to make sure it's tucked away safe and sound in there, but I actually hold the leash for at least half the steep climb up Liberty hill this time.

When we get back, we boot up Will's laptop, try to reopen all our important articles, but the browser doesn't cooperate. That's how we notice the great and untimely death of the Cortez cable modem.

"Oh, no," Will says before trying to go to a new page.

Chrome just spins and spins some more, and then: "You

are not connected to the internet."

Will tries to argue out loud with the computer, shout-ing, "We are too connected!" as she peeks behind it, looking for loose wires where there aren't any. We're using Wi-Fi, and we're on battery.

In a panic, we scramble down to the basement. Gustavo pecks at our shoes while we drag the modem out from its hidden corner and mess with it some (man, the face Will makes when I suggest unplugging and plugging it back in for the third time). It's just that, without the internet and our articles, we're sunk.

But no matter how hard we wish for it, this modem is not coming back to life. Papa C. jumps on the phone for us and gets some Spanish-speaking help, but all he does is unplug and plug it back in another five times.

We're stuck.

"How's your internet speed?" Will asks me, and I can't dodge it anymore. If we want to finish this project in time, we're going to have to continue working at my house. And somehow avoid the watchful eyes of the head council-woman herself.

We wait until Monday, so that Mom isn't home at least. But of course, like every day in summer, Dad is. I don't know what's worse: Having a teacher-father in winter—where he's always just down the hall . . . at school . . .

underfoot. Or having a teacher-father in summer, where he's always just down the hall . . . at home . . . underfoot.

To make things worse, Dad's questions about why I'm spending so much time over at Will's have really picked up speed. It's almost like he knows what we're up to, and he's trying to squeeze it out of us. To stop us, I guess. Report us to Mom maybe. Which is why I make sure to stay strong and not mention anything about the dog park plan or our visit to Ms. Opal. I'm starting to run out of maneuvers, though.

I know Dad's seen us leaving occasionally to walk this dog or that one. Both he and Mom have been a little more cheerful and a lot nicer to each other these past couple days. Maybe they think my switch has flipped, that old, dog-walking Mortimer is back again.

And you know what? After seeing Ms. Opal again, I wonder if part of old Mortimer *has* returned. At least, he's lurking around somewhere. But the other half of me understands there is no going back to who you were before. Things happen, and those things change us.

"Hey, neighbor," Dad says to Will when she steps through our door for the first time. He wipes the screwdriver in his hand on the front of his shirt. Something in Mom's office apparently needed tightening. "Hanging out here for a change?"

"Yeah, our internet is down," Will says.

I wince when Dad gets an especially interested look on his face. "Oh, yeah? What do you need the internet for?"

"It's just a project," I say quickly. "No big deal." I feel Will shift on her feet nervously. She knows she's made a mistake.

Dad hesitates. "All right then. Just let me know if you need anything, okay?'

"Let me know if you need anything" turns out to be Dad's go-to phrase that entire afternoon. Like Grandma Cortez, he keeps popping in to check on us. But unlike Will's grandmother, he never brings us any food or soda. Instead, he keeps craning his neck, hoping for a peek at what's on our screen. We cover it—and our papers—with our arms and hands every time he shows up.

"What is this project of yours again?" he finally asks point-blank during his third visit.

"Okay, just let me know if you need anything," he replies much more slowly when Will and I both echo, "Just an idea. It's nothing really."

"Let me know if you need anything" becomes "If you need something, just holler," which turns into "I'm right downstairs, you know." Through it all, we keep our lips sealed.

"This isn't like planning a dog-walking business," Will groans. "There are so many laws and clauses and standards and—"

She continues to complain for a while. I let her. Feels like it's something she has to get out of her system. And also . . . she's right.

What were we even thinking, taking on this kind of project? What was Ms. Opal thinking, dumping it into the laps of two kids? No adult to help, no experience or idea of what we're doing. I start to think we might need to stop by Queenie's or Mack's. Anybody older than twelve who has some kind of life knowledge that goes beyond the best locations for poop bag pickup and drop-off points. Near the entrance, of course. Probably on the opposite side, too, in case of emergencies.

But I keep my doubts to myself. I'm too busy getting that stuck feeling all over again. Freezing up. This time, though, it's not just about me crashing and burning in class. The consequences are way bigger. All of Townsend Heights could go down in flames with me when I stand up at the meeting. Me and my sweating neck and my dry mouth.

By the time Dad visits for the fifth time that afternoon, it's getting late. Won't be long before Mom gets home. I start to close the laptop lid but Will's hand darts in, stopping me. I give her a look that warns her my father will see our screen if she doesn't let me finish closing it, but she only nods at me firmly.

"Still don't need anything?" Dad asks behind us,

sounding the tiniest bit more hopeful this time.

Will gives me a pointed look, her lips pressed together tightly, and I get it. She's been thinking we need an adult, too. Only she's considering someone I never would've thought to invite. She waits a beat, giving me one last chance to stop her.

Slowly, I peel my fingers off the laptop. Once she's in complete control again, she opens it and spins it toward Dad, so that he has a full, unobstructed view of it.

"Actually, Mr. Bray, what do you know about dog parks?"

As soon as we finish revealing the secrets we've been hiding for days, telling Dad all about what happened with the vacant lot and Carter's General, this strange, far-away look takes over his whole face. He starts to rub his chin.

Worry fills me. Because Dad doesn't seem all that surprised by our shocking secrets.

"That's awful," he does finally say quietly. "It . . . it makes some sense, though." He glances around the room, like the history of this house, the whole neighborhood even, is written on the walls surrounding us.

"So you knew?" I can hear the accusation in my tone.

"Of course not!" Dad cries, leaning away from me like

I've stabbed him with something sharp. "I'm just saying it explains a lot. Like how none of the home ownership in the Heights seems to go back generations. That sort of thing."

I sigh with relief. The offended look on his face stops me from asking my next question, because it's another accusation. *What about Mom? Does she know?*

Will and I finish up by listing out the progress we've made on our plan so far. We stumble over our words, and it becomes even more clear how in over our heads we are. Even though I'm still kind of afraid of what Dad might say, I'm grateful for the possibility of some real guidance from an actual adult.

Dad listens for a while, reads for a while—our proposal, what there is of it, the Frenchie Bulldog article, even George and Henrietta's deed, which Ms. Opal let us borrow to support our research—and listens some more.

The whole time, he's crouching like a catcher in front of the laptop screen on the floor. The room's been utterly quiet—except for Cinnamon, who we wake up with all our animated discussions—nervously squeaking round and round and round in his wheel.

Dad stands up straight. Gets this really distant look on his face. Starts to pace so suddenly, Will jumps.

Maybe this was a bad idea after all. Maybe, instead of helping us, Dad's trying to dream up the right punishment.

After all, now he knows for sure where Papa C. took us. Which means he also knows we went to visit Ms. Opal and I never told him. I'm sure he realizes I avoided his question that day—okay, he knows I *lied*.

Maybe Dad's going to suggest telling Mom, getting the council involved. Maybe he's going to tell us that what we're trying to do can't be done. Especially not by two twelve-year-old kids.

I chew the inside of my cheek. So hard it hurts, but it's nothing compared with the agony of waiting for Dad to say something. *Anything.* When he finally stops pacing in the very spot he started, though, his reaction ends up being none of those bad things running through my head.

In fact, what he ends up saying makes complete sense, especially given the way he's spent his entire summer so far.

"We need to fix it," he says.

Fix it. Of course. Classic Dad.

"We need to *stop* it," I say. "Stop him. Brewster. Stop his project before it destroys the whole neighborhood."

Only foundations left. Clumps of concrete and scattered grass.

A wave of temporary people rushing in every morning. Ebbing back each night. Dragging all the good stuff, the things that make the Heights the Heights, out of our streets with them. Creating a void we won't be able to refill.

Come on, Dad, you see it, don't you? You were the one who taught me about waves and tides that day at the beach.

I go back to chewing my cheek. Mom has forbidden any and all discussion of Brewster Station in our house this past week. But I keep remembering, with hope in my heart, how angry Dad was outside her office on Poop Boy Day. The afternoon Brewster came over with his plans.

He even tried to kick Brewster out. So now that I think about it, I'm pretty sure he's been on our side from the beginning. But with each second that passes without him saying anything, my doubts and worries double.

Dad gestures at Will's laptop screen, requesting control. She leans out of the way. He crouches again, reaching out to scroll up and down, crying out nonsense as he does. Names of neighbors, like Mack, Queenie, and a few others.

"You say Opal suggested this?" It's his first full sentence in at least a minute.

"Sort of."

"We came up with it together," Will says more firmly.

"Well . . ." My heart skips another beat as Dad scratches his chin. "It's a brilliant idea. And I think we can help finish this proposal."

I rise to a kneeling position. "Awesome! But who's we?"

Dad glances between us, lowering his voice like he's letting us in on a secret. Which turns out to be exactly what he's doing. "There's a small group of us. Not on the council. Other neighbors. Concerned ones. We've been talking, emailing each other, mostly, trying to find a way . . ."

That secret call in the driveway, as soon as Mom left for the meeting the other day. He wasn't talking to her, and he wasn't talking about me, either. That call probably came from someone in his secret group.

Dad's been fighting for the neighborhood all along. Trying to do something about what's been happening. He even started long before Brewster Station.

My father grabs the back of my head, pulls me toward him. He kisses my bangs. I resist, embarrassed, but when I check on Will, there's no sign of mocking in her expression. She's smiling at both of us.

There's a long silence. I feel off-balance. A few minutes ago, I wasn't sure I could trust Dad with this project. Now he's . . . kissing my forehead? Looking excited? About to . . . help us? My insides go for a spin, like they're in the dryer on high.

"So what are we waiting for?" Dad shouts. "Let's get to work!"

It's hard to believe how fast things start to move. Dad makes a bunch of calls. He asks Will if we can go back to her house. I'm betting he's worried about Mom walking in on us, just like we were worried about him seeing what we were up to before.

Using his phone for a hotspot in dead-modem-Cortez-ville, Dad takes over Will's laptop. He walks us through everything he's doing, all the information he's researching and why. The neighbors he mentioned, the hidden committee opposed to Brewster's plan, start showing up at the Cortez place, too. One by one at first, looking over their shoulders to see who might be watching them arrive. Then in packs.

Papa C. and Grandma Cortez seem equally thrilled and shocked to have so many people in their house at once. It occurs to me it's probably the first time they've had company from the neighborhood. Grandma carries plate after plate of pastelillos down to the basement. All movement and brainstorming stops every time she arrives with a new batch.

I'm amazed all over again how quickly Will comes up with a nickname for this pack of concerned neighbors who arrive to help us. There are nine of them, so naturally she refers to them collectively as "Gustavo's Fine Nine." The new name sticks really quickly. Soon the Nine are even using it themselves as they help work out the details for our proposal.

I've never seen Mack and Mr. Chung, Frankie's neighbor, say more than two words to each other, but they act like old chums as they pace out measurements in the backyard, planning enclosure sizes, discussing safety precautions. As soon as they think they have a plan, they head up to the lot to measure things there, too.

Another Townsend Heights newcomer, Mrs. Dawkins—

no dog, if you can believe that, so I've never met her—visits as well. She used to work in local government in another state, so she's able to help us get the format of our proposal right. She's also the one who loves Will's nickname the most. Every time someone uses it, she tries to add a secret way they can identify themselves as members, but all her attempts are too loud, too flamboyant, or both. She starts with a chicken wing dance ("Please no," Dad objects), wriggles her fingers over her head and gobbles ("Why are we doing turkey impressions?" Mack asks), cups her hands together and blows a birdcall into them (everyone covers their ears with both hands to block the piercing whistle).

All nine neighbors seem to have some kind of important suggestion to make, and Dad writes every single one down. He uses an empty wall in Papa C.'s basement to tape up his sheets of scribbles and brainstorms, organizing them for our document.

"That should do it," Dad says, clicking save one final time. "Best we're gonna do on short notice anyway." We're at the table in the laundry area. It's getting late. All the other neighbors have gone home. It's just Will and me and Dad now.

Oh, and Gustavo. It's impossible to ignore the stir he's been causing behind the curtain in the next room. He's been hearing all the talking out here and has wanted out for hours now.

I guess Dad's been so focused he hasn't noticed all of

Gustavo's scratching and clucking, because he glances that way now with a surprised expression. "Don't tell me. Is that . . . ?"

Will nods and finishes his thought. "Gustavo? Yep." Her eyes light up at my father's interested expression. "Want to meet him?"

"Are you kidding? He's a local celebrity!" We move together into the smaller room next door. Dad watches as Will approaches Gustavo's hidden closet-home in the far corner. I stare up at his fascinated expression. He's been a completely different person from the one I've been around all summer, the one who seemed to only care about home improvement repair jobs. The one who snapped at Mom whenever the neighborhood disagreements came up. The one who did his pre-dawn countdown in the dark hallway outside my door in light I could barely see him in, then seemed almost afraid to talk with me the rest of the day. Like I was a bomb about to go off—or a poop-encrusted sneaker, maybe, that needed to be handled just right. Cautiously. Carefully.

This new Dad, though, this Happy Dad, is filled with energy and curiosity rather than irritation and worry. I see him more clearly now, how dedicated he is to helping the neighborhood. *Our* neighborhood.

It makes me think about all that other helping all summer long. The vacuum, the faucets, the toaster oven. I start to get the idea none of it was about what I thought it was about. My dad is just a doer, not a talker—frankly, the exact kind of person I need right now.

A familiar sound makes me jerk my head up. Will peeling back the thick curtain, the hooks screeching along the metal pole. I'd heard Dad agree to meet Gustavo, but I was so lost in thought, I didn't fully comprehend what it might mean. Not until the room erupts in feathers and squawks, falling wings, clawed rooster feet.

And a very high-pitched scream. It takes me a second to realize it's coming straight out of my own father's mouth.

Will chases the oversized rooster around and around the little basement room. Every time she seems about to catch him, though, Gustavo speeds up, staying a fingernail out of Will's outstretched reach. She finally gives up, resorting to forming a human wall between the rooster and Dad, her arms spread wide, feet sliding to prevent the bird from charging us with his sharp claws extended.

I've been through this once already. So maybe I'm not screaming like Dad, but I do sort of hide behind him the whole time.

Gustavo's even worse than the day he and I tussled—a rooster possessed, bouncing off the walls and the table, sending the tools flying, papers fluttering. His claws clang off the old metal water heater, rip at the duct tape covering the equally ancient furnace. In a last-ditch effort, he flaps hard, awkwardly rising off the floor and over Will's shoulder. She tries to block him, ending up in a half split, like a hockey goalie missing the puck. Gustavo stretches his rooster neck forward, heading straight for Dad's ducking head, barely missing him before slamming into several bags of dog treats stacked on a shelf behind us.

Dad and I move again, falling into each other as we shuffle away, toward another corner of the room. My heel bumps into something. I turn around and see that it's the back of an old mirror. I get an immediate idea.

I'd lift it myself, but one of my arms is still in a sling. "Dad," I say, nodding at the mirror. "Help me."

He has a question in his eyes, but it doesn't come out of his mouth. Instead, he nods and follows my lead. We each grab one side of the heavy old mirror and slide it in front of us at the last possible second. Gustavo's recovered from his encounter with the dog treats; he's heading for us again. We crouch down behind the mirror and hold our breath. In hardly a moment, the sound of Gustavo rushing toward us stops.

I peek over the top of the mirror and find what I expected: Gustavo's halted in his tracks and is staring at himself, just like before when he saw his own reflection in the water heater. Except this time his view isn't distorted.

Gustavo actually struts back and forth in front of his reflection, his open admiration of the image of himself clear.

"That was close," Dad says. At the sound of his voice, though, Gustavo seems to remember what he was in the middle of doing. He starts to get worked up again. His wings flap. He squawks loudly.

There's been so much noise and commotion, Papa C. must have heard it from all the way upstairs. He rushes into the room, shouting in Spanish. Pointing and directing, though none of us—well, maybe Gustavo—understands his instructions fully.

This is the first time I've seen Papa C. near his special pet when Gustavo's acting all aggressive like this. Once the two of them finally lock eyes, Will's grandfather turns out to be the actual rooster whisperer. He just gives the bird this intense stare and doesn't break it, saying some more commanding-sounding words in Spanish. Gustavo seems to understand them, even hangs his head a little, and settles down for good this time. Almost like he's been hypnotized.

Papa C. picks up Gustavo and holds him close. He begins to stroke his feathers the same way I've seen Will do. Like on the porch after the Poop Boy incident.

"Sorry. Sometimes he just needs a little love," an out-of-breath Will explains to Dad. She strokes the rooster's feathers, too.

My dad, who a moment ago was screaming like he'd been cast in *The Walking Dead* finale, begins to laugh. He brushes a few stray feathers off the front of his shirt.

"No harm done," he says as together we push the mirror back to where we found it. "In fact, you should sell tickets to that thrill ride. Most excitement I've had all summer."

I let out a breath of relief. After all his out-of-character snapping at me and Mom, I guess I thought this rooster incident might put him over the edge, make him storm back to our house. But instead, Dad's super cool with it, even cracking jokes.

Out of nowhere, I chuck him in the shoulder.

Dad fakes being injured, bending at the waist, mock-stumbling forward while clutching his arm. He glances at me from the corner of his eye, suddenly noticing the arm I used for my half punch is the same one that's been imprisoned in a sling for the past week.

He straightens up. "Hold on now. Look at you!"

Look at me is right. My shoulder actually feels kinda normal. So normal, I used that arm to smack him without thinking about it. I decide it's time to shrug out of my sling completely.

The initial movement over my head is awkward—first time in a while I've swung my arm up that far. So awkward, in fact, I lose my grip on the sling after removing it. It falls to the floor. Dad bends to pick it up.

For a long time, that thin strip of cloth felt like armor and a prison at the same time. Protecting more than just my shoulder, keeping *all* of me safe. Locked up, yes, but also safe.

Now, though, I see this thing I depended on for days and days for what it really is—just a loose strap really, some flimsy clips, a cheap bit of Velcro. It flaps harmlessly in Dad's fingers, and I almost can't believe I ever needed it.

"No sling!" Dad cries. "How's that shoulder feel?"

"Doesn't hurt at all anymore."

And it's actually true. I feel so much better. Not just my shoulder. My whole . . . me. How long have I been hiding how hurt I am? From both Dad and Mom. From everyone, I guess.

"That's awesome, Mortimer," Will adds from across the room.

"Really good," Dad agrees, holding his hand up. I slap it five. Even when I rotate my shoulder up fast like that, I don't feel any pain at all.

Everything heals, if you give it time.

"¡Muy bueno!" Papa C. agrees with a smile. He's still stroking Gustavo's feathers, hugging the bird tightly to his chest, like he's trying to hear his rooster's heartbeat. Or maybe let Gustavo, who's completely calm now, hear his. Papa C. lowers his pet to the concrete, sending him off in the direction of his closet-home.

We all head upstairs. Papa C. and Dad lead the way, striking up the best conversation they can have in some form of mutually understood, rapidly invented, broken Spanglish. Will and I hang back.

"That was crazy, huh?" I ask. "With Gustavo."

Will seems subdued. "Yeah. Crazy."

Out in the garage, Papa C. starts showing off his big yellow truck to Dad. It takes about ten seconds for him to end up sitting in the driver's seat, playing with every dial and knob within reach.

"You'd think they've known each other forever," Will says. Now that we're outside, in the sun, she seems to have cheered up a little. So I keep walking and so does she. Eventually we drift down the driveway, almost to the street.

"Or that they at least speak the same language," I add.

"Right?"

A chain jangles, and we both look up. It's Frankie. On the other side of the street, almost straight across from the Cortez place. The DiNuccis' husky, King, is on the end of the leash he's holding. They're both just suddenly there; I can tell from the look on her face Will didn't hear them approaching, either.

It doesn't really make sense for Frankie to be walking King out this way. It's not on the way from or back to the DiNuccis no matter how you calculate it. Still, here he is looking totally shocked. And maybe . . . sad?

For a few seconds, nobody talks or moves. The three of us stare at each other in the most awkward of awkward moments. King is the one who finally can't stand the quiet. He starts to stamp his feet, lifting his head in a getting-ready-to-howl motion.

But before King can get going, Dad appears out of nowhere.

"Hey, you kids up for a celebratory dinner?" He drapes one arm around my shoulders, the other Will's. "I think I know the perfect place."

He pauses when we don't answer, tries to make it sound more enticing. "There's this Puerto Rican restaurant—"

Dad stops himself. I feel him lift his head to look at what our gazes are fixed on.

"Oh," he says. "Frankie." I guess he hears his own surprise, too, because he tries to steady his voice. "How ya doin', bud?"

But as soon as Frankie hears his own name, he snaps out of whatever trance he was in and takes off, walking away so fast he could almost be running. He pulls at King, who's more interested in continuing to watch the three of us in the Cortez driveway. Eventually, though, the leash goes taut, and the husky has no choice, forced to break into a trot to catch up with Frankie.

I think about running like that, up and down the streets

of the Heights, with dogs like King.

With Trevor.

Something near my belly button gets sharp, stabbing me, and I almost double over.

"You guys still on the outs?" Dad asks me.

I nod. It was so weird, seeing Frankie looking that shocked, feeling just as surprised myself. Sensing the static in the air, like some kind of electricity was drawing us toward each other while pushing us apart at the same time.

"Well, you're going to have to fix that, too. At some point." Dad stares after Frankie's rapid retreat. "I would've invited him. Do you think he wanted to join us? Should I—?"

I shake my head.

"You can, you know," Will assures me. "I don't mind."

"No," I say, a little too forcefully. I look up into Dad's face. "Everyone's coming?"

"Papa C. said he'll drive. He and Margarita are getting ready. Will, you go ahead inside and get ready, too. Mortimer and I will just change quick and come right b—"

"I mean *everyone*. As in Mom?"

Dad straightens and pinches his ear, down to the lobe. "I texted her. She was on her way home from work, but some kind of special council session got called, something about tomorrow night's hearing, I think. . . . It doesn't sound like she's going to be able to make it."

Deep down, I know Mom coming to dinner would also mean her hearing about why we're celebrating. Finding out about the plan I was so careful to keep hidden from her. Still, it feels like she's been missing a lot lately. And another mystery council session doesn't help.

Dad must notice my hesitation. He pats my shoulder again, turns up the fake enthusiasm. "No worries. It'll have to be just us."

Mi Isla—turns out those words mean "My Island" in Spanish—ends up being a hole-in-the-wall Puerto Rican café smack in the middle of an ordinary-looking strip mall. It's wedged between a Best Buy and a family shoe store, and even though it's small, the sign just about shouts an invite for us to eat there, with all its bright yellows, greens, blues, and reds.

I can't get over how fascinated Will is by everything. The shape of the tables, the colorful, surf-themed murals on the walls, the accent of the hostess who seats us.

"Are you from Puerto Rico?" Will asks her as we weave through the tables, following her and the stack of menus in her hands until she reaches one big enough for our group.

"I am," the woman answers with a smile. It fades quickly, though. "But I'm afraid I haven't been back for many years now."

Will's so distracted, she doesn't hear me when I ask if she wants to sit next to me. We end up across from each other instead.

Papa C. and Grandma Cortez gaze around the restaurant with wide-eyed wonder. Watching them closely, Dad seems overjoyed. Matter of fact, he's been happier all day today than I've seen him in forever. First planning the dog park with us, now getting ready to celebrate with new friends. Somewhere along the way, Dad's switch definitely got flipped.

We order, and when Will points at the picture of pernil trifongo on the menu and pronounces it *perneel*, her grandparents start to chuckle softly.

Will's face reddens, and she looks between them, searching for the joke. Dad leans close to her. "I think it's pronounced *pernil*, pal. The 'i' is short," he says, tapping the word.

"Oh," Will says, looking down and taking a couple of deep breaths as the red in her cheeks deepens. I can't figure out why botching pronunciation would bother her so much. She's usually so confident.

"I'll have the perneel, too," I shout, purposely mispronouncing it the same way she did.

"Yes!" Dad cries, catching on quick. "Perneel for every-one!"

The whole table laughs together, and I wonder if I'm the only one who notices that, when the waitress walks away, Will's grandmother leans over and helps her learn how to pronounce every single word on the entire Mi Isla menu.

I'd never been to a dinner like the one at Mi Isla. Dad told stories about the Heights. Papa C. matched each one with memories from Puerto Rico, both of them in halting Spanglish that no one understood completely. Yet, somehow, everyone laughed anyway.

We're all still laughing and wiping our eyes as Papa C. swings a left off Townsend Ave., bringing us back to the Heights. Dad had just finished imitating his own expression when he took the first bite of a chorizo dish he hadn't realized he'd ordered. The spice of the sausage had shocked him, and he'd been forced to gulp down both his water and mine so fast some of it spilled out the sides of his mouth.

Normally I pay close attention to the way our car

immediately tilts up Liberty hill. Tonight, though, I hardly notice it. I think I'm enjoying the sound of Dad's laughter a little too much. But soon we reach Cromwell and take the same right turn as always, and at first I think we must somehow be on the wrong street. Because, even though our houses are less than a block up, they aren't actually visible right away. The evening air shimmers with bright flashes of red to blue, blue back to red, a constant glimmering that fills our vision.

The laughter in the truck slows and then fades completely. It takes a full second for my eyes to adjust to the wash of surprising colors. Half a moment more to recognize the blinking lights are coming from . . . police cars.

I take a sharp breath. Because the last time I saw police lights on a Townsend street was the night Opal left in that ambulance.

I can't utter the question that immediately floods my brain. *Where's Mom?*

I can't.

Is this what I get for letting myself get distracted?

Papa C. places two suddenly serious hands on the wheel. He slows the truck's progress forward, navigating around cop cars parked in strange angles. We maneuver past one that seems to be trying to block the whole street and I can see for the first time that some of the flashing lights aren't from cop cars at all. Not regular ones anyway.

They don't say Sheriff on the side. No, these read . . .
Animal Control.

My heart leaps into my throat.

So it's not Mom, but now there's another memory flashing in front of my eyes. Another scene I never wanted to
see again. One I'll never forget, either.

Because all these lights, the strange people wandering
around, authorities corralling onlookers back onto the sidewalk . . . it feels so familiar. Looks familiar. Almost exactly
like the day, that afternoon, the one when Trevor . . .

The driver of the car that struck him sitting on the curb
in shock, staring ahead at nothing. Me kneeling on the
opposite side of the street, my face buried in my hands.
Mom prying my fingers off my forehead one by one.

The same dread that consumed me on both those days
squirms its way up my back now, prickling the hairs on my
neck. Making sure I understand *something* is wrong.

And, soon enough, *something* is wrong will become
everything is wrong.

Which eventually turns into *nothing will ever be right
again.*

There's nothing you can do about whatever's happening, a voice inside my head assures me. You're helpless,
powerless, just like last time, and the time before that . . .
and the next time, too.

I blink. Shadowed figures loiter on both sides of the

street. People craning their necks along with me, all of us trying to get a better view of what's happening at the Cortez place.

My vision blurs again. It keeps coming and going. But somehow, in all this mess, Dad sees Mom. He calls out to her with the truck windows still up. No chance she hears him.

As soon as I see her standing there safe, all the breath leaves my body.

She's at the end of the Cortez driveway. Same exact spot Will and I were just a couple of hours ago. We were staring at King and Frankie, but Mom is doing something very different.

I start to inhale all over again when I notice Mom's talking with Brewster. Calmly! With Brewster! My own mother standing right next to that man talking. Not yelling. And now I see that's not all they're doing. They're both sort of directing traffic, pointing up at the Cortez house, their porch, shouting instructions to the cops.

My slow inhale turns into a gasp.

More onlookers arrive. Some still in their work clothes, ties tugged low around their necks. Others already in pajamas and robes, arms wrapped tightly around themselves or each other to stay warm. It's summer, but the nights are always chilly up here in the hills. Even though I'm still in the heated truck, my skin prickles with goosebumps.

I finally manage to choke out a couple of desperate words. "What's happening?"

I ask no one and at the same time everyone even though I'm starting to think I might already know the answer. Maybe I hope I can somehow prevent my guess from being true by pretending I never guessed it in the first place. But it feels too late for that.

"¿Qué pasó?" Papa C. asks. The alarm in his tone makes me wonder if he can read the sides of those two Animal Control SUVs, too. If he has the same guess about what's happening that I do.

A new Animal Control officer comes into view, stomping across the Cortez front yard from somewhere out in the gloom. He's holding a familiar metal-wire cage.

Even from this distance, even with the shimmering lights clouding my eyesight, I recognize Gustavo inside his cage. The rooster flaps and squawks, banging into the cage walls. He extends his neck and pecks at the nearest side, trying to reach the officer's exposed fingers. No luck, so he flaps again, squawks again, tries the other side. Each new movement more frantic than the last.

The cage trembles in the officer's hands. He almost drops it, grimacing as he barely maintains control.

From the opposite side of the street, barking erupts. Teddy gets a glimpse of his rooster friend, and the boxer immediately strains and pulls at his leash, yanking Frankie's arm along with it. Cantaloupe soon joins in. Then King. Then every other dog brought out to check out the commotion lighting up Cromwell Street tonight.

Papa C. slams the brakes on his truck—we were only inching forward anyway—barely throwing it into park before thrusting his door open and rushing out. He's seen Gustavo, too. "¡No! ¿Qué pasó? Stop!"

It's the last word that's so jarring. Papa C. yelling "Stop!"—in English—as he hurries around the front of his precious truck, up his driveway, straight for the officer struggling with his rooster. I dart out after him. Dad's right behind me.

Papa C.'s so focused on Gustavo, he doesn't even glance at Brewster as he passes right in front of the man. But our big neighbor doesn't miss pointing at Papa C. accusingly.

"That's him," he says. With each word, he voice rises in volume. "Right there. You left that bird of yours out to attack anyone walking by. They should take you away with him, far as I'm concerned." He glances around for support from the crowd. "Am I right?"

There's so much barking and other shouting, though, I don't think anyone hears him.

Besides . . . *left him out*? That doesn't seem possible. I'm almost positive that before we left for dinner, Gustavo was safely back in his little curtain-enclosed cupboard in the basement.

"Easy, sir," one of the officers says to Brewster, his tone stern. He's got a long face, and a weird mustache that runs down the sides of his mouth toward the bottom of his chin. "The animal is secure. That's all we were called here to do." He glances at Mom. "Correct, ma'am?"

Before she answers, Mom's gaze finds mine. We lock eyes long enough for me to recognize her big, guilty expression.

What did she do? What did my own mother *do*?

This must've been her special council business, the reason she couldn't come to our dinner. She *knew* where we were all going. Dad had told her. *Invited* her. She—my own mother—must've passed the information to Brewster so he could . . . so they could . . .

I can't believe it.

I can't. I can't. I can't.

And yet . . . actually, I can.

This was the perfect night to sneak in and take Gustavo away. To pretend he'd been left out. That he was a danger. Some kind of menace threatening the neighborhood. A problem to be solved.

Papa C. tries reaching out for the cage. His sharp movement causes two more officers to appear. They grab Will's grandfather, carefully at first. Things get rough fast, though. They bend his arm backward and he cries out. They force him to his knees.

"Leave him alone!" Dad shouts. He starts to rush forward, but backs off with his hands up when one of the officers moves toward him in response. "That—" He points wildly. At the officers. At Papa C. At Gustavo. Dad looks like he wants to say so much. He settles for, "That rooster was *not* left out. I know he wasn't. I was with the family when they put him away a few hours ago."

I was so sure of it, too. But the way Brewster lied to those officers, without even blinking . . . I'd started to question my own memory. I feel better hearing Dad's recollection matches mine. That I'm not losing it.

I mean, I guess I've been losing it for a while now. Just not tonight.

"A lot can happen in a few hours, sir," a stocky female officer assures Dad over her shoulder, her other suspicious eye still fixed on Papa C.

"I've been with them ever since!" Dad says. "All night!"

"Mom," I plead with her, pointing vaguely at Dad arguing with the cops, Papa C. being held back, Gustavo struggling inside the tiny caged prison.

How can she do this? She *has* to make it stop.

"Not now, Mortimer," she replies with that annoying calmness, holding a hand up, a signal warning me to back off. "Let these officers do their job."

"What job? Being jerks?"

"Olivia, please," Brewster says, gesturing at me like I'm being ridiculous.

"Oh, will you just shut up, Reggie?" Mom shouts, and the way Brewster steps back from her might bring a smile to my face if I weren't so furious.

From the ground, Papa C.'s heavy, struggling breaths turn into sobbing. "¿Qué pasó?" he keeps asking. "¿Qué pasó? ¿A dónde lo llevan? ¿Qué pasó? No . . . Gustavo . . . Gustavo . . . por favor . . . stop!"

"Look what you're doing!" I shout at Mom while gesturing to Papa C. The old man's shoulders are hunched from the pressure the officers are still applying, his head hung low.

"¿Qué pasó?" he moans again.

His voice is so desperate, I feel tears coming to my eyes. "Mom, you have to know this is wrong. Gustavo's not a menace. He's just . . ."

My shoulders droop, almost matching Papa C.'s. From the corner of my eye, I see Will and Grandma Cortez approaching arm-in-arm, supporting each other. Will wipes away tears, too.

"You can't do this," I insist, again addressing Mom, even more desperate than before to get her to listen.

But by the grim look in her eyes, I know she won't.

Because it's not my mother looking back at me right

now. Not *just* Mom, anyway. It's Head Councilwoman Bray.

And the fact is, Head Councilwoman Bray decides what happens on the streets of Townsend Heights. She has for years now.

The fact is, I couldn't be more ashamed of my mother right now.

CODE OF ORDINANCES—TOWNSEND HEIGHTS

Sec. 14-35—Cruelty to animals; fighting animals

(c) No person or persons shall:

(1) Own, possess, keep, or train any animal with the intent that such animal shall be engaged in an exhibition of unlawful fighting.

(2) Build, make, maintain, or keep a pit on premises owned by them or occupied by them, or allow a pit to be built, made, maintained, or kept on such premises, for the purpose of an exhibition of animal fighting.

(3) In any manner encourage, instigate, promote, or assist in an exhibition of animal fighting.

(4) Charge admission to, be an assistant, umpire, or participant at, or be present as a spectator at any exhibition of animal fighting.

Sec. 14-35*—Cruelty to animals and neighbors and sons, all at the same time

Dear Mom,

I'll never forgive you for letting Brewster take Gustavo away from Papa C. Whose side are you on, anyway?

Signed, Mortimer

Happy Dad's comeback lasts only a few hours. The other Dad, the one always snapping at Mom, is back in full force. Not that the shouting downstairs is a one-way street. Mom's giving it right back to him.

Honestly? Part of me wants to go down and join in, to show Mom how angry I am about Gustavo. Most of me, though, can't bring myself to fight with my mother right now.

Because I can hardly look at her.

Cinnamon hears their arguing, too. My hamster gets in his wheel and starts spinning and spinning and spinning.

I crouch down next to his cage and whisper: "There's nowhere to go, buddy. We're both stuck here."

The whole night is such a blur, I'm not sure if Will and I even talked. I think we didn't. She and Grandma just took each other to Papa C.'s side in silence. Tried to calm him down as they all watched Animal Control slide Gustavo's cage into the back of a waiting SUV. Helped him to his feet, supported each other as they went into their house, like some kind of sad three-legged sack race, only without the sack.

Honestly, I remember only flashes, still images of the shocking night, like paintings slashed out of a palette of those shimmering reds and blues. Gustavo's wide eyes just before the SUV door shut and he disappeared. Papa C. kneeling in the grass, dogs yelping, straining against leashes, the uncomfortable shifting of the human onlookers.

More flashes. The stern, resolute expression on Mom's face, the gleeful joy on Brewster's. The police cars doing three-point turns and pulling away. The Cortez family mounting their porch and disappearing into their house. Mom, Dad, and I crossing the yards toward ours. Heads down, all of us, staring at our feet.

In silence, but only at first. It wasn't long before Mom and Dad ended up in the kitchen at the same time. Mom was in the middle of a cup of tea, trying to calm her nerves. That was when all the shouting between them started up again. That was when I decided I'd rather be up in my room than in the middle of it.

I whip my useless sling across my room. It lands in my desk chair, rocking it backward an inch or two. Just today I'd felt like a huge weight had lifted off my shoulders—at least, *one* shoulder—when I discovered I didn't need to wear the stupid thing anymore. Tonight, though, surrounded by more of my parents' bickering, overwhelmed by seeing all the council complaints about Gustavo become real action, everything feels . . . tighter. Like the world is closing in, squeezing me more than that thin black strip of cloth and Velcro ever did.

Police cars! Actual police cars, showing up in the night. Waiting until an innocent rooster was alone, and pouncing to take the poor thing away from probably the only people in the whole world who actually care what happens to him.

It's all so confusing. They kept saying Gustavo was outside. Suggesting that he was some sort of danger to our neighbors. I know we put Gustavo back in his little closet, but those cops—and Brewster—made me feel like I could be wrong.

Every once in a while, the voices downstairs drop to normal volume. Sometimes they stop entirely, only to pick up again a few minutes later. More yelling. A few shouts. I don't hear everything they say, but the names they use . . . those jump out at me.

There are a ton of "Mortimers."

"Opal" rings out one or two times.

There's a "Will" and a "Gustavo" and at least one "Cortez."

Even a "*Trevor.*"

I keep thinking my door will spring open any second. Or someone will knock. But no one ever does. I sit on the floor, leaning against my dresser, slowly banging my head against one of its round knobs.

Above me, Cinnamon never stops racing round and round his wheel, and in my chest, my heart never stops hammering away at almost the exact same pace.

Squeak, squeak, squeak.

Thump. Thump. Thump.

Thump.

The next morning, I get the knock I expected the night before. No idea if it's Mom or Dad, but it doesn't matter. The small amount of sleep I got hasn't changed my mind. I don't want to talk to either of them.

I pull my sheet up until it covers my head. "Go away."

Mom ignores my . . . well, let's call it a request. She opens my door, takes a step inside. I lower the sheet so that I can see her holding her own cell phone out.

"I can't talk to you right now, Mom."

She purses her lips. "What about Opal?"

I sit up.

"After all, she went to all the trouble to call." Mom

steps deeper into my room. She approaches my bedside, sets her phone down on my nightstand. I see the screen light up. "Opal" at the top, the red hang-up symbol glowing at the bottom. The clock ticking away, reminding me the council meeting's tonight. That time's running short.

"Her second surgery is over. She's started rehab already. She wanted to give you all the details." Mom pauses and meets my eyes. "You know, everything that's happened since the day of your *visit*?"

I try not to blink. But in my head, I'm running through all the stuff I haven't told Mom, the sneaking around I've done. Hearing Ms. Opal's name during her argument with Dad last night. Starting to think by now my mother probably knows everything I thought I'd kept secret.

I reach for the phone, but before I can bring it to my ear, Mom adds, "Downstairs." She nods at the phone. "When you're done and dressed."

As soon as Mom shuts the door behind her, I snatch up her phone. "Hello?"

"Mortimer! There you are. You ready for the council meeting? It's tonight, right?" Ms. Opal's voice is like a warm blanket. She sounds so excited, like she knows for sure I'm going to march in there, beat Brewster, and save Townsend Heights. She has no idea that, just last night, I couldn't even keep Mom from helping him steal Gustavo.

Ms. Opal has no clue that Mom's not going to let me

present anything tonight. I'm amazed my mother's even allowing me to talk to her right now. Mom's probably downstairs wringing her hands, worried Opal's riling me up with council business. Which . . . is kind of exactly what's happening, now that I think of it. It's just not working.

"I guess," I say with zero enthusiasm. The other thing Ms. Opal doesn't understand is that I've pretty much given up already.

She doesn't reply right away. I know I should try to sound more positive. It's just that everything has gotten so jumbled. So I change the subject and ask her how her surgery went. That's what she called to talk about, right?

"The doctors say my operation went exactly as planned this time. So I'm hoping this particular new hip ends up being my rest-of-life hip."

Ms. Opal chuckles, but it's a nervous one, and for the first time I get the idea she might be afraid of what will happen to her if this second hip fails like the first one did. If there's another bad infection.

"They had me at rehab first thing this morning. It went so much better than the day after my last surgery. You know, I'll still need the walker for a while . . . but come on, this must be boring you. Tell me about your proposal! Do you feel good about it?"

I wish I could come up with something new to say, but I can't. "I guess."

"Mortimer." If I were in front of her, she'd reach out and lift my chin. But she's not here. She's miles away. So my chin stays fixed to my chest. "What's wrong?"

"Nothing. It's . . . I . . ." I can't find the words.

"Take a second."

"O-Okay." I launch into a blow-by-blow of the past several days. I begin slowly, but soon my words start rolling as if they were going straight down Liberty hill. Working on the proposal, the dinner celebration, Animal Control showing up in the Heights. How they took Gustavo away.

Doesn't feel like all those things could've happened in just one weekend. Seems like it must've taken months.

"The worst thing is, Mom planned the whole thing. She did exactly what Brewster asked her to do. And now Gustavo's missing."

"Oh, Mortimer, are you sure? I don't think your mother would—"

Suddenly I do want her here lifting my chin. "Can you come home? I mean . . ." It's not her home anymore, my brain reminds me. But those are just details. "To Townsend Heights? Like, now? Or at least tonight, for the meeting? Can you—"

"Mortimer, I'm not . . . no, I'm sorry, I can't travel so soon. My hip still isn't . . . Listen, you—"

"But you *have* to. How can you stay *there* when the meeting is about to happen *here*?"

I heave a breath. How can I explain all this in the time we have? Mom's bound to burst back into my room any second. Come to think of it, she might even have her ear to my door out in the hall. My mind races. Have I already said something I shouldn't have?

"Let's go one step at a time," Opal says. "Maybe you'll feel better if you help your friend get her grandfather's rooster back. Where did they take him?"

She's right. Of course, Ms. Opal's always right. That's what I should be worrying about. They took Gustavo, sure, but it doesn't mean we can't try to get him back.

"I . . . I don't know." But I do know someone who does. "I'm sorry, I have to go."

"Well . . . all right," she says after a second's hesitation. "Listen, Mortimer, just slow down, take a deep breath. I believe in you. You know that, right? The whole neighborhood does." She sighs so loudly I almost think I feel her breath whoosh into my ear. "I just wish I could help you more."

We hang up. I rush to get dressed so I can wash up quick. I want to stay positive, but I can't stop hearing Ms. Opal's voice. Her tone. Her words. Her pauses.

When the conversation started, she'd been excited.

By the time it ended, though, all that remained was worry.

I can't fix that. But what I can do is exactly what she suggested.

Find Gustavo. Bring him back.

One step at a time.

Downstairs, Mom's drinking her morning cup of coffee, sitting at the kitchen table. There's no sign of Dad anywhere.

I march in, determined, and slam her phone down right in front of her. From the way her brow furrows and her eyes darken, it's possibly not the best move.

"Where is he?" I demand. "Where did they take Gustavo?"

32

"**T**hat's *not* on my list of things we need to talk about," Mom says. Her expression doesn't shift. There's no light in her eyes, no hint of a smile on her lips. On any other day, I'd slowly back out of the room, give her the morning—or maybe most of the week—to get over whatever's made her that angry.

Not today, though.

Today I stand my ground.

"Well, it's on mine." I point next door, at Will's house. "Where did you and Brewster tell them to take Gustavo?"

"Me and . . . Brewster? Mortimer, what—"

I refuse to let her talk circles around me, so I interrupt.

"Do you have any idea what you're putting their family through? How awful—"

"Sit down, Mortimer." The calm way she peers at me over the lip of her mug as she takes another sip of her coffee spikes a splinter of fear into my chest.

Still, I push at the back of the already-pushed-in chair. Doing my best to make it clear that I have no intention of pulling it out and sitting down.

Outside, a strange echo rings out. Almost sounds like it's coming from next door. But it couldn't be Gustavo. Not after last night. In fact, today was the first day in forever I didn't get woken up by the rooster's 5:00 a.m. serenade. Though it didn't matter much. I was lying in bed wide awake anyway, same as always.

"Okay," Mom says slowly, eyeing the chair. "I actually *don't* know where he went, Mortimer. The Cortezes were provided with the steps to follow to regain custody of the . . . of Gustavo." Mom looks down at her hands, watching them spin her mug once all the way around. "Animal Control's required to do that. And let's remember, they're the ones who took him away, not me. And whether the Cortezes are able to actually get custody back or not is up to the courts now. *Not me*."

She leans forward and keeps going. She wants to get this last bit in before I have the chance to interject again. "But

Mortimer, these are not things a twelve-year-old should be worrying about. You've had . . ." She sighs. "Things have been rough for a while now."

I look away from her. She takes my inability to meet her eyes as agreement. "You really don't need any more stress. I want you to stop thinking about Gustavo and the vacant lot and Mr. Brewster's project, okay? I know Ms. Opal—" She stops herself. "Just . . . try to relax. You *know* what happens when you get too worked up."

"This has nothing to do with Ms. Opal, Mom," I half shout. The words feel true leaving my lips, but are they? Isn't Ms. Opal the one making me do all this? The idea for the dog park came from my visit to the nursing home, for sure, but was it my idea? Will's?

Or was it Ms. Opal's?

It's hard to separate one from the other, which makes me feel even less in control of what's happening. Still, I can't agree with Mom. Doing nothing is . . . well, it's doing nothing.

"And you want me to relax?" I take a step back from the table. "How can I relax?"

"Mortimer, please."

"Where's Dad?" I ask, looking to each side and over my shoulder, as if I might spot him standing there, when I already know he can't be home. Because if he were, he'd have heard us by now. He would've *done* something by now, at least showed up to referee. Definitely wouldn't be just *talking* about doing something. Or doing nothing at all. *Relaxing.*

"He said he needed a few minutes alone. Went somewhere. Probably to the hardware store."

"He's been trying to help, you know. He wants to fix . . ." I gesture wildly, huffing, not really sure of what I'm trying to say. "All this. He's trying his best. You should've seen how excited he got when we asked him to help us with our proposal."

"Ah, yes. The proposal. Your father tells me it's going to fix everything. That I should give you a chance to stand up in front of all those people and present it."

She says it like all our work is a big joke—just some silly idea Dad and I cooked up together. And do I even disagree at this point? The low heat at the base of my neck starts rising toward my face. I fight it back, hearing her words from only seconds ago, about what happens when I get "worked up."

"Telling me not to present—I suppose *that's* on your list?" I know I should've sided with Dad, defended our proposal as much as it sounds like he did last night, but it's hard for me to fake it like that. Truth is, I think our idea probably will turn out to be a huge flop. A big waste of everyone's time.

"Yes, actually. Mortimer . . ." Mom sighs again. "Do

you really think this plan of yours has any chance of working? With the . . . struggles you had at the end of the year . . ." She doesn't finish. She doesn't have to. Everything rushes back again, that fast, taking over my whole body this time. The sweat on my face, the change in my voice, my dry mouth. And that was in front of my friends, a class of not even thirty other kids. Not the entire neighborhood, not the whole council, not the special VIPs from City Planning and Development.

"Mortimer, that meeting tonight . . ." She shakes her head, searches her fingertips for words she's obviously having trouble conjuring up. "It's not for . . . young people. And your idea . . ." More headshaking. "The city isn't going to want to hear about putting a dog park on that lot. You have to understand how lucrative a project like Mr. Brewster's is. How beneficial it will be for the people of this neighborhood. The whole city, really. A dog park simply can't compete with all that."

I'm so tired of hearing her call him "Mr. Brewster" while she sides with him. Like he's her boss or something.

"The city doesn't want to hear it? Or you don't?"

"I've already told you that this is not about me, Mortimer. It's not my role to—"

"To do what? The right thing? What *is* your role, then? What's anybody's role, if it's not to do the right—"

"Stop!" Mom slams her hand flat on the table. Her

phone jumps. Her coffee mug rattles.

Everything goes silent. I hear the echo again, clearer this time, like a siren or something, right behind our house. From the way she turns her head, Mom hears it, too. But she blinks and frowns. She's working hard to convince herself whatever we're hearing isn't important enough to interrupt this particular talk.

"Mortimer, I know you care very much about the people who live here, these streets, the houses. I know that's what Opal . . . I know it's important to her, and I know she's important to you. Very important." She sniffs. "Dad even told me about her grandparents' store. All that, it's very terrible. It should never have happened. But you have to understand I only want what's best for *you*. I'm on your side here."

Mom reaches out across the table, as if I'm going to meet her halfway, put my hand into hers. But I don't move, only stare at her open fingers.

She leans back into her seat again and her slowly softening expression hardens once more. "I admire your passion so much, Mortimer. Really, I do. But I want you to think about how much you care about Townsend Heights." She meets my eyes until I relax my posture. "Now multiply that times one thousand. Because that's how much *I* care about *you*."

I'm not quite sure what she's saying.

"And . . . well, because of that, I can't let you put your-self in front of all those angry people to talk about putting a dog park on that lot." She says the words *dog park* like they're completely ridiculous. "Not with the year you've had. Not after all your struggles."

"That's what's wrong with me according to you? That my brain is . . . you think I'm broken, don't you?"

I stop myself when I see the shocked look on her face. Maybe that was going too far. I steady my breathing, level my voice, try to focus less on my emotion, change the sub-ject to something she can hold, look at, touch. I think it's easier for both of us. "Did you even read the proposal? Did Dad show it to you?"

Mom exhales again, the longest one yet, like this whole discussion is making her tired. No, not just tired. *Exhausted.* "I don't need to read it to know what's going to happen, Mortimer. I'm sorry. I won't have you humiliated like that."

Humiliated? Does she think I'm that . . . I can't believe she would say . . . I can't even respond.

Mom fills the silence. "I'm trying to help you, honey—"

"So you'll tell me where Gustavo is?"

"Come on, Mortimer, I told you I don't know."

"At least admit you were the one who told Brewster that the Cortezes wouldn't be home last night."

"Told who . . . what . . . ? Mortimer, where are you

getting—" she says, clenching her teeth and glowering harder at me. She takes a deep breath, clearly giving herself a second to calm down before finishing. "I was only out there to make sure nothing bad happened. That's it."

"But something bad did happen! They took Gustavo!"

As my raised voice dies in the air, we hear it again. The noise behind us. Clearly now. It sounds like . . . like some kind of howling.

Mom can't ignore it any longer. She pushes her chair back and stands. "What in the world?"

I follow her out the back door. From our deck, we can see over the tops of the fences behind us, and next door, too. The Cortez yard, usually full of so much activity—a clucking rooster and a puttering old gardener and sometimes even Will playing with one of her dog customers—is completely quiet this morning. But over the back fence, on Brewster's deck, Teddy sits alone, staring longingly into space.

The boxer lifts his head into the air, straight up, and releases the most miserable-sounding howl I've ever heard come out of a dog. It splits the still morning air.

The noise rattles heavy in my chest, settling there. This was it, the sound we kept hearing inside, muffled compared with how it sounds out here.

Mom stares forward with an empty expression, tilting her head like she's trying to figure out what she's looking at. Hearing. Teddy's lived behind us for years. Sometimes he'll do a bunch of barking, maybe race around his yard in ever widening circles, kicking up dirt like a madman, but he's never howled like this. No way.

I whisper a theory. One I'm pretty sure is true. I think it's the way he's staring at that hole in the fence he and Gustavo used to have their little chats through.

"He misses him."

Mom turns to me. "Who misses who?"

"Gustavo. Teddy misses him. They were friends." I let it sink in for a minute, wait for her to see I'm right, before adding, "Imagine how Papa C. feels."

Mom reaches out to the deck railing, gripping it with tight fingers. She nods slightly.

Suddenly Brewster's back door opens and he stumbles out, looking left and right. That's when Teddy lifts his head to start another sad, longing howl.

"What the—" Brewster starts before rushing forward, hands outstretched.

The large man slides his fingers beneath Teddy's collar, halting the dog mid-howl. He's grabbing him in the identical spot I did in our front yard, and uses his grip to yank the boxer hard, pulling him backward across the deck. I feel the pain in my shoulder even as I watch Teddy trying to dig in. But there's no soft grass this time; his paws slide on the slick wooden surface. His nails skitter wildly.

Brewster cranes his neck left and right again, clearly checking to see if anyone's noticed that it's *his* animal disturbing the neighborhood peace this time. I can tell it's what he's thinking by the panicked look in his eyes. They're so wide I can see the whites in them from almost two yards away.

He lets up on his dog when he sees us standing there. Brewster straightens his posture. With a final jerk, he swings Teddy in the direction of his still-open back door, giving him a smack on his rump as it passes by. The boxer disappears inside with a sharp yelp.

His eyes never leaving us, Brewster shifts his shoulders, like he's trying to pretend we didn't just see what he knows we just saw. Then he follows his dog inside, and before the door shuts again, we hear his shouting starting up all over. Is he blaming Chester? Or just yelling at Teddy some more?

Mom looks down at me. Her eyes are dark. But not the same kind of dark they were before, that flame-like anger lingering behind them. This is a different shadow, an exhausted sort of grayness.

"I'm telling you the truth, Mortimer," she says. "I don't know where they took Gustavo. I didn't think to ask last night. There was so much—"

She pauses, and I open my mouth to issue another pro-test, but she continues before I can get the words out. "I can probably find out, though. Give me a few minutes to make some calls." She swallows hard. "You can go help your friend and her grandfather, at least tell them where to visit. As long as you forget about tonight, your dog park thing. Let me handle Mr. Brewster, okay? Do we have a deal?"

She isn't giving me much of a choice. I *have* to help Will and her family. Because Ms. Opal was right—as much as I want to fight Brewster Station, nothing will feel worth doing if we don't get Gustavo back first.

So even though I really don't want to keep having to lie to my parents, I nod back slowly, cross my fingers behind my back, and give her the answer she wants. A promise I have no intention of keeping.

"Deal."

hardly look up from Mom's handwriting as I rush out the door. It took her three calls, but eventually she got the answer I was looking for. She wrote down the address for the Stuyvesant County Animal Shelter on this powder blue index card in my fingers, and now I'm protecting it like it's etched in gold. I march my legs as fast as they'll go across the yards. Before—I don't know—a strong wind blows it out of my hands and the precious info is lost forever.

I'm so intent on the card, I hear Frankie's voice before I notice him standing right there in my own yard. "Mortimer?"

"Not now, man."

He's got a desperation in his eyes, but no leash in his hands. He isn't here because he's on a walk. He came all on his own this time.

Frankie's gaze shifts downward. I go back to hurrying toward the Cortez house. Instead of taking the hint and heading home, though, I hear his footsteps as he follows me across the grass. I consider spinning around to tell him off again, but just then Will and Papa C. pop out of their front door.

Will hesitates for the briefest of moments when she spots Frankie behind me. But she's not about to let him stop her. She marches down their steps, Papa C. right behind her.

"We need to talk to your mom," she demands. "The city's Animal Services Department is saying they don't know anything about any roosters." She gestures at Papa C. with a thumb over one shoulder. "He's losing his mind not knowing where Gustavo is."

Papa C.'s glancing all around the yard like his missing pet might appear from behind a nearby tree at any second. His facial features are as drawn as Mom's were on our deck twenty minutes ago. This whole deal is wearing everyone out. It's equal opportunity exhaustion around the Heights these days.

I raise the card over my head. "The city doesn't have him. Not sure why, but they sent Gustavo to the county shelter instead. It's farther away, but not by much."

Glancing at Frankie cautiously, Will grabs the card from me. She reads the address out loud, and then whips out her phone and types it there, too. Once she has it mapped, she shows the result to Papa C.

"Aquí," she says.

The light returns to her grandfather's face. "¿Gustavo?" he asks excitedly.

"Yes."

"Sí, sí," Papa C. says. "Vámonos." He turns and heads toward the garage and his shiny yellow truck.

Frowning, Will looks Frankie up and down. "So what's *he* doing here?"

"I need to talk to you guys," Frankie says. "It's really important."

Behind Will, Papa C.'s truck rumbles to life. No dusting it off for twenty painful minutes today. Not when Gustavo is missing. I figure Will's going to chase Frankie off but I'm shocked when instead she says, "Then I guess you'll have to tell us about it on the way."

For the first part of the drive, the only talking comes from the front, Will once again navigating for Papa C., reading the English directions from her phone out to him in that same combination of Spanglish, hand gestures, and body language.

I watch intently, part of me worrying that we're already

too late. What if, by the time we pull into the shelter parking lot, someone has already moved Gustavo to a new place?

If we don't get Gustavo back, if we don't beat Brewster and his dumb station tonight . . . I'm just not sure I can handle those two back-to-back disasters.

Maybe Mom is right. What's the point of presenting some random dog park proposal? As if the city will listen to what two twelve-year-old kids have to say. Especially if one struggles to string two words together.

I glance up at Will, confidently directing her grandfather across town. I'm so glad she'll be up on the podium with me tonight. Matter of fact, I should let her do all the talking. Most of it, anyway.

I almost forget Frankie's sitting in the back of the truck with me. I jump when he leans over and whispers. "I saw a map."

"What are you talking about?"

Will shouts a sudden change of direction. Papa C. barely has time to make the turn. Frankie's attention is momentarily captured by the commotion. Once he sees it's all under control, though, he whispers an answer meant just for me. "A map of Townsend Station."

"You mean Brewster Station," I say, lowering my tone to match his.

"No, I mean *Townsend* Station."

I shake my head. "Start over. You saw a map where?"

"At the Brewsters' house. The old man's office. Sometimes . . . I've been going over there."

"You don't have to whisper it, dude. I know you're hanging with Chester now," I say. "I've seen you guys around."

Frankie leans back in his seat. Away from me or away from the truth, I'm not sure. "I was angry at you, okay?" He scratches the back of his head. "I did some stupid things. Stuff . . ." Frankie inhales. "Stuff I should apologize for."

He bites his lip. I wait. So *is* he apologizing? I'm not exactly sure.

Frankie shakes his head and meets my eyes again. "I'm really sorry, Mortimer. But maybe something good came out of it? Because I saw that map. It's . . . Brewster Station, the vacant lot . . . it's only the start of the real plan. Later on, it'll be the whole neighborhood. So they can build what they really want to build: Townsend Station."

He pauses, waiting for my reaction. Townsend Station. That's what Ms. Opal had called it, the train station the city was planning to build over sixty years ago.

But they wouldn't try that again, would they? They couldn't. It . . . it failed already. Shouldn't that mean you're not allowed to . . . I mean, no do-overs, right?

When I still don't respond, Frankie tries to explain. "I think it's supposed to be a station, with stops. For the train." He nods his head to one side, as if we're still in the Heights, and he's indicating the tracks on the north end, where the trains rumble across our high ridge several times a day. "And something else, like a transit line? You know, sort of a subway. Except above ground. Straight down Townsend Ave. It was all right there, on the map."

"The map you saw. At Brewster's house. Hanging with Chester."

Frankie nods and hangs his head, like Brewster's plan is his fault somehow. "Mr. Brewster kept saying how important it was to get in there first. 'All the money's in being first.' Must've heard him tell five different people that, about ten different times. Not really sure what that means."

I still can't put words together. I'm picturing the plan that Frankie's describing, comparing it with what I remember from Ms. Opal's files. As far as I can figure, they're almost exactly the same.

Didn't Mr. Holloway teach us something like this in social studies last year? The whole history-will-repeat-itself-if-you-don't-learn-from-it thing?

I guess I thought it was teacher-speak, not an actual thing. But if Frankie's right, Brewster Station's only the first step of a much bigger plan. An old plan, coming back from the dead, like a giant-size zombie rising from the grave. *Townsend Station.* And that means Brewster and his team don't just need one big, empty lot. For Townsend Station, they'll need the whole neighborhood.

"We're here," Will announces and I notice we've stopped moving. Truck doors are open. She's leaned the seat forward, waiting for us to climb out. Her grandfather is halfway to the front door of the Stuyvesant County Animal Shelter, gesturing at us to hurry up.

A chorus of barking—plus a bunch more yelping, whin-ing, huffing, and gruffing—welcomes us as we step through Stuyvesant's front door. After some negotiating with the shelter manager, who looks like she's just emerged from wrestling a Great Dane and doesn't have much fight left in her, a tall, pimple-faced teenager named Brett is nominated to lead us back through the kennel area.

We follow Brett as he pushes through the swinging doors on the back side of the lobby. We stay right behind him as he lopes down the long, straight hall, past a couple of examining rooms. For a second, the place falls silent. I sense the hush of anticipation.

Brett fiddles with his keys, doesn't explain a thing we're

seeing. Honestly, he isn't the best tour guide.

We turn a corner and there they are. The dogs. The source of all that noise from earlier. And, as soon as they see us, we're hit full force with a new stanza from Stuyvesant's canine choir. We sweep past cages on the left, more on the right. Some dogs are alone, but most share their tiny shelter prisons with groups of two and three others.

As we pass by each of their cages, the dogs stop making all their noise long enough to stare at us hopefully, or stand on hind legs so they can stick their noses between the bars, checking out our scents.

They remain mostly silent for those few seconds, like they're holding their breath—trying so hard to be good boys and girls—right up until the moment it's clear we aren't going to stop to pet them. That's when the barking, whining, and yelping erupt all over again.

We march past them, like horses with blinders on, but it's really hard *not* to stop. Especially, I can tell, for Will. She clenches her fists at her sides with each cry she hears. But she forces herself to keep going forward, for Papa C.'s sake.

Because somewhere ahead, Gustavo's waiting for us to find him.

Even as, to our left and right, the dogs continue barking. And barking and barking and barking.

I've been walking dogs too long, I think, because I feel

like I actually understand them. What's probably just noise to everyone else reaches my ears as if it's not barking, but clear English begging.

"Hey, what about *me*? Come back and pet *me*! Take *me* home. I'll be so good. I *promise*."

Someone's written names and descriptions of the dogs on cards. They're taped near the top of every cage. Halfway down the hallway, Will starts reading every single one out loud. It's as if, since she knows she can't stop and meet them the way she wants to, she's at least acknowledging each dog exists by speaking their names and breeds.

"Hi! My name is Zoey! I am a terrier. Hi! My name is Paco! I am a chihuahua. Hi! My name is Hank! I am a rottweiler!" Her voice grows softer and more desperate with each card. All those sad faces wearing her down. Wearing us all down.

I make the mistake of meeting the eyes of Hank the rottweiler. His are huge and longing, and they stare at me without blinking. I'd done such a good job of avoiding the gazes of the other dogs, but now I can't turn away from this one's deep, soulful gaze. I've never seen a rottweiler in person before. Hank is as ginormous as the rumors I'd heard. His eyes are telling me stories already, and at the same time promising he has a ton more from the same place they came from. This dog has a whole life to share with someone, if they'd just stop walking past him. If they'd only give him a chance.

If *I* would only give him a chance.

Because he isn't even glancing at Frankie or Will or Papa C. Hank stares straight at me, like I'm the only one in our group.

I'm so distracted by the way he's looking at me, I forget to keep walking for a second. Frankie, his attention stolen by an Airedale terrier bouncing up and down like he's on a pogo stick—"HiMynameisPeter,HiMynameis-Peter,HiMyname" I swear I can hear him say—bumps into me. We almost tumble down to the concrete together. Holding each other up, Frankie and I untangle and rush to catch up with the rest of our group. Hank whines and barks after me, but just once.

"This is awful," Will whispers when we pull even with her.

Papa C. must hear, because, despite his rush to find Gustavo, he pauses long enough for Will to reach his side. He puts one arm around her shoulders, hugging his grand-daughter tightly.

For the entire, long walk past the rest of the cages, Frankie's expression is vacant. He looks around, open-mouthed, at the dogs, the prison bars, the friendly signs in bright cursive that seem out of place in the middle of all the crying and whining. Maybe I'm doing the same, because it *is* awful. All these dogs, caged. Barking at me, yelping at me, begging for my help.

I try to stop looking. Stare at the floor instead. It's better if it's only noise, if I don't see the faces that belong to all that carrying on.

There are drains every twenty feet or so, and I notice the cement floor slants slightly toward each one. We step around random puddles, little accidents where some pup or another couldn't quite make it outside. Hoses pop up at random spots, wound around a holder or lying jumbled on the floor. Probably the way they send all those puddle mistakes toward the drains when they need to.

Brett nods recognition at a few other teenagers who pass us with more dogs on leashes, about to take them out for a walk around the yard. They nod back at him, but mostly they stare at us, probably wondering what three kids and an old man are doing here, in this back part of the shelter with so many Staff Only signs hanging from every wall and door.

Papa C. pulls away from Will, straightens, and gets Brett's attention by asking a question in Spanish.

I can't tell if Brett understands it or if he's just faking it, but he turns toward us as he points ahead. "The fowl area is out back. Just around the next bend."

"There's a whole fowl *area*?" Will asks.

Brett nods enthusiastically. "Oh, yeah, for sure. It's mostly just chickens, though. We have one guinea fowl.

And the rooster who came in last night."

Will and I meet each other's eyes knowingly. *Gustavo.*

Brett shrugs at us. He pushes another door open and morning sunlight streams in, forcing us to lift our hands to our faces to block it. Outside, a half dozen chickens wander around the edges of a tight cage, pecking at scattered feed, dipping their beaks into a water dish. Next door, the tallest bird, gray with a sort of powder blue face none of the rest have, stands up straight, perking up at the sudden appearance of so many newcomers. The strange chicken with his red beak and jowls takes a breath before stretching its neck up. It starts to squawk.

I guess that's what you'd call this awful noise. Actually, it sounds more like a goose than a chicken, more of a honk than a cluck. Only when you hear geese, they're usually flying way high overhead. This weird, blue-faced dude is two feet from us. If it's possible, it sounds worse than Gustavo's 5:00 a.m. crows. Louder, more grating.

Frankie covers his ears. "What is that? A car alarm?"

"Told you we had a guinea fowl," Brett snickers. He points toward a woman standing outside the last cage. All the way at the end, beyond the chickens, past the guinea fowl. She's wearing a big floppy hat, kind of like Papa C.'s safari one, except, well . . . floppier. Her rolled white socks peek out from the top of her tan work boots. She has cargo shorts on, and a blue button-down shirt tied near the waist.

There's a rooster in her arms. As she turns to face us, we see him more clearly.

Clear enough to know for sure. She's holding Gustavo.

The woman's in the middle of whispering to Papa C.'s pet. He's pressed against her chest, the same way I've seen Will and Papa C. holding him, too.

"That who you're looking for?" Brett asks.

Papa C. practically leaps forward, extending his arms. "¡Gustavo!"

But the woman spins away from him, blocking Papa C.'s reach. "Can I help you?"

"He's ours," Will tries to explain. "We're here to take him home."

The woman pushes her hat back so quickly it falls off her head, dangling at the middle of her back, held in place by the string that had been under her chin but now catches at the base of her neck. "You're responsible for this bird?"

Will stands her ground. "Yes. Like I said, he's ours."

"Please." Papa C. stretches his arms toward the woman.

Floppy-hat lady backs away some more, cradling Gustavo protectively. Her piercing eyes send daggers toward Papa C. "Please keep your distance, sir."

She seems angry, but I don't get why.

I turn to see if Brett might offer some clue, but the teenager's gone. Must've just left, too, because the door hasn't quite finished swinging shut behind him yet. *Super helpful.*

"Eduardo Cortez?" When my eyes find her again, I see that rooster-woman has unfolded a piece of paper, probably pulled from one of those hundred pockets in her shorts.

"Sí," Papa C. says excitedly, as if his name being written there proves Gustavo is his. And I bet it does, just not in a good way.

"And you are?" Will asks, stepping in before the lady can say more to her grandfather. It's kind of cool how she protects Papa C. wherever we go.

"My name is Kaitlyn Cooper," rooster-woman says with a dignified nod of her head. "I'm with Fowl City Rescue. The shelter sometimes calls us in for cases like this one. Our job is to examine the bird, to help determine—"

"Gustavo," Will interrupts.

"I'm sorry?"

"His name is Gustavo."

Kaitlyn gazes at Will a moment, and then nods slightly. "The shelter called me here to examine *Gustavo* and determine what type of care he needs, and make a recommendation on who should administer it. The presence of the prior owners—the people responsible for . . . Gustavo being here in the first place—this is highly irregular. I think it would be best if you—"

"They're not responsible," Frankie blurts.

"Excuse me?" Kaitlyn asks.

"It's not their fault Gustavo's here." Frankie steps forward. "It's mine. It's all my fault."

He glances around, taking in the cages first, the big yard beyond them next. Two of the teens we saw inside are way out in the distance now, walking their assigned dogs.

Frankie takes another step toward Gustavo, and Kaitlyn doesn't spin away when he reaches out his hand.

"I'm so sorry, buddy," Frankie whispers as he strokes the rooster's head.

Frankie pulls his hand back. He turns around to face us. "I'm the one who told Chester you guys were going to dinner. It was just . . . I don't know. I guess I didn't think . . ."

"*You* told them?" Will snaps. "Why would you do that?"

Frankie hangs his head. "I'm really sorry."

Will isn't satisfied. "Well, you're right about one thing," she continues. "You didn't think at all, did you?"

"I didn't know he would tell his dad, okay? I didn't know they were waiting for Gustavo to be alone. I didn't know they'd let him out, call Animal Control, make it look like—I just didn't think that anyone could actually do . . ."

There are tears in my friend's eyes as his words pick up speed. Papa C. sees them, and despite the fact he hasn't been able to touch his pet since he arrived, despite Kaitlyn Cooper the rescue woman looking at him like he's the devil himself, he doesn't allow Frankie to cry alone.

Papa C. embraces Frankie, burying him in his arms. Overwhelmed, the old man starts to sob, too. Will watches them together, and before long her tears come. Sniffing and blubbering, she joins the group hug.

Kaitlyn, still holding Gustavo tight to her chest, slowly rocking him to and fro, watches the spectacle for a few seconds. I watch her watching.

Her angry eyes seem to settle. She licks her lips, processing what she's looking at. Finally, she turns to me, the only one of our group holding it together, standing apart, though I'm not exactly sure how I'm doing it, because my insides are bubbling and boiling over, too.

The woman from Fowl City Rescue sighs and shakes her head. Her expression says she's just now realizing things are much more complicated than what she'd first assumed.

Things usually are.

"I think somebody ought to fill me in on what, exactly, is going on here."

Will starts with the obvious. "It's kind of a long story."

"I think I've figured that much out." Kaitlyn makes a show of glancing at her watch. "Good thing I have plenty of time to hear it. Trust me, I really don't want to go back to what I was in the middle of doing before being called out here."

"Well, it's not actually *that* long," I say. "Gustavo's kind of in the middle of a neighborhood squabble." I explain as much of what's going on in Townsend Heights as I can. The emergency council meetings, the debates over 5:00 a.m. rooster crowing, the vacant lot, Brewster's plans for it, our proposal, the meeting tonight.

It's good to talk about it with someone new. If only

because it somehow helps organize everything that's happened in my brain, keeps me focused on the conversation in front of me. That way, I don't think about Frankie's confession, or all the accusations I sent Mom's way earlier today and last night. False accusations, I realize now.

Kaitlyn rocks Gustavo while she listens. She raises her eyebrows suspiciously when I finish. Almost like she thinks I'm purposely excluding something. But I can't think what, so I just finish with, "I think that's about everything."

"Is it, though?" Kaitlyn asks, but she's not talking to me. Her gaze shifts from Will to Papa C. "Is it everything?"

"Pretty much," Will answers quickly, but I also notice how fast she averts her eyes.

Kaitlyn opens her mouth, but Frankie pops in before she can ask her question again.

His words come out slow, like he's also figuring some stuff out. "What were you in the middle of?"

"What's that?"

"You said you had time to listen to our story because you didn't want to get back to what you were in the middle of doing," he says. "What was it?"

Kaitlyn sighs again. "I was packing. We're losing our farm."

"You run a farm?" Frankie asks.

It's funny how interested Frankie seems all of a sudden. Must be because he feels bad about how Gustavo ended up here. I think about Mom again—how she had nothing to do with Animal Control coming to the Heights last night. And how, after finding out it was about to happen, all she really did was her best to keep things from spinning completely out of control. Which is exactly what she told me she was trying to do. So why hadn't I believed her?

Kaitlyn shifts Gustavo's weight, raising one knee to get a better grip. Makes me wonder if she's ever handled a rooster as big as him before.

"Well, not a farm, exactly. I run a rescue organization. Animal rescue. That's what Fowl City is. We started with a focus on birds, but now we handle all sorts of animals. We're located on a farm south of the city. Or . . . we were. The owner let us use a corner of his acreage—that's where we house the animals, care for them, provide medical attention, nurse them back to full health. We don't need that much room. But now the farmer has decided to sell his land. Somebody wants to build a subdivision there, and the money he's been offered is just too much. He's always been so generous before, but now . . ."

Kaitlyn shrugs before continuing. "We're about to be homeless. I was in the middle of packing things up. That and calling around, trying to find a new place for Fowl City Rescue to go. It hasn't been very easy. People aren't exactly clamoring to house animal rescues. Even most farms. I've sent almost all our animals out to other rescues across state lines, but there are a few that we haven't found new homes for yet."

Kaitlyn gestures at Gustavo, resting so peacefully against her he almost looks like he might fall asleep. "I would've loved to help this one, too. Such a sweetheart." She stares at Papa C., assessing him with new eyes. Without warning or saying anything at all, she hands Gustavo over to him.

Papa C. can hardly settle down long enough to cradle his rooster in his arms again. He purses his lips and coos at his friend, stroking his back, holding him close. So close, the rooster starts to squirm away.

Kaitlyn makes a clucking noise. "Uh-oh, not so tight," she warns.

Papa C. nods emphatically, smiling huge, and clearly Kaitlyn's worried he doesn't understand. She seems to sense Will is going to be best at translating, so she turns toward her.

"Loving him is good, it's just that . . . I know it sounds strange, but too much love, squeezing him too hard, it can do more harm than good. It might only make Gustavo want to run and hide from you. And that's not what you want, is it?" She smiles at Papa C., speaking directly to him again. "They've had tough lives, these birds. Which means they need us, but they also scare easy."

"He knows that," Will says defensively. She doesn't have to pass the message on to Papa C., either. He's already loosening his grip, holding Gustavo close, but not as tightly as before. The rooster settles into his arms.

The whole time Kaitlyn Cooper talks about holding on too tight, I keep hearing Mom's voice. Repeats of conversations we've had all summer, avoiding the hard times. Going back to what used to be easy.

And just like that . . . I get it. Just like that, I get *her*.

For the past few months, Mom hasn't been trying to *stop* me. She's been trying to *protect* me. Only she's been squeezing a bit too hard. Which wasn't exactly her fault. But it wasn't exactly mine, either. And it wasn't my fault I squirmed a little under all her tight pressure to be the person I was before.

I think it's about time, though, that I stop running from change.

It's time to stop hiding from myself.

36

The four of us walk back to Papa C.'s truck in silence. In the end, although Kaitlyn Cooper allowed him to hold Gustavo for nearly an hour, she couldn't let his pet rooster leave the shelter with us. Her hands were tied by the legal process.

"The best advice I can give you is to head on home. They'll take good care of Gustavo here. I'll keep checking in on him, too." She pointed at the bunch of forms she'd given Will. "Make sure you file all that paperwork on time. Maybe look for a rescue that will take Gustavo in. I'm sorry I can't offer more than that right now. But with us losing our home . . ."

Will had already searched for other rescue groups

around town. Besides Fowl City, there wasn't one that handled roosters for hundreds of miles in any direction. There were a few way out in California, and the topic of trying to move both Gustavo and her grandparents closer to her mom and dad came up again, but Papa C. shook his head no. He didn't even want to discuss it.

Even after all the trouble we'd put him through, he still hoped to find a way to make things work in Townsend Heights. He wasn't going to give up on our neighborhood. Not without a fight.

There were tears in Papa C.'s eyes when he was forced to hand Gustavo back to Kaitlyn. They started to fall as he watched her return the rooster to his lonely cage, separated from even the chickens and guinea fowl.

It's the middle of the afternoon by the time we leave the shelter. Which means tonight's council meeting is that much closer. As we march toward Papa C.'s truck, Will grabs my arm, stopping me. Frankie and Papa C. don't notice; they just keep walking.

"I have something to tell you," Will hisses at me urgently. "About tonight."

"I've been thinking about the meeting, too. You should go first. I'll come in eventually. Unless you're holding their attention, and then maybe you could just keep—"

"Mortimer, stop a second." Her eyes dart ahead, making sure Papa C. still hasn't turned around. "I-I'm sorry, but . . . I don't think I should present at all tonight."

I'd been pulling against her grip, but now I stop in my tracks, even take an actual step back from her, my shock is so strong. "What do you mean? The park is as much your idea as it is mine. We wrote the proposal together. We need to present it the same way."

"I know, but . . ." Will's hand drifts to the back of her neck. "There's something you don't know. About Papa C. and Gustavo . . . about the reason he left the island." She takes a deep breath. "See, he found out the farm he was working on was training some of their roosters."

"Okay," I say slowly. "Training them for what?"

Will bites her lip. "Cockfighting."

"Wait. You're not . . . are you serious? Isn't that, like—"

"Awful? Yes, of course it is. Which is why we don't talk about it. Imagine how people would treat them if they knew about that, too. Everything would be that much worse. But I swear, Papa C. wasn't involved. He didn't know it was happening at all. Once he found out . . ." She peeks ahead at her grandfather again. He still hasn't turned around, but he's almost reached his truck. "Listen, there's only time for the short version of this, and he can't know that I told you. Promise?"

I nod, shock taking over my whole body, stealing any words I might've had.

"I don't think I know the entire story anyway. What I

do know is that once he found out his bosses were using the farm for that kind of training, Papa C. got really upset. His job was to take care of the roosters and chickens who weren't involved. Every once in a while, though, one of the roosters would just disappear. It really bothered him, because he was careful to account for them all. Anyway, that's how he found out. One day it was his favorite, Gustavo, who they took. And when he searched for him, he found out what they were doing. He had to do something to stop it."

"Which was?"

"Papa C. couldn't . . . he had to . . ." Will breathes out. "He set them all free."

"The roosters?"

Will nods hard. "He took Gustavo home, but the rest . . . there were too many. I'm not sure he thought it all the way through. But he got in really big trouble for what he did. So much trouble, he and Grandma weren't safe there anymore. They had to leave."

"Which is why they came to live with you."

She nods. "Exactly."

"So what does that have to do with the council meeting?"

Will points back at the shelter. "That woman—Kaitlyn—she knows. I'm sure of it. She must have rooster-sense or something. Whatever examination she gave him . . . I don't get how, exactly, she just knows. And I'm afraid if it gets out, if Brewster were to find out, no one would listen to the proposal. The whole meeting would end up being about Gustavo and Papa C. and . . . well, even me. Not what it should be about. You and Brewster Station and the future of Townsend Heights."

"But you don't know for sure that's going to happen."

"No, but we can't take the chance. Listen, you can do this. You don't need me up there with you."

She doesn't know about my freeze-ups in class. She doesn't get that what she's suggesting—sending me up there alone—will never work. I'm trying to find some way to explain, but Papa C. has finally reached his truck. He's turned around, clearly wondering why we're hanging so far back.

"¡Vámonos!" he shouts back at us, holding the forms in the air. Will had explained what they were for, and I'm sure he's eager to get home so he can start filling them out.

I wait for the freeze-up I know must be coming. Full panic mode. But something's different.

I'm not sure if our proposal's going to work, or if I'll be able to present it all by myself, but I know it's what I need to do. I know it's the next step, the one waiting in front of me. And I finally understand that maybe that's all you can really do—figure out what the next step is, see that it's right and take it, even if you're scared. No hesitation.

Maybe that's all that trying is, when you break it down into smaller pieces.

Will's already on her way toward her grandfather. "Remember," she hisses back at me. "Not a word, okay?"

I nod. Point my body in the direction Will's going. Pick one foot up, put it back down again. Move myself in the direction I know I have to go. Trust that the rest of the steps I'll need to take are lurking somewhere right behind this first one.

CODE OF ORDINANCES—TOWNSEND HEIGHTS

Sec. 155-75—Dead Ends

(1) A Dead End sign shall be placed on the right side of the dead end roadway just beyond the intersection. The Dead End sign shall be posted to permit the road user to avoid the dead end by turning off, if possible, at the nearest intersecting street.

(2) One or more Dead End signs may be placed before the end of the road.

(3) All Dead End private roads must terminate in a cul-de-sac so emergency vehicles and equipment are able to turn around.

THE RIGHT DIRECTION

How do you know you're going in the right direction?

Sometimes I think there should be Dead End signs in the world, so you know not to turn down certain roads. It sure seems like that would make things a whole lot easier.

But maybe big decisions aren't supposed to be easy. You're not always going to be right, and that's okay.

What you need to remember is if you do go

the wrong way . . . well, turning around may not always be easy, but it's never impossible.

—From the secret files of Mortimer Bray

37

Will might not be presenting, but that doesn't stop her from helping me get ready. Both she and Frankie work with me nonstop all afternoon. We print and we stack and we sort. Three copies of our proposal, just in case. Some of my color hamster-care sticky notes added to the most important parts, trying to make sure I won't forget to highlight them when I'm up there.

The three of us form a fast, efficient team. We hardly even talk while we turn our detailed proposal into a summarized presentation.

It comes out more perfect than I could ever imagine.

But it shakes in my hands anyway.

I'm sitting in the back of the meeting room, where I

always am, but only because Queenie and Mack saved us seats. We arrived late—there had been maybe a bit *too much* printing, stacking, and sorting. Not to mention the color-coding.

The auditorium is so packed when we get here, the other latecomers have to stand along the side, or cram into the very back, near the doors. Lucky for us, Queenie flags us down. I take in the huge crowd as I lead my friends over to my usual row.

"The entire neighborhood's here," I say to Will as we sit.

"Not just the neighborhood." Queenie points up front. "See the bald guy? That's the head of the city planning committee. The rest of those suits all came with him."

I knew the planning people would be here, if only to put their official stamp of approval on Brewster Station, but I figured maybe two or three would show, like the last time. Tonight, though, there are nearly a dozen of them up front, all wearing similar suits. They look more like a single, dark shape than actual, individual people. A few are busy helping set up the council table, which has been extended to fit more VIPs. The bald guy from the last meeting is right next to Mom. His tie is bright purple.

Newspaper reporters mill about, too. Photographers and camerapeople take up positions wherever they can.

Our little Townsend Heights council meeting is suddenly a newsworthy event.

Mom's going crazy up front, trying to accommodate all the extra people at her table, warning a photographer he can't be so close to the stage, fielding complaints from regular attendees about their usual seats being occupied by strangers.

She stops for a second, swiping that familiar lock of hair away from her forehead the way she always does when things aren't as orderly as she likes them to be. But her quick breather is short-lived. Mr. Purple Tie gets in her face, asks a question, and before long she's back at it. Organizing, helping, directing. Trying to make everybody happy. Keeping the peace.

Dad's here tonight, too. It's the first time in forever he's made it to a council meeting. He and the rest of Gustavo's Fine Nine are gathered about halfway down on the left side. Most of them, including Dad, end up standing, leaning against the wall for support.

A late-arriving photographer tries to squeeze into a spot in the reporter area. As I allow my eyes to focus on his negotiation with the other camera-wielding newspeople, bloggers, and podcasters, the proposal shakes even harder in my hands.

I mean, as if I wasn't already going to have trouble speaking. People will be filming me? Taking pictures?

Writing down whatever words I manage to sputter out onto their little notepads?

My stomach churns. My sense of certainty from earlier, the confidence Will and Frankie helped me conjure, starts to waver.

I can't do this.

I can't. I can't. I can't.

And honestly, Mom might not let me. Nothing's changed about our deal, because I didn't even have time to talk to her about it today. In fact, I hardly saw her at all. I spent the entire afternoon over at Will's. All that prepping, plus the occasional moments I thought I was being sneaky with the different ways I tried to get Will to change her mind about presenting with me.

"You're still sure?" I lean over and whisper-ask her again now, for about the hundredth time today. "I really don't think anyone will—"

Her gaze shifts, and I follow it to see what's caught her attention. A young couple passes by, making their way toward the front, squeezing past neighbors. The husband sees Frankie and points him out to his wife. They both smile, even start to wave, but then they notice Will sitting on the other side of me.

Smiles disappear. Brows furrow. A few rows later, they wedge in next to the DiNuccis, settling into saved seats. They never look back at our group again. It's like we aren't worth any more of their interest or attention.

"I'm telling you, it's too risky," Will whispers right back at me. "Half these people don't like me." Those words hang in the empty air for a moment. "Anyway, it doesn't matter. You don't need me up there. This is going to work, promise. You got this."

It's the same thing Queenie said to me when we first arrived. "You got this, Mortimer." I really don't understand what makes everyone—Will, Ms. Opal, Queenie, the Fine Nine—so sure I can do this when *I'm* not even sure I can do this.

If only I could look ahead somehow, see that it's going to go well. If only I could know the future, at least predict it a little bit while I'm sitting here waiting.

But I can't.

I can't know what's going to happen next any more than I can change what's already happened.

I remind myself that all I can do, really, is focus on taking the next step. Remember the bad things from the past. Understand why they happened, and how they happened. Try my best to keep them from happening all over again.

It's simple, really. If I stop Brewster Station, I stop Townsend Station, too. Just like Grandpa George did all those years ago. Remembering it's been done once before propels me. At least carries me from this breath to the next one.

Will notices my shaking hands for the first time. She reaches out and grips the one closest to her, steadying it. Now my leg wants to join in beneath our linked fingers, but I blink hard and concentrate on keeping it still.

The front rows finally settle down. The cameras, the boom mics, the phones with recording apps all zoom in on Mom and Purple Tie and the rest of the council up onstage.

Mom—Councilwoman Bray—bangs the gavel. I close my eyes entirely now, working to keep the trembling from starting up again. Will's focus is drawn to the stage, where all the action is. Her hand drifts away from mine.

It takes a lot more bangs of the gavel than usual to get the auditorium to quiet down, but eventually the talking becomes murmuring. I open my eyes back up.

The murmuring in the packed rows of seats becomes whispering and, eventually, the whispering becomes silence. The most important council meeting I've ever attended has officially started.

And I can't help it—our proposal starts shaking in my hands all over again.

Brewster is called up to the podium first. It makes sense, you can't hear counterproposals until the proposal itself has been presented. His presentation is even more polished and detailed than it was the first time, with updated charts and diagrams showing the benefits of Brewster Station.

The core message? Everybody will be better off once the new construction is completed. Not only the neighborhood and our community, but also the entire city.

But there's no mention of Townsend Station, the bigger plan that would steal away the houses of most of the people in this room. Could Frankie have misunderstood?

Purple Tie nods his way through the entire presentation. Maybe this isn't the first time he's heard this version of Brewster's pitch. Maybe Purple Tie was one of those people in Brewster's home office from the very beginning.

The city commissioner isn't the only one nodding along. Lots of other Townsend people are. The ones hoping for a nice coffee shop around the corner, a yoga studio up the next street, maybe even a fancy new restaurant at the top of Liberty hill.

And, I mean, *of course* they're nodding. The way Brewster presents the project—all upside, not a single downside in sight—who could possibly disagree with it? Seriously, why are we even here?

Why am *I* here?

The room spins. My eyes are cloudy. This whole meeting's flashed by in a rush already. I'm running out of both time and chances.

And the proposal in my hands shakes and shakes and shakes.

"I want to sum up by thanking *you*, Councilwoman Bray," Brewster finishes. "And also the city planning commissioner." He nods so hard at bald Purple Tie it makes me think he might end the motion with a literal bow. "I'd be honored to field any questions you might have, Commissioner Stevens."

Everyone at the table looks at each other, shaking their heads. There are no questions. I'm more convinced than ever that this Stevens guy has heard Brewster's speech before, already seen his fancy charts and diagrams. Already approved them. Or helped to plan things, whatever. Point is, this was never a real decision at all.

Stevens looks over at Mom. She stares back at him, shrugging slightly. Mom doesn't argue or debate. She's still in peacekeeping mode. Sometimes that's smart. Sometimes it's totally the right thing to do, getting people to agree with each other, breaking up fights.

But sometimes it's not. Sometimes compromise and talking isn't enough. Sometimes, you have to do more. You have to at least *try*.

"Such a well-organized proposal," Commissioner Stevens finally says. "Excellent work, Reg."

Reg, not Reggie or Reginald. Definitely not "Mr. Brewster." I'm more positive than ever. They *do* know each other. This whole meeting's been a sham from the word go.

Sensing an ending, the room starts to stir. Whispers turn back into murmurs. Mom bangs her gavel. "Are there any questions from the community, any objections to this proposal, or especially any"—she clears her throat—"counterproposals?" Mom pauses again. She looks straight at me. Is it because she wants me to stay seated? Or stand up? "If so, now is the time to bring them forward."

Will nudges me from one side. When I don't move, even though I know lots of people are waiting for me to, Frankie shoulders me from the other. I'm bouncing between them, like a pinball.

What should I do? I search Mom's eyes for an answer, but she's not looking my way anymore. She and Brewster are answering a question about timing for the project when it gets approved. Brewster's saying words like "sooner than later."

When, not *if*. Sooner, not later. Has my chance already vanished?

I tell myself to stand, I really do, but suddenly I'm all sweaty again. Queenie and Mack twist around. They clench their teeth, trying to tell me to get my butt up there.

Everyone around me is wearing these worried expressions, these now-is-the-time looks on their faces. But I can't move.

The last time I felt this paralyzed, I was standing in the middle of the street. Frankie was yelling at me. He had to come out and get me, drag me across to the other side. If he hadn't done that, I might've stayed there forever.

Here I am, lost again. Paralyzed again. Stuck in another freeze-up. I swore I was done with them, but maybe it's not up to me.

This time no one's going to come for me. No one's going to grab my arm and pull me up to the front. If I can't do it myself, it isn't getting done.

I'm sitting stock-still, hardly moving a muscle, but

somehow it feels like I'm running. Running from change. Hiding from myself. And hadn't I already decided to stop doing those things?

I stand up.

The room is so still, the creaking sound my chair makes as my weight leaves it must sound like a siren going off. Everyone looks around at me. I gulp, but I'm only the center of attention for a moment, because the double doors in the back suddenly bang open. Half the crowd, including me, jumps. A bunch of people even let out tiny squeaks of surprise. They stop looking at me, moving their eyes to the doors instead.

The first person through is Papa C., and he looks super strange because he's coming in backward. Next is Grandma Cortez, reaching ahead to help hold the door for her husband. Seeing the elderly couple, a big man who had moved out of the way comes back again, takes the weight of the heavy door from her. Grandma Cortez nods a thank-you.

It makes more sense why he's walking backward when I see that Papa C. is pulling a wheelchair over the doorway's threshold. Once he gets all the way through, he spins the chair so it's facing forward. The middle aisle slopes toward the stage, and when he turns the chair around, he has to tighten his grip to be sure Ms. Opal doesn't go barreling straight down it.

Papa C. engages the wheel brakes, whispers something

in Ms. Opal's ear. Behind them, Grandma Cortez stops, too. She's holding a folded-up walker. Opal's walker. It still has the streamers hanging from the handles.

Nodding, Ms. Opal raises one finger. Mom's mouth drops open. It takes her a second to bang her gavel again, quieting the room so everyone can actually hear what our old neighbor, whose voice isn't quite what it used to be, came here to say.

Opal lowers her hand as silence descends, as if she's the one, not Mom's gavel, controlling the room. She takes a deep breath, summons her strength. She glances around at all the eyes on her, every single one in the auditorium. A whole neighborhood's worth of eyes. A city's worth.

"Well," she says. "I hope I'm not too late."

Several long moments of awkward silence are followed
by a few seconds of shocked voices, all of them hushed.
I use the time to glance toward Ms. Opal's hip, the injury
that was supposed to keep her away tonight. I can't tell if
it's better or not. Except, well, she is in a wheelchair.

So Ms. Opal might've made it here, but it doesn't look
like it was the simplest thing to pull off.

I exhale so deeply I'm not sure there's any air left inside
me. I'm already standing, and I was ready to head toward
the podium, but it still didn't feel right. Now, though . . . I
know for sure that this is it, the moment I've been waiting
for. My sign.

"Ms. . . . . Opal," Mom says into her microphone, slowly,

her voice filled with surprise and concern. For some reason, Mom glances at me. Does she think I'm responsible for Ms. Opal being here? I don't know if she can see me or not, but I shrug back at her. It's true; I had no idea this was going to happen. I didn't even consider it a possibility. Ms. Opal had said she couldn't come, and I believed her.

That was that.

Papa C. starts to wheel Ms. Opal down the center aisle. It occurs to me to check on Will. Did she know about this? The way she raises both her eyebrows answers my question. I shake my head and smile at her. However they did it, she and her grandparents made sure I got just the kick in the pants I needed, exactly when I needed it.

Mom leans in closer to the mic and corrects herself. "Ms. *McKenzie* is a long-time resident of Townsend Heights. In fact, her family goes way back in this neighborhood. Generations."

Papa C. reaches the base of the sloping aisle. He turns to the right, passing Brewster, still standing on the podium. Grandma Cortez trailing a step behind the whole way, they cross in front of the rest of the city people next—that dark, singular blob. Finally, Papa C. wheels Ms. Opal's chair into an empty handicap spot at the end of the first aisle.

"I . . . see," Commissioner Stevens says, regaining his composure. For a second there, he looked a bit panicked.

"Welcome. So, Ms. McKenzie, are you here to . . . did you want to . . . are you going to speak tonight?"

Ms. Opal repositions her blanket over her legs, flattening some of its wrinkles. "Oh, no," she says, loud as she can muster so the room can hear. Then she twists, looking out across the audience, her eyes finding mine. She holds my gaze long enough for me to wonder if my mouth has dropped open or if I've got some food on my face or something.

Then she finishes her sentence. "I didn't come here to speak, dear. I came to listen."

Everyone looks back at me again, like they all know exactly who Ms. Opal expects to be listening to. Maybe because I'm the only person standing up in the middle of my row of packed seats.

I nod at . . . well, all of them, I guess. This time there's no hesitation at all. And the proposal is entirely still in my hands. It doesn't shake even a tiny bit.

"Objection!" Brewster shouts from the podium.

He glowers at Ms. Opal. "We've had our battles, but tell me you aren't serious with this." He glances up at the council next. "What's the point of bringing a ten-year-old up here? If you think we're going to have sympathy for—"

Mom cuts in so fast and hard, Brewster actually makes a sort of chirping, mid-sentence put-on-the-brakes noise.

"My son is twelve," she says before catching herself. Because she must've heard the same thing in her own voice that I did. A tone almost sounding like she's in *favor* of me presenting. That can't be right, though.

Can it?

Mom coughs into her fist, a move I've seen her do with Dad when she's about to say something she knows she'll end up regretting. When she finally continues, it's with a new tone. A more factual one. "Which I'm quite certain you're aware of, unless you don't know your own son's age. Our boys are in the same class, Reggie."

Brewster emits another stammer that isn't quite made of words, making me think maybe he actually *doesn't* know how old his own son is.

It gives Mom time to straighten to full Head Councilwoman Bray stature. She holds Brewster's gaze long enough to win their brief staring contest. "And I don't know about anyone else, but I didn't come here tonight to just rubber-stamp this proposal. If an interested party has something to say, then I, for one, would like to hear it."

She meets my eyes. For the first time in a long time, hers have no warning in them. Nothing that looks or feels like a stop sign. The imaginary stoplight that's been hanging in front of my eyes flips from red to a bright green. I almost can't believe it.

"Of course," Commissioner Stevens, eager to be the

next voice heard, replies. "By all means. That's definitely why we're here." He makes a gathering motion to show that everyone up on the stage is on the same team. "We're all eager to listen to anything and everything the Townsend Heights community has to say about this project. It's critical everyone understands the benefits."

Mom stares straight at me again, clearly waiting expectantly. Almost . . . eagerly. In fact, just about the whole room is looking right at me, I suddenly realize.

The sweat on the back of my neck and forehead returns ten times worse than it's ever been. My mouth's the Sahara. My lips crack and stick to each other, like they're trying to protect me from opening my big flap and saying something stupid.

But how can I say something stupid? I'm an interested party. And it's time for interested parties like me to share what we think. Mom said so herself.

And . . . interested doesn't cover it, actually. I am way more than just interested in what's going on in my own town, and what's happening to my neighbors.

It's my job to rep all these other people. Everyone in Townsend Heights.

And this neighborhood isn't just interesting. It's home.

Townsend Heights is home, my home, and the people here aren't just my neighbors.

That's how I stumble my way into Ms. Opal's secret.

In that moment, I realize that she wasn't doing all those projects for herself or even for us. All the ways she made Townsend Heights a better place to live. All the times she made sure the rules followed the people, not the other way around.

Those moments, those efforts, all those roll-up-your-sleeves projects it seemed no one else wanted to take on—they were for her grandparents. Her grandparents and their neighbors, their friends, all the people who gathered on the concrete benches outside their store every night, back when she was a kid.

Those people were *her* people. Ms. Opal's family. Everyone who lived in Townsend Heights sixty years ago. All the friends and relatives and neighbors who had their homes taken away back then, right out from under them.

And this strange mix of friends and neighbors and relatives surrounding me now? Rooting for me? Giving me the space I need to do what has to be done, to take the next right step?

These people are *my* people. My *family*.

I look around the room, taking them all in. Feeling their energy and hope encouraging me. When my gaze falls on the Fine Nine, wedged together tightly along the auditorium's side wall, Mrs. Dawkins wriggles her fingers above her head. She stops herself from making the gobbling noise that went with it before, but the silent motion reminds me I'm a member of their group now, too. Or maybe it tells me we've always been members of the same group. Neighbors, sure, but even more than that. People who want the same things for the same place.

The secret Fine Nine sign only she seems willing to use is what ultimately gets me moving again. I squeeze past the knees in my row, muttering apologies as I head for the center aisle.

I start walking down it, in the same direction Papa C. wheeled Ms. Opal.

Step-by-step, I follow the identical path she did, not even a minute ago. That's the easy part; I've been following Ms. Opal for years.

Mr. Brewster leaves the podium before I get there. He tries really hard not to be seen sneering at me while he steps down, but I still detect it in his sideways glance at me as I grow closer to him.

At the base of the tall wooden platform, I hesitate. It's like I'm about to climb Mount Everest and not a couple of short, wooden podium steps.

"Are you . . . ready?" Mom asks. The entire room seems to be holding their collective breath with my every pause.

One more inhale. The sweat on the back of my neck cools. My saliva, some of it anyway, returns to my mouth.

Mom's open, welcoming gaze feels like the time I was lying in the front yard a few days ago. Dad, loosening my grip on Teddy's collar so he could take the pressure off my arm. Off me. Mom, patting my back hard when I couldn't catch my breath suddenly.

Remember to breathe.

I feel like I must be nodding *yes* to her as I take the first big step up and then another. I did it. I'm on the podium.

I'd be looking straight at Mom, only . . . this podium's definitely not designed for twelve-year-olds, especially remarkably short ones. My eye level is even with the shelf where you're supposed to set your work. But if I do that, the pages of our proposal will be over my head. And I'll be so far from the mic, even my deepest, surest voice will probably come out as a faint whisper.

"Someone get that kid a box!" I recognize Mr. DiNucci's joking tone. Laughter erupts from his buddies. That young couple who glowered at Will. A bunch of others. The sweat comes back to my face, full force this time. I'm drenched. It's as if DiNucci's words turned on a shower above me. My mouth goes immediately dry again. I can't do this.

I can't. I can't. I can't.

I start to turn around and leave, but as soon as I do, I

come face-to-face with Dad. He's carrying a chair. Just an ordinary, wooden chair he pulled from gosh-knows-where. The seats here are all bolted to the floor, so it's an honest-to-goodness mystery, but not one I can spend any time puzzling through right now.

"Wish I had time to run home and grab my ladder," Dad says in a hushed voice. Then he asks me the same question Mom did. "Ready?"

"I think so." I move to one side so he can slide the chair in. "Thanks, Dad," I say to him, and it's for more than just the chair. He tests the footing by putting pressure on the seat with his flat hand, even helps me step back up, first to the podium then again higher, feet up on top of the shiny wood.

I rest our proposal on the shelf, pull the mic, now the perfect height, a little closer. The chair wobbles because I move too quickly.

"Careful now," Dad warns in my ear. "Here, I'll stay with you." He crouches down, grabbing the chair's two back legs. "Make sure you don't fall."

Mom watches our exchange. I'm not sure I've seen a smile that big on her face this whole summer.

While Dad helped me, the room had started to murmur again. I wonder if I should go ahead and start talking or if it would be better to wait for everyone to quiet down.

Mom solves my problem for me. She bangs her gavel down so hard I see a dust cloud float up into the air, and the auditorium goes entirely silent.

Townsend Heights is ready for me to begin.

I swear I can feel the sweat dripping down my neck. I keep my head down, focusing on sifting through this big pile of paper. Agonizing seconds pass. Everyone's waiting for me again. Waiting for Mortimer Bray to get on with things.

The chair shifts under my feet, as slightly as possible, almost not at all. A message from Dad. Pushing at the legs just hard enough to remind me he's back there. Spotting me. He's not going to let me fall, not after working so hard to finally get me to this place, this moment. This here. This now.

"Take your time, son."

I raise my head, almost not believing those words come

from who they come from. Mom. Calm and steady, hands laced in front of her, she nods so slightly maybe no one else sees it. But I do. I see it and I understand it completely, too.

She's repeating those same words, just with body language this time.

Take your time.

It's a different message from the one I've gotten from her all summer. Showing me pictures of dogs up for adoption, trying to get me to pick one out, some Trevor-replacement. Urging me to return to the dog-walking business I gave up, get back to hanging out with Frankie, desperate to see me just . . . go back. Come back. Move forward. Anything but staying stuck where I've been, paralyzed in place.

But I'm pretty sure that's not how it works. I see that now, and I think maybe Mom does, too. The only *when* I can be is right now, the only *where* I can be is right here. The only thing I can do is the next, best thing. The right thing. The one coming straight from my gut.

And that's presenting this proposal.

Mom's been waiting for me all summer. Waiting for weeks and weeks and months. Until now. Now, exactly when she should be feeling the pressure of the important commissioner sitting next to her, of Brewster's impatience in getting the approval he's so sure is a mere formality, when everything's that's happening should be rushing her to rush me, she tells me the very opposite.

Take your time.

Maybe that's what *I've* been waiting for from her. Permission to not have to be ready. Because suddenly I *am*.

So I take a deep breath, count to three, and . . .

In . . .” I have to clear my throat, but it’s not because I’m freezing up. I think . . . maybe . . . am I excited?

“Back in 1957, the city wanted to build something called Townsend Station. It was supposed to be in the exact spot where Townsend Heights is now. It was going to be a train station. High-speed rail, too. They were going to replace the trolley that used to run along Townsend Avenue with a new system, and Townsend Heights was going to be one of the main stops. The station was going to have to be huge; they needed the entire hillside. People were living there then, like we do now, but the city claimed most of their homes using eminent domain.”

I pause, and look out at the crowd. All those faces

staring back at me. Will someone chuck an eraser at my head again? Bracing myself, my confidence starts to deflate. Maybe this is a mistake. Quickly, I turn my eyes back down to the pages in front of me.

Keep going, I tell myself. *Don't stop now.*

"They started by knocking down a store called Carter's General. It was on the corner of Liberty and Prince. The spot we know as the vacant lot. What we've been talking about all night. Once upon a time that corner was somebody's whole life. Their dreams and their hard work and all the money they had in the world went into building the store that was there."

I decide to leave the part about Carter's General belonging to Ms. Opal's family out. I don't want my argument to seem too personal.

I can already hear a lot of whispering around the room. I try to block it out, look only at Mom. Because, in the end, I'm not telling this story to the room. I'm telling it to her. It's not that different from the way I used to come back from a walk and be so eager to recount all the crazy stuff my dogs had gotten up to. The way she would patiently listen to every detail, even though she probably didn't care that much about *what* I was saying. I think she cared a lot more about *who* was doing the saying.

Mom's eyes are intent on me. She's not glancing at Commissioner Stevens or at Brewster, not even at Dad.

For the first time in a while, I feel like she's listening to me and only me.

"This is probably news to most of you," I continue. "Townsend Station doesn't exist, right? The rail system doesn't exist. But that's only because, back then, the community rose up to stop it. They got together, worked together, and even though a lot of people still lost a lot of things, Townsend Heights exists today, the houses on these hills are still standing for all of you to live in, because of their efforts."

I turn a page of the proposal over, replace it with the next one. The room is so quiet, when someone drops their pen on the table up front, it practically echoes.

"But nobody talks about any of that. The easiest way to make the past repeat itself is to pretend it didn't happen." I'm not entirely sure where that came from. It seems to cause a lot of shifting butts in seats up front, though.

"Ms. Opal," I take a moment to meet my old neighbor's eyes. She smiles at me. "She's always loved this neighborhood. Me, too. It just took me a while to figure out why. To be honest, I thought it was all your dogs I loved so much."

Laughter rolls through the auditorium. It makes me pause. Then smile. Then keep going. "But it wasn't just them. Not really. It was all of you. The people." I steal a second to take in all the smiles I get back.

"I met you when I would come and get your dogs for walks. I know who you are. Who you really are, not just who you become in this meeting room. Remember the blizzard we had two years ago, how that big group went driveway to driveway until everybody's walks were cleared and their cars were cleaned? We didn't worry about how big the job was. We just cleaned the driveway in front of us. Then the next one. Then the one after that. I never had so much fun in all my life. Or worked so hard, either, which I guess probably sounds weird."

"Not at all!" somebody yells, but I don't turn around again to check who. I just keep going.

I give a bunch of other examples of how the people of Townsend Heights have always stuck together over the years, until I feel like I might be pushing the point a little too hard. It's just because the list in my head is so long.

"Ms. Opal used to welcome every neighbor. And it wasn't just her! A ton of folks would bring treats and gifts over whenever someone new moved in. We used to have those huge block parties, too. Remember all that?"

"When am I going to get another one of those burned hot dogs, Mack?" someone else shouts. The crowd erupts again. Yet another voice shouts, "Hey, the man likes 'em well done! Give him a break!" When I turn around, Queenie's grinning over the way Mack is blushing.

"So what happened?" I ask, and the laughter and joy

settle down a little. "This summer, we had a new neighbor move in, to Ms. Opal's house, even." My glance in Ms. Opal's direction is meant to catch the eyes of Papa C. this time. "The Cortez family. New people, but in the end people just like us. Actually, once they move in, they're supposed to become more than just people, aren't they? At least that's the way I remember it. I thought people were supposed to become *neighbors* as soon as they moved into the Heights. No matter who they were, or where they came from. Was I wrong about that?"

I take another break. Turn around again, looking for someone to answer. Even the DiNuccis and their side of the room stay quiet.

"Because I didn't see anybody stop by the Cortez place with cookies or cupcakes. I didn't see anybody stop by at all, come to think of it, and I live right next door. That goes, by the way," I continue, turning back toward Mom, "for me and my family, too. I wasn't . . . we weren't . . ." I breathe out heavily. My eyes cloud up. "I was having a tough summer, I guess."

Mom's face loses its fragile composure, as if the simple act of me saying those words forces us both to relive everything from the past few months all over again. Ms. Opal leaving, Trevor dying, freezing up at school, giving up the dog-walking business I loved so much. Giving up almost everything I used to love so much.

But now, I realize, I'm done letting the things I love go.

"I love Townsend Heights," I say without planning to. "And I won't give it up without a fight."

That's when Brewster bolts to his feet. He's finally had enough.

Give it up?" Brewster cries. "Townsend Heights isn't going anywhere. We're making it better." He looks straight at Commissioner Stevens. "I don't know why we have to sit here and listen to some kid complain about his own neighborhood. I ask you, what does this have to do with the proposal at hand?"

"I'm afraid I have to agree, young man," the commissioner says. "I don't really see what you're getting at." He checks his watch. "And I'm afraid we're running out of time. There may be others who wish to—"

"The young man," Mom says pointedly, "will speak until he's finished. However much time that might take. This is an important issue for our community. Are we keeping you from something, Commissioner Stevens?"

The commissioner flattens his hand on the table, so that his watch is out of view. "Of course not."

"What I'm *getting* at," I say, continuing, "is that we need to protect Townsend Heights. How do you know that Brewster Station isn't just the first step? All those years ago, when they first tried to build Townsend Station, people had to sell their houses and move away. They had to find somewhere else to live. How would you like to have that happen to you?"

"So let me get this straight. You want to protect . . . what, exactly?" Brewster scoffs. "There's nothing on that lot but dirt. Do you know what vacant means, son? I think the adults in the room realize this project is a no-brainer." He addresses the crowd next. "What it'll do for everyone's property values alone—"

I inhale, dare to interrupt him. "Townsend Heights is supposed to be about more than dollar signs and having a Starbucks close by. We're supposed to be a family."

Now it's me imploring the audience. "So let's be one then. It starts right here, right now, with us coming together. When big things happen, when everything's changing, isn't that what families are supposed to do? Come together instead of drifting apart?"

When I face back forward, Mom's composure vanishes

again. Her lip trembles. I can tell she's overcome with emotion all over again.

I press on, stacking the pages in front of me into a pile. Quickly, haphazardly. A few stick out at awkward angles, but I ignore them, lifting the whole stack up over my head.

"I walked dogs in this neighborhood for a long time. Almost every one of you has one. My friend Will says she's never seen anything like it. But when I walked them, I never really had anywhere to take them, just up and down our steep streets, until we were all so tired we could sleep for hours. I bet a lot of them probably did when I finally got them home to you."

More scattered laughter from behind me. I thrust the pages up higher.

"Our idea is that the real, true value of the Townsend Heights vacant lot is in how we can use it to help each other—and that includes our animals. And maybe . . . other animals, too. This proposal"—I bring the stack down to eye level, lower my voice so it sounds more reasonable—"This proposal has all the details about what a bunch of us think should be done with the corner of Liberty and Prince streets. We don't want a giant office complex or a shopping center or a live-and-work whatever it is. We think . . ."

I take one final deep breath. This is it. The sentence

that might get me drummed out of this room. Run from the building. Maybe chased away from the whole neighborhood.

"We think the vacant lot should be turned into a dog park. A dog park . . ." Something had been bugging me since the shelter visit, since we met Kaitlyn Cooper and heard about her organization losing their home. Now I understand what it is.

"A dog park and an animal rescue, too. Think about it. We have the space. Space the city needs. There's an open space standard they haven't been following. Everyone should look it up." I raise my pages over my head again, as if they're evidence of the city's park space requirement. I lower them again quickly, though, because, yes, the requirement's mentioned in our proposal, but I'm pretty sure that doesn't count as evidence. "The space we have, it's not just in the vacant lot. We have space in other places, too. Like our hearts. We can come together and protect what makes the Heights the Heights before it's too late. Just like those other people who lived here before us did. And what makes the Heights the Heights isn't stores or offices made out of cold steel, windows so shiny you can't see the people inside. I think we're more than that. Don't you?"

The final words are barely out of my mouth before the room erupts. I can't tell which voices are agreeing with me and which are opposed, but it seems half and half again, and despite being proud of myself for getting through my whole speech without passing out or throwing up, I kinda feel like I've accomplished nothing. Townsend Heights is as divided now as it was when I started talking. Judging by all the back-and-forth shouting behind me, it could be I've even made things worse.

Mom's gavel and Brewster's booming voice emerge from the mess of noise at the exact same moment. The big man is back to standing near his easels now, facing the room, not bothering with any microphones.

"Neighbors, please! This is ridiculous, and it needs to end now. We're supposed to give up this lucrative project for a dog park?" Brewster guffaws and looks at me. "And what exactly would we be rescuing? Tell me this," he says, his eyes landing on Will. "Does it have anything to do with that rooster ruining our mornings?" he starts, but I notice Stevens sending him a zip-it, stay-on-point glare. This isn't supposed to be one of Brewster's rooster-complaint sessions.

He shifts on his feet and backtracks. "Are you suggesting that all these good folks who have lived here for so long should give up a fortune in increased property values for this Mexican?"

Brewster points accusingly at Papa C. Townsend Heights' newest resident shrinks back, as if he's trying to blend into the wall behind him, like a chameleon. Grandma Cortez reaches up to touch her husband's arm at the elbow, calming him.

"He isn't Mexican," I say, pulling Brewster's attention back to me with the power of my mic's volume. "He's American. From Puerto Rico." I turn toward the crowd. "And what does it matter, anyway? Mexican, Puerto Rican, American . . ." I fight back emotion I didn't expect to feel. My voice lowers as I choke up a little. "What does it matter?"

Brewster snorts out his next words. "Whatever this Cortez person really is, whatever he's really up to, the fact is we don't want it here. The people of Townsend Heights know better. You can't fool us. This isn't that kind of neighborhood. Am I right?"

He starts gesturing out to the crowd, picking out Mr. DiNucci first. "Dave, you wouldn't mind the value of your house doubling, would you?"

DiNucci stands to respond, but Brewster doesn't allow him the time. He points around the room some more instead. "Of course you wouldn't. Listen, I don't think any of you understand how lucrative that lot is. How valuable all your lots are. Kid wants to turn prime city real estate into a toilet for dogs and chickens and God knows what else . . ."

"Probably a few goats," I suggest seriously, and Mom barks out a laugh so sudden, her hand flies up to cover her mouth. Too late, though. She gets dirty glances from both Brewster and the commissioner. She pulls her hand away from her face and holds her palm out in apology, but she still looks like she might erupt at any second.

Brewster's still talking to the crowd. "Do any of you realize how much the city is about to offer you for your homes?"

Commissioner Stevens sits up straight. His eyes go wide. The room is silent for about a second as everyone processes Brewster's question.

Even Brewster seems to realize his own mistake. "What I mean is—"

"Wait. I'm not selling my house to the city," Mr. DiNucci, already standing and clearly flabbergasted, shouts. "Why would that even be on the table here? Why would you ask . . . you are building this station on the vacant lot *only*, right, Reg?"

"Sure," Brewster starts. "Of course, Dave. Don't be . . . what I meant was—"

"No," I say. "Brewster Station's only the first step. My friend saw their map." I look over my shoulder at Frankie. When my eyes find him, he's already nodding, so I tell everyone what he told me.

"Brewster Station is only the beginning of a much bigger project. Eventually, they're going to build Townsend Station, the same idea people like them had all those years ago. It'll take up the entire neighborhood. All of Townsend Heights. Only now it won't just be a distant memory that you don't have to think about if you don't want to. This time, it'll be you. All of you will be forced to sell. And the people stomping through that huge station a few years from now will think about you about as much as you think about the people who lived in your houses sixty and seventy years ago."

"This is . . . You're mistaken," Brewster says, his voice disturbingly calm, his posture oddly straight. He turns to the council and the city commissioners to explain. "I don't know what this boy is talking about. There's no such map. I've already presented all the maps." He gestures behind him. "They're right here. This proposal is for Brewster Station. On the vacant lot. That's it."

"He's lying," Frankie shouts and points from the back. "There is too a map. I have pictures of it."

Frankie raises his phone into the air. The woman next to him snatches it, looks at his screen, turning it over to see things better in landscape mode. The people next to her join in, peering over her shoulder. A few take their glasses off to squint harder at the images they see there. Next comes all the nodding and whispering and general agreement. When the crowd waiting to get their own look grows too big, the phone starts being handed around. First

Queenie's row, then the next. One by one, until everyone sees the truth.

Pictures don't lie.

I never thought to ask Frankie if he had any actual evidence. I just believed him.

"The city was in that meeting, too," Frankie shouts, pointing at Commissioner Stevens. "That guy, right there. I didn't see him, but I recognize his voice. He knows all about the other map, too."

Mom turns to Stevens. "Is this true, Commissioner?"

"Of course it's not true," Brewster insists. "As I've already explained, this project is confined to the vacant lot only."

Mom doesn't even glance Brewster's way. She stays focused on Mr. Purple Tie.

"Is this *true*, Commissioner?" she repeats, more slowly this time. "Is there another plan, a different one from what Mr. Brewster has shown us here? And before you answer, I suggest remembering that a lot of us here in the Heights are extremely conscientious voters. I believe we sit in the very center of your district, do we not?"

Commissioner Stevens stammers. "Well, you see, it isn't so cut-and-dried as all that. We, um, well . . ." He wipes the back of his neck, and I recognize the motion. Trust me, that's the perfect spot for nervous sweat to pool.

Funny how my own neck feels pretty dry right now.

"All plans e-evolve," the commissioner continues. "Th-The responsible thing for the city to do is to cast one eye toward growth while—"

"Not over our houses, you aren't gonna grow," DiNucci shouts.

"That's right. I ain't selling my house to the city," Mack yells, standing to point at Stevens. "I ain't selling to anyone. Don't you even think about using your eminent domain again, neither."

Soon dozens of neighbors are standing, shouting out similar protests, gesturing at Brewster and Stevens over and over, sometimes in ways that aren't as polite as mere pointing.

Everyone's finally together. All of Townsend Heights. The entire neighborhood sees the truth now: the potential for history to repeat itself. They've heard how the people before them stopped this project once, saved the houses on our hills so they'd be there for our families to buy and move into, to raise their kids inside, spoil their dogs inside.

Those once lonely, empty houses became our homes. And not a single person here is giving theirs up without a fight.

Townsend Heights is talking in one, single voice again. First time in forever. Saving the Heights all over again. For themselves, and the people who will come after them, too. Maybe the people who come after us will have to stand strong before some new Brewster—because, let's face it, there's always a Brewster, isn't there? Maybe the next Townsend Heights will read or hear about what this Townsend Heights did, the way I heard about what the Townsend Heights of Ms. Opal's childhood did. Maybe they'll be inspired by it. By us. Maybe they'll end up fighting—trying—all because we did.

Maybe that's all there is—winning the battle in front of us while making sure to leave a trail behind for the next set of people to follow. A lit path. One to follow when they have to fight their own battle. One foot in front of the other, the next step after the last. Over and over. Always and forever.

I feel Ms. Opal's smile before I see it. She rests her hand over her heart. We're too far away from each other for words, but that's okay. We don't need them. She told me I could do this, as long as I trusted my gut. She was right.

Mom's banging her gavel again. It takes about twenty good thwacks for the room to finally quiet down enough for her to speak. As she does, she grins at me widely.

I return it, full force. Welcome back, Happy Mom. I promise to stick around if you do.

And I think she will, because, eyes never leaving me, she says, "Do I have a motion to call for a community vote?"

Dozens of hands shoot straight up into the air. Including Dad's. Including Will's. Papa C.'s, Mack's, Queenie's. Even Mr. DiNucci's. The entire membership of Gustavo's Fine Nine.

And, of course, mine.

THE NEXT SUMMER

To tell you the truth, nobody actually *likes* the name the city gave our dog park. It's way too long and official-sounding. But we weren't about to complain— especially not when our dreams were coming true right before our eyes.

After what happened with Brewster and Commissioner Stevens at the council meeting, the mayor felt the need to smooth things over with Townsend Heights. There were too many reporters in attendance that night, too many journalists who all wrote articles about the pint-size twelve-year-old who took down the blustery business- man's secret plans. Mayor Evans couldn't pretend they were going to go away on their own.

I guess maybe he was thinking about the next election, because the city ended up donating a bunch of money to help finish our project in record time. They even paid for and installed the big, fancy sign at the new park's entrance.

The big, fancy sign with the big, fancy name, the one that was way too long. The one nobody liked. The one that, now that it was posted, we couldn't change.

TOWNSEND HEIGHTS CITY DOG PARK AND PETTING ZOO
UNDER THE GUIDANCE OF FOWL CITY RESCUE

Will still impresses me with the way she can organize a complicated thing in her head and shrink it down to its most important parts. Like the Frenchie Bulldog article. Or this, the city's way-too-long dog park name.

She grabbed the "Under" from the beginning of the second line. The "dog" part was pretty obvious. And "city" actually shows up twice on that huge, unnecessary sign.

So now everybody in the Heights refers to the most popular spot in our neighborhood, the corner of Liberty and Prince streets, by the same name. The nickname Will came up with.

It's not the vacant lot anymore. No more ghosts.

It's *Underdog City* now. Constantly filled with life.

And today we're heading up Liberty hill, straight for it. Will and her grandparents. Me, Mom, and Dad. Also

Hank, the rottweiler I met at the Stuyvesant County Animal Shelter. The dog we adopted about a week after I stood up on that podium.

The very next morning, I'd begged Mom to take me back to the shelter. She asked, "Are you sure?" about a million times. Said the same thing a bunch of different ways, like "We don't have to rush, you know" and "You can take as much time as you want."

Take your time.

That's a big thing in our family now. We take our time with each other. Dad doesn't snap anymore. Mom doesn't roll her eyes when he starts fixing something. She gets why he does it now.

Not that I don't hope he'll eventually stop "fixing" our appliances. At least while we still have a few left in the house that actually work the way they're supposed to.

"¿Estás listo?" Will asks Hank, bending down and ruffling his ears. Hank gets excited, pulling at the leash in my hand, tugging my arm, dragging me up the hill.

After I get him back under control, I peek over at Mom. She still worries about my shoulder, especially after I picked out such a huge dog. Thing is, I think I needed a new friend big and strong enough to support all my old weight. The heaviness that still sometimes threatens to overwhelm me when I'm thinking about Trevor too much.

Mom's staring at me like I knew she would be, but when

we lock eyes, she widens hers and makes a zipping motion over her mouth, promising not to bug me about Hank pulling too hard. She makes that wordless promise to stay quiet pretty often now. It means a lot to me, because it's her way of letting me know she's learned to trust me more.

It's been good to be responsible for something besides Cinnamon again. And guess what? I don't need any sticky note reminders to know when my new dog needs to be fed or walked. When his water bowl needs to be filled or he should have a bath.

Come to think of it, I'm not even sure where my color sticky notes are. Guess I haven't been using them for Cinnamon, either, and he's doing just fine, too. No squeaky wheel from my hamster as far back as I can remember.

Sure, Mom trusts me more. But maybe what's more important is I've learned to trust myself again.

"Hank doesn't speak Spanish," I remind Will.

"Right," she says, index finger shooting into the air as if she really did forget that my dog isn't bilingual.

She repeats her question in English. "Are you ready? Are you?" She ruffles Hank's ears again, and he gets excited again but doesn't pull on the leash this time.

It's amazing how much Spanish Will speaks now. I didn't see her all school year, but we FaceTimed a bunch and texted and wrote about seven thousand emails back and forth. She'd told me she was taking a Spanish class three times a week, but I had no idea she'd come back practically fluent. She looked so proud of herself every time she spoke a full sentence in front of her grandparents.

Will and Dad and Papa C. were having some lively conversation as we marched up the hill. That's right—Dad spent a big chunk of his winter learning Spanish on some app, too. And a bunch more time fawning over Papa C.'s truck and hanging out with the Puerto Rican man next door. The two of them are so different, but they don't let it stop them from being friends.

I didn't catch all of what they were saying—I mean, I'm apparently the only one left in this neighborhood who *doesn't* speak Spanish (yet)—but I definitely heard Dad describing the wide variety of sausages we picked out at Townsend Meat Market this morning. My stomach rumbles.

Frankie waits for us at the top of the hill, just outside the entrance to Underdog City. He's dwarfed by the huge sign, standing almost directly beneath it like he is. His Weimaraner, Einstein, tugs at the end of the leash as soon as she sees Hank, and both Frankie and I fight to manage our dogs' excitement.

These days, Frankie never forgets to walk Einstein.

We meet up, our dogs jumping and yelping. Maybe he's been waiting a while, because Frankie's bouncing on his toes, clearly itching to head into the park. And we're about to follow him there, too, until Mom speaks up behind me.

"Will you look at that," she says, her voice filled with wonder.

We all freeze, and we look, really look, at Underdog City. It's been commandeered today for the first block party Townsend Heights has had in forever. A huge blowout that's just about to really get going.

Mack's working three grills at once. His hands move fast, turning hot dogs, flipping burgers, poking sausages. Queenie's right there next to him, but just as I notice her, she starts to wander away from her old friend. She pats Mack gently on the back before leaving him to his work.

Monty the bulldog trots alongside Queenie as she ambles along, heading straight across the park. Past the petting zoo, where all of Townsend Heights' younger kids are, chasing after the roosters and petting the goats and talking to the guinea fowl and the chickens and watching Cinnamon, who I brought up earlier this morning, spin round and round and round his wheel.

Another group of kids are down on all fours on yoga mats, giggling as baby goats—more kids, just of a different kind—gleefully climb onto their flat backs.

Goat Yoga. It's an actual thing.

I've even tried it myself, after Mom found out it helps with anxiety. And maybe it has helped. I'm not totally sure. All I know is that it's a ton of fun, and I don't sweat on the back of my neck or get dry mouth when I'm doing it. I haven't stopped freezing up completely, but to be honest, I can't remember the last time it happened, either.

Queenie waves at Gustavo, cradled protectively in an eight-year-old's arms. The rooster doesn't squirm an inch. A few of the Fowl City people are close by, guiding the kids, showing them how to pet and hold and comfort the birds. How to love them without suffocating them at the same time.

Trust me, it's a fine line.

Queenie and Monty continue their slow march. Past the mini-zoo. Past the Goat Yoga. Past Gustavo.

Past Teddy, who's chasing a fluttering group of chicken friends in a pen, big grin on his face, tongue flapping in the wind as he changes direction after them. One of the chickens decides to turn the tables on their canine friend, spinning around a hay bale and emerging from the other side on the offensive. The big boxer slams on the brakes, kicking up dust. He heads in the opposite direction, the suddenly aggressive chicken hot on his heels. Before long, all the chickens join in, giving Teddy back a bit of his own medicine.

Past Chester Brewster, who brings Teddy up to Underdog City more than he'd probably admit to us. He's as drawn to hanging out in this spot as the rest of us are. Same way Ms. Opal's family always was.

Chester's leaning against the back fence, staring at his phone, still wearing his Beats, but today, at least, he has a blue poop bag in his hand.

My earth science–teaching Dad's always reminding me that it took the Colorado River 225 million years to form the Grand Canyon. And that, on the very same planet, we also have tornadoes that can sweep through and wipe out a whole town in thirty seconds flat.

Time is weird. You can't make it go backward. There's no fast-forward button, either. Lots of real smart scientists have dedicated their whole lives to studying time. If you ask me, though, I think the best idea is to try not to think about it at all.

Because if you think about time too much, you end up dwelling on things that are completely out of your control. Like the fact it took Chester Brewster nearly a year to understand he's responsible for cleaning up his own dog's poop.

A Frisbee lands at Monty's feet. The bulldog jumps back from it like it's a bomb, but King, the DiNuccis' husky, is on it like lightning, snatching it up and prancing proudly back to his humans with his prize.

Queenie and Monty veer around the DiNucci family. They pick up their pace as friendly waves are exchanged.

Past Dave DiNucci tossing a Frisbee to his dog. Past the rest of the dogs and neighbors running in circles, or twisting in the air on the rings of the Underdog City playground. Past all of Townsend Heights, really. Because everyone's here. I hope that's how it is for every block party we ever have, but I also know it takes a lot of work to keep a family this big together. More than you think. Good thing I've had Ms. Opal showing me how to do it for so many years.

On the Liberty side of the park, Kaitlyn Cooper wrestles with another goat, corralling it off their truck toward the petting zoo. Brett from the animal shelter is right behind her, carrying one more blue-faced guinea fowl. The waitress from Mi Isla follows them both, lugging a heavy bag of feed.

All these random lives, twisted together into this odd sort of shape. A shape that has a lot of different names. Community. Neighborhood.

Family.

I see where Queenie's headed now. The auditorium built into the hillside. Because that's where Ms. Opal is. She's up front, sitting on one of the stone benches, presenting to the newly formed Townsend Heights Historical Society. The outdoor auditorium was her idea. Once she saw the city working so hard to appease the neighborhood, to help the Heights any way they could, she sneakily added the hillside theater no one knew she'd been dreaming of to our plan.

She wanted it to look like something the Greeks or Romans would've had. She wanted it to become the platform her grandfather should've had. The podium Townsend Heights always deserved.

I must've had six kids in my class do presentations on what happened with the first Townsend Station project, back in the fifties. They all bugged me for Opal's contact info, so they could interview her about it. She didn't even mind telling them the same story over and over again. Carter's General, her grandparents, the whole thing.

Ms. Opal says once people finally start listening, it's important to keep talking.

And she turns just then, my Opal, sitting on her stone bench, built in almost the exact spot the old bench was. The one on the side of her grandparents' store, the one her people gathered at and sat on all those years ago. They walked up these hills every night to be with each other. To share their stories and advice and love.

It was where and how they first formed this community. Where and how they built this neighborhood up from nothing. The rest of us wouldn't have what we do if it weren't for them. There could never be a *now* without a *then*.

Ms. Opal's people had to bring their own chairs up the hill, just in case there wasn't room on the bench when they arrived. But now, there's a whole theater of benches. Plenty of seats, enough for anybody who wants one.

She catches sight of our little group. Ms. Opal takes up the cane at her side, pushes herself up to stand. She still favors her replaced hip, but the infection is gone.

With a big wave of her arm, she invites us to join her. Queenie notices the gesture and turns to join her friend in making it. Both of them, calling us forward.

And finally, finally, I look up at Mom. "It's pretty amazing, isn't it?" she asks me.

I'm not really sure at first which part she means. All of it, I guess.

"Yeah," I agree.

Mom smiles at us then, Will and me and Frankie. "Well? What are you waiting for?"

Our dogs lead the way, running at full speed. Panting and drooling and being dogs. But me and my friends aren't far behind.

We race into the park we helped create. We sprint through the city. Our city.

Feeling like we're on top of the world. And here, at the top of the Heights, we kind of are. Still, as big as we might grow, I don't think we'll ever stop being underdogs. And that's okay, because underdogs have always existed.

The underdogs are the ones who have to try the hardest.

We're the ones who close our eyes and tackle the problems in front of us. And when that first problem is done and gone, we move on to the next one. And the next one after that.

Never stopping.

No hesitation.

That summer, on a Tuesday, a sign appeared on every available Townsend Heights telephone pole. It was the first of many, swapped out for a new one each and every day. The signs were all perfectly placed. No one could remove them without breaking Ordinance 16-8— the unlawful removal of properly placed bills, posters, and dodgers. Not that anyone would've dared anyway.

Sometimes the quotes came from Ms. Opal. A few times it was something Will might've said. Or Mom or Dad. Once or twice even something Frankie said.

But the first one? On that Tuesday? It came from a teacher. Sort of. Before the teacher, the quote had come from somebody else. Somebody famous. A historical VIP.

The words on that first sign had been hidden in Mortimer's secret files for a very long time. Ever since last year, when Mr. Holloway was talking about the U.S. Civil War in class and wrote them on the board. They'd just struck Mortimer the right way. Even if at first he wouldn't have been able to tell anyone why.

By the summer of Underdog City, though, Mortimer understood the words a lot better. He knew, at least, exactly what they meant to him. And that made him want to share them with the rest of the Heights. Because if something means a lot to you, you shouldn't hide it. You never know who might get inspired by a good thing you say. Or do.

TOWNSEND HEIGHTS QUOTE OF THE DAY
FROM MORTIMER BRAY

The best thing about the future is that it comes one day at a time.
—Abraham Lincoln

ACKNOWLEDGMENTS

I owe a great debt of gratitude to several editors at HarperCollins for this book, starting with Elizabeth Lynch, who once again was the one to give it a chance to be what it could be and then take it there. Sarah Homer and Tara Weikum graciously picked up the reins afterward, never wavering through final edits and more logistics than I probably even know happen. You're so appreciated.

Constant and eternal thanks to my agent, Alyssa Jeanette. Only she and I know how very different the original idea for this book was from the one you're holding in your hands. Her honesty and forthrightness helped isolate its true heart before we ever showed it to anyone else. No one could have done that better.

I spent the year and a half leading up to the release of this book at countless bookstore signings and events with Rosalind and Maggie Bunn. Their selfless friendship and fellowship, the way they adopted me into their supercool book-writing family, is a kindness I'll truly never forget.

Nicole D. Collier critiqued this project at several crucial points. I am grateful for her steady, wise, and dependable voice. It's one any writer should wish to have in their corner.

I read very early excerpts of this book to a few critique groups. Thank you for the comments that helped set it along its proper track to my Next Level Team, the Forsyth County Library group, and my Roswell friends as well.

Special thanks to the coffee shops and restaurants around Atlanta that gave me space to work on this book, especially the Matt Highway Laredos Taqueria. Your friendly faces and good food became much-needed fuel for this project.

I am grateful every day to my sisters for many things, including listening to my first stories about neighborhood dogs. Some of the quirkier elements of *Underdog City* were inspired by my Grandpa and Grandma Negron, who were from Puerto Rico and sometimes hard for me to communicate with. Yes, Grandpa really did keep a rooster behind a curtain in his basement, though the references as to why in this book are completely invented. Thank you also to my parents for giving me everything I needed early in life and for always being there.

Townsend Heights is not a real place, and you may notice I don't even name the city it's a part of. That's because it's built from pieces and parts of all the homes I've ever had, including New Haven, CT. I owe a huge thank-you to my wife, Mary, for more things than I can count, but in the case of Townsend Heights and *Underdog City*, it's for introducing me to her city and to her family and their history, which includes grandparent-owned stores and eminent domain.

And, finally, thank you to all the kids. Not just for reading my work, though I admit that is a very cool thing for you to do. No, I want to thank you for moving from one day to the next with a smile on your face and hope in your heart.

I see you working hard to make the world around you a better place. I see you being the voice of reason when adults spend too much time arguing. I see you ignoring the things that make us different and focusing on the ways we're the same.

I see you coming up to me at the end of a talk and shaking my hand and thanking me and calling me sir, even though that's totally unnecessary. I see all your smart questions, your boundless curiosity. I see you sneaking a book to my table and asking me to sign it to your mom instead of yourself. I see you showing me the picture of one of my characters you drew for your little brother. I see how excited you are not only to read my stories but to explore your own.

I see all of it.

I see all of you.

—Chris Negron
April 2023